W9-BRJ-638

CITY
OF
SECRETS

Center Point
Large Print

Also by Victoria Thompson and available from
Center Point Large Print:

Murder in Murray Hill
Murder on Amsterdam Avenue
Murder on St. Nicholas Avenue
Murder in the Bowery
City of Lies
Murder on Union Square

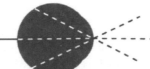

**This Large Print Book carries the
Seal of Approval of N.A.V.H.**

CITY
OF
SECRETS

A Counterfeit Lady Novel

VICTORIA
THOMPSON

CENTER POINT LARGE PRINT
THORNDIKE, MAINE

This Center Point Large Print edition
is published in the year 2018 by arrangement with
Berkley, an imprint of Penguin Publishing Group,
a division of Penguin Random House LLC.

Copyright © 2018 by Victoria Thompson.

All rights reserved.

This is a work of fiction. Names, characters, places, and
incidents either are the product of the author's imagination
or are used fictitiously, and any resemblance to actual
persons, living or dead, business establishments, events,
or locales is entirely coincidental.

The text of this Large Print edition is unabridged.
In other aspects, this book may vary
from the original edition.
Printed in the United States of America
on permanent paper.
Set in 16-point Times New Roman type.

ISBN: 978-1-64358-029-6

Library of Congress Cataloging-in-Publication Data

Names: Thompson, Victoria (Victoria E.), author.
Title: City of secrets / Victoria Thompson.
Description: Center Point Large Print edition. | Thorndike, Maine :
    Center Point Large Print, 2018. | Series: A counterfeit lady novel
Identifiers: LCCN 2018045945 | ISBN 9781643580296
    (hardcover : alk. paper)
Subjects: LCSH: Swindlers and swindling—Fiction. | Large type books.
Classification: LCC PS3570.H6442 C585 2018b | DDC 813/.54—dc23
LC record available at https://lccn.loc.gov/2018045945

To my wonderful editor
Michelle Vega,
who is godmother to
the Counterfeit Lady series.
Thanks for making it better!

CHAPTER ONE

Elizabeth had to tell more lies on a Sunday morning at church than she ever had trying to cheat a mark out of fifty thousand dollars.

"Lovely hat, Mrs. Snodgrass."

"So nice to see you, Mr. Peabody."

"Good sermon, Reverend Honesdale."

But when she glanced over and saw the way Gideon Bates was looking at her, she decided it was worth it. If she was going to marry him, she would have to live in his world, and if that involved lying, at least it was a skill she had already mastered.

"Lizzie!" Anna Vanderslice cried, pushing her way through the worshippers who had lingered after the service to chat. She took Elizabeth's hands in hers and gave them an affectionate squeeze.

"Anna, I'm so glad to see you." Finally, she got to speak the truth. "How are things going at home?" she added in a whisper.

Anna's eyes sparkled with mischief. "David finally admitted to me that he was the one who broke your engagement and he only allowed you to take the credit to save your reputation."

Indeed, if word got out that Anna's brother had found Elizabeth unworthy, no other gentleman in New York would dare make her an offer of marriage. Not that Elizabeth wanted to marry any of the other gentlemen in New York. "He's very kind," Elizabeth said with a straight face.

"I told him so, too," Anna said. "Even though we both know he was saving his own reputation with his *kindness*. No debutante in the city would trust him if he threw you over. How on earth did you convince him it was his idea?"

Elizabeth couldn't explain how she'd gotten David to break the engagement she'd previously convinced him to make, even though he'd never actually proposed to her—at least not while they were standing in a church aisle. She simply smiled mysteriously. "Are you coming to the salon this week?"

"You know I am." Anna hadn't missed a single one of the weekly gatherings held at Elizabeth's aunt's house since Elizabeth had introduced her to them.

"We can talk about it then."

"Anna, how lovely to see you," Gideon's mother said, having wandered over from where she'd been greeting some friends. "Is your mother here? I didn't see her."

"She has a cold, so she stayed home today."

"Nothing serious, I hope," Mrs. Bates said.

Anna's shrug reminded them both that her mother was something of a hypochondriac whose ailments were never serious. The three women chatted for a few minutes before Anna took her leave to find her brother.

Mrs. Bates scanned the dwindling crowd with the shrewdness of a business tycoon determined to transact a multimillion-dollar deal. Or rather with the shrewdness of a society matron determined to find a social advantage for her only son, which made her even more ruthless than a tycoon. Since her only son needed a wife who was completely acceptable to society, and since Elizabeth was the wife he wanted, Mrs. Bates had her work cut out for her.

At the moment, Gideon's mother was limited to introducing Elizabeth to whatever illustrious individuals happened to have lingered to chat after this morning's service. Judging from her expression, she didn't see anyone left who was worth pursuing.

"Is Priscilla here?" Elizabeth asked, naming the one woman she'd actually become friends with so far. "I didn't see her."

"I thought . . ." Mrs. Bates scanned the auditorium again. "Yes, there she is, up front. Oh dear, I hope she's not ill."

Indeed, Priscilla Knight was still sitting in one of the front pews, staring straight ahead and making no move to chat with any of the ladies clustering nearby.

"I'll make sure she's all right," Elizabeth said, hurrying toward the front of the church.

Priscilla had recently been widowed for the second time in her young life, and Elizabeth knew she carried a heavy burden. As she approached, she saw that her friend looked more distressed than ill.

"Priscilla?"

Priscilla looked up and smiled when she recognized Elizabeth, but the smile didn't quite reach her eyes. "Oh, Elizabeth, you startled me."

"You did look like you were deep in thought. I didn't know whether to interrupt you or not." Elizabeth slid into the pew beside her. "Is everything all right?"

"No," she said softly. "No, it's not."

Which was not what people usually said unless something was very wrong indeed. "Can I help?" Elizabeth heard herself say, although she usually wasn't the least bit interested in getting involved with other people's problems. But she really did care about Priscilla, which was somewhat of a shock to realize.

"I don't know if anyone can help."

Before Elizabeth could respond to this terrifying statement, Daisy Honesdale, the minister's wife, arrived. Her handsome face was a mask of concern. "Mrs. Knight, are you all right?"

This time Priscilla raised her head and smiled the determined smile of a woman with no intention of giving in to despair. Then she rose to her feet. "I'm perfectly fine, Mrs. Honesdale. I was just praying. For Endicott, you know," she added, naming her most recently deceased husband.

"Of course," Mrs. Honesdale said a little uncertainly, glancing at Elizabeth, who had risen as well. "I'm glad to see you in church today, Mrs. Knight. It's important to see one's friends when one is in mourning."

If that were true, then why were widows who were still in mourning forbidden to socialize in all but the most restricted ways? But Elizabeth wasn't going to take this particular opportunity to challenge society's strictures. Instead she took Priscilla's arm, sensing her friend didn't want the minister's wife inquiring into her problems. "Mrs. Bates wanted to say hello to you, Priscilla. Let me take you to her."

They nodded their farewells to Mrs. Honesdale, and Elizabeth escorted Priscilla down the aisle to where Mrs. Bates waited.

"Could you . . . ?" Priscilla whispered.

"Could I what?"

"Could you come to see me?"

Elizabeth could not mistake the desperation in her friend's eyes. "Of course."

Daisy Honesdale watched Priscilla Knight and her friend as they made their way out of the church. They were practically the last to leave, and she waited, knowing Peter would come to

11

find her when he had shaken the hand of the last parishioner and closed the front doors.

He came down the aisle slowly, his clerical robes flapping around his long legs. He was a handsome man, just as she'd been promised, and not particularly bright, which had sealed the deal. She had made a good bargain, and soon she would have everything she had always wanted. How nice it would have been to share her victory with a beautiful man like Peter. He had worked just as hard as she to earn it, after all. But the truth was, she could no longer stand the sight of him.

"What do we know about that girl who's been coming with Hazel Bates?" she asked when he was close enough.

Peter's perfect face creased slightly with the effort of thinking. "Her name is Miles. Elizabeth, I think. She's one of Mrs. Bates's suffragette friends."

"She's gotten awfully friendly with Priscilla Knight."

He glanced over his shoulder as if he could still see them. "I did notice they walked out together."

A miracle. "Where did this Miles girl come from? Do we know anything about her?"

"I don't think so. She just showed up with Mrs. Bates a few weeks ago."

"Gideon seems smitten."

"Does he? She's quite lovely."

Of course he'd noticed that. "She's smart, too."

"How can you tell?"

12

"Mrs. Bates wouldn't waste time on her if she wasn't."

"Oh." He considered. "I suppose you're right."

Of course she was right. She was always right. "We need to keep an eye on her."

"Why?"

Daisy managed not to sigh. "Because she's taken an interest in Priscilla, and Priscilla will soon discover her true situation, and she might confide in the Miles girl."

"What could she confide?"

"Peter, darling, there are lots of things she could confide. She can, for example, remember the role you and I played in her most recent marriage."

"We were only trying to help her. You said so yourself."

"Of course we were, and we had no idea of Mr. Knight's true nature. We are as shocked as Priscilla will be."

"Then why do we need to keep an eye on her?"

This time Daisy allowed herself to sigh. "Because we don't know what trouble she might cause, and we need to be ready."

Finally, he seemed to grasp the significance of the situation. "What can we do to be ready?"

She favored him with a smile. "I don't know yet, but opportunities have a way of presenting themselves, don't they?"

He smiled back. "Yes, almost as if they fell from heaven."

• • •

"Who is Priscilla Knight?" Gideon asked.

Elizabeth had waited until they were enjoying Sunday dinner in the Bateses' dining room and the maid had withdrawn before telling Mrs. Bates about Priscilla's strange request.

"Priscilla *Jenks,*" Mrs. Bates told her son. "You remember, DeForrest Jenks died suddenly a little over a year ago. Priscilla remarried rather quickly, to Endicott Knight."

"That's right," Gideon said. "I remember now. I also remember wondering why on earth she'd married Knight."

"He was . . . rather attractive," Mrs. Bates allowed.

Gideon leaned over to where Elizabeth sat to his left and stage-whispered, "The way a cigar-store Indian is attractive—very noble but without much conversation."

"You shouldn't speak ill of the dead," his mother scolded.

Gideon feigned chagrin and Elizabeth bit back a smile. "She must have been thoroughly charmed if she remarried so quickly. Or maybe she just didn't care much for her first husband and didn't see any point in mourning him too long."

"Oh no, she adored DeForrest. They were devoted to each other," Mrs. Bates said. "And Gideon is right. Endicott wasn't . . . Well, let's just say it's unlikely he *charmed* her into marrying him."

14

"I heard it was money," Gideon said.

His mother stiffened. "Was DeForrest a client of yours?"

"Certainly not. I couldn't gossip about him if he was. And I didn't gossip about him at all, come to that, until this very moment."

"But someone gossiped to *you* and said Priscilla married this Mr. Knight for his money," Elizabeth guessed.

Gideon winced a bit. "Something like that. Someone hinted that DeForrest had left Priscilla destitute and she needed to remarry to provide for her girls."

Elizabeth glanced over at Mrs. Bates and saw her own disgust reflected in her expression. "How awful for her," Mrs. Bates said.

"But a very familiar story," Elizabeth said.

"And now she's been widowed twice in a little over a year, and she's barely thirty." Mrs. Bates shook her head. "No wonder she's distraught."

"So you're going to see her?" Gideon asked Elizabeth.

"Of course. Except for the women I met in jail, she's the only female who has shown any interest in being my friend."

"And only a few of the jailed women live in New York," Mrs. Bates added. "So of course Elizabeth is going to see Priscilla."

Gideon shook his head in mock despair. "I just realized I'm probably the only attorney in New

15

York eating Sunday dinner with two convicts."

"Two convicts who happen to be your mother and your fiancée," Mrs. Bates reminded him.

"I'm not his fiancée yet," Elizabeth reminded her right back.

"That's right," Gideon said. "It's bad enough that I'm stealing my best friend's girl. I can't be seen to do it too quickly."

"Is there a specified period of mourning for a lost fiancée?" Elizabeth asked. "Where is Mrs. Ordway's book? I must check the etiquette on that so you can inform poor David." Mrs. Edith B. Ordway and her book *The Etiquette of Today* were considered the ultimate authorities on such matters.

"I'm very sorry to inform you, but David is not currently mourning the loss of his fiancée," Gideon said gravely.

"You can't mean it!" Elizabeth said in mock despair. "I thought I'd merit at least a month of grieving."

"I believe it's been almost a month," Gideon said. "Nearly. Close to it, anyway."

"It has not! I'm terribly affronted. And insulted."

"I don't know how to tell you this, but he's actually relieved to be shed of you," Gideon informed her.

Mrs. Bates was laughing now. "He told you this, I assume?"

Gideon managed to maintain a straight face. "Yes, this morning. Not in so many words, of course. A gentleman never besmirches a lady's character to another gentleman."

"Horsefeathers," Elizabeth said. "I shall sue him for breach of promise."

"No one does that anymore," Gideon said in the ponderous voice he used to offer legal advice, or would use if anyone ever asked him for it. "That's what engagement rings are for. The jilted lady can sell the ring to reimburse herself for her injured pride."

"But I returned the engagement ring to him, so I can't sell it."

"You returned it because it was hideously ugly and you didn't want it," Gideon reminded her. "And because you're the one who called off the engagement, you can't sue him for breach of promise in any case."

"Can he sue me?"

Gideon wagged his head. "Men are made of sterner stuff than that, Miss Miles. We don't ask the courts to salve our broken hearts with financial settlements."

"That's enough of your nonsense," Mrs. Bates said, although she was still smiling. "We shouldn't be making fun of poor David. He probably did care for Elizabeth, at least a little."

"And I'm sure Elizabeth deeply regrets tricking him into becoming engaged to her," Gideon said.

"Yes, I do," Elizabeth assured them. "And I never would have abused him like that except to save my life, which some people might consider selfish of me, but I considered vitally important, at least at the time."

"We all considered it important," Mrs. Bates assured her. "I'm sure David would, too, if he knew."

"Perhaps we should tell him," Gideon said.

"Perhaps we should," Elizabeth said. "Especially if you want him to be best man at our wedding."

In the end, Mrs. Bates decided to go with Elizabeth to visit Priscilla Knight that afternoon, for which Elizabeth was grateful. For all her varied life experiences, she'd never had to comfort a young widow.

"Oh, Mrs. Bates," Priscilla said when the maid had escorted them into the parlor. "I didn't expect to see you, too. Thank you both for coming."

She looked even more distressed now than she had in church. Her face was pale and her eyes bloodshot, either from weeping or lack of sleep. Perhaps both. The unrelieved black of her outfit didn't flatter her fair coloring, either.

When they were settled, Elizabeth said, "You sounded so desperate this morning, we decided we needed to come right away."

"Desperate? Yes, I suppose I am."

"I can't imagine what you must be going through, to lose two husbands in such a short time," Mrs. Bates said.

"I . . . Well, I don't want you to think I'm grieving for Mr. Knight. I . . . Actually, I hardly knew him."

Elizabeth and Mrs. Bates exchanged a glance. "We know you had to marry him," Elizabeth said, "to provide for yourself and your daughters."

Priscilla frowned. "What? Where did you get that idea?"

Elizabeth glanced at Mrs. Bates again and saw her own confusion mirrored there. "Someone said your first husband left you penniless, and that's why . . ."

"Oh no," Priscilla said, shaking her head vehemently. "DeForrest left us very well situated. I never would have wanted for anything."

Could that be true?

"I know you were devastated when he died," Mrs. Bates said tentatively.

"I was! I cried all the time, for weeks. Some days I couldn't even get out of bed. When I look back, I don't know how I survived, but Mrs. Honesdale was so kind to me. She visited me every day and never let me completely surrender to my grief."

Elizabeth frowned. If that were true, Priscilla would be deeply grateful to Daisy Honesdale. Why, then, had Priscilla been so eager to escape her this morning? "She takes her position as the minister's wife very seriously." She tried to see how Priscilla would respond.

"Yes, she does," Priscilla said sharply, with what looked like anger sparking in her pale blue eyes. "And after a few weeks, she took it upon herself to convince me I needed a man to look after me."

"Why did she do that?" Mrs. Bates asked.

"Because she believes that a woman alone is in danger. Anyone might take advantage of her if she has no man to protect her."

"Don't you have any family?" Elizabeth asked.

"No, I . . . I was an only child and my father died years ago. My mother and I lived with an uncle, but he passed away before I married, and my mother is gone now, too. I'm quite alone."

"So you decided you did need to remarry," Elizabeth said.

"No, I didn't," Priscilla said, shocking them both. "I never decided that at all. Reverend Honesdale brought Mr. Knight to call on me a few times. I wasn't in any condition to entertain visitors, but I didn't object. That would have seemed churlish after all the Honesdales had done for me."

"Then did meeting him make you change your mind about remarrying?" Elizabeth asked.

"No, I told you. I never changed my mind about that."

"Then how . . . ?"

"How did I end up marrying him? I honestly don't know," Priscilla said, her voice shrill with frustration.

"What do you mean, you don't know?" Mrs. Bates asked, frowning now with the same determination that had kept Elizabeth and the other women focused when they'd been jailed almost two months ago.

"I mean much of that time is . . . well, 'foggy' is the only word I can think to describe it. I was prostrate with grief and I wasn't paying much attention to anything else. I just remember Mrs. Honesdale telling me how much I needed a man to look after me. Mr. Knight called here, but he hardly ever spoke to me, and I honestly have no memory of him proposing to me. All I know for sure is that one day the Honesdales and Mr. Knight arrived with another man I didn't know and Reverend Honesdale married me to Mr. Knight."

"How could they do that, marry you to someone against your will?" Elizabeth demanded, outraged.

"But I must have agreed," Priscilla said. "They couldn't . . . they *wouldn't* do that unless I'd agreed, would they?"

In Elizabeth's world, people got bamboozled all the time, but she didn't think those things happened routinely in Gideon's world. Maybe she was wrong about that, but Mrs. Bates looked baffled, so probably not.

"I can't imagine anyone—and certainly not a minister—marrying someone against her will," Mrs. Bates said, although Elizabeth could tell she wasn't as certain as she was trying to appear.

"So you see, I must have agreed, but I felt so guilty afterward. I know people wondered why I remarried so quickly, as if I couldn't be bothered to mourn DeForrest, who had been the love of my life."

"No one thought that, my dear," Mrs. Bates assured her, although Elizabeth was pretty sure she was lying. Elizabeth hadn't known any of them then, but she knew enough about human nature to be fairly certain that if people had a reason to gossip about someone, they would.

"And apparently, people thought you needed a husband to support you," Elizabeth added, earning a black look from Mrs. Bates. Mrs. Ordway's book said talking about money was always frowned upon in polite society, but Elizabeth thought Priscilla would rather be thought penniless than heartless.

The grateful smile Priscilla gave her proved her right. "That would have been a justification, I suppose, although I don't know how a rumor like that got started. I had a very nice dowry when I married DeForrest, and he was quite comfortable as well. And Mr. Knight was quite well off, too, or

22

at least that's what everyone thought, but now . . ."

"Now?" Elizabeth prompted.

"Now my solicitor tells me I really am penniless or nearly so."

"What!" Mrs. Bates exclaimed.

"How could that be true?" Elizabeth asked.

"I have no idea, and even worse, it appears this house is mortgaged and I have no way of paying that, either. The girls and I will have to leave, although I don't know where we can go."

"There must be some mistake," Mrs. Bates said. "Fortunes don't disappear overnight."

Elizabeth could have disagreed. In her experience, that's exactly the way they disappeared, and often they disappeared into the hands of one of her family members. She herself had been in the midst of cheating someone out of his fortune when she'd first met Hazel Bates and her son, Gideon.

Mrs. Bates knew all about her past now, of course, so Elizabeth had no trouble at all reading her thoughts when their gazes met across Priscilla's parlor. Could Mr. Knight have lost Priscilla's fortune to a con artist?

"I thought it must be some mistake, too," Priscilla was saying, oblivious to the undercurrents. "I told my banker that, but he was certain he was right."

"Did he know what happened to your money?"

"He claims he does not, and I don't have the

slightest idea of how to find out myself. I'm sure he's wrong or has made some terrible mistake or—and I hate to say this, but I'm sure it does happen—that he has stolen the money himself. But no matter what happened, how will I ever find out?"

"And of course you don't want to be making such serious accusations with no basis in fact," Mrs. Bates said, "even if you're just accusing him of making an error."

"I don't care about the money for myself, you know, or the house, either," Priscilla said. "But my girls . . . What kind of a future will they have if . . . ?"

"Now, now, don't borrow trouble, as my dear mother used to say," Mrs. Bates said. "We'll get this sorted out."

"Will we?" Priscilla asked. "I wouldn't even know whom to ask for help or whom to trust at this point."

"Would you trust Elizabeth?" Mrs. Bates asked, giving Elizabeth a look that made her sit up straighter.

"Elizabeth? Of course I would, but what—"

"Elizabeth has a rather unique family history that . . . Well, let's just say she might be able to figure out what happened to your fortune and who was responsible." Mrs. Bates's expression asked a silent question that Elizabeth was only too qualified to answer.

"I just might at that," Elizabeth said. "Would you allow me to look through Mr. Knight's papers? I think that's the logical place to begin, and I might be able to figure out something."

"If you think you could, of course. I'd be very grateful, although I don't know what you might find."

Elizabeth knew, though. She also knew the questions to ask Priscilla and anyone else who might know something about Mr. Knight's financial dealings. If Endicott Knight had been cheated out of Priscilla's fortune, she could find out who had done it. She might even know them by name. The chances of recovering the money were slim, but at least Priscilla would know the truth, and Elizabeth might—just might—be able to prevail on someone's conscience to help a poor widow.

"I could come tomorrow morning, if that's convenient for you," Elizabeth said.

"Every day is convenient for a woman in deep mourning," Priscilla said sadly. "I can hardly ever leave the house."

"Do you think he could have been . . . cheated?" Mrs. Bates asked as she and Elizabeth huddled together under the lap robe in the back of the taxicab. The winter sun was setting, and it was too cold to walk back home.

"It certainly sounds like he was," Elizabeth

said. "How long was she married to this Knight fellow?"

"Let me see . . . About nine months, I'd say. That's not much time to dispose of a fortune in the usual way."

"What is the usual way to dispose of a fortune?"

"Spending it, I suppose," Mrs. Bates said, shaking her head. "I've never had the luxury of trying it, but I'm told it's possible."

"And I suppose you could do it rather quickly if you put your mind to it, but what would he have spent it on?"

"Maybe he was a gambler, although I can't say I've ever heard a whiff of gossip about him. People do talk, and it doesn't seem likely the Honesdales would pair Priscilla up with a gambler or someone with similar expensive vices."

"Would a minister know if someone had vices?"

Mrs. Bates gave her a pitying look. "Ministers tend to know everything. People confess their shortcomings to ministers in hopes of getting help, and of course others are only too eager to tattle about their neighbors' shortcomings."

"So whatever Mr. Knight was doing, he managed to keep it private."

"Which is what made me think it might be something like the way you got Oscar Thornton's money."

26

"We call it a con," Elizabeth said sweetly. "And Knight wouldn't necessarily even think what he was doing was illegal, so he'd have nothing to confess."

"Exactly. Will you be able to find evidence if that's what happened?"

"Probably, but I also probably won't be able to get the money back, if that's what you're thinking."

"I don't hope for miracles, but I would like to give Priscilla some explanation for what happened."

"What I don't understand is why the Honesdales were so anxious to get her remarried," Elizabeth said.

"That does seem strange, doesn't it? Of course, some people are always deciding they know what's best for someone else. Maybe the Honesdales really did think Priscilla needed a man to look after her and were only trying to help."

"I wouldn't consider it helping if someone tricked me into marrying a man I hardly knew."

Mrs. Bates nodded. "Neither would I, especially if he squandered all my money, but of course they couldn't have known he'd do that."

No, they couldn't, could they? It seemed unlikely. Still, they'd assumed a lot of authority over poor Priscilla. Elizabeth hadn't really formed an opinion of the minister and his wife one way or the other. Her limited exposure to them hadn't given her much opportunity. She'd have to pay more attention.

"Are you going to tell Gideon what we found out?" Elizabeth asked.

"Not yet. I was thinking you should just go straight home so he can't ask you anything this evening, and I'll just say it ended up being a condolence call."

"What if we're right and Mr. Knight was conned?"

"Then we'll tell him, of course," Mrs. Bates said impatiently.

But Elizabeth wasn't fooled. She knew Mrs. Bates was trying to protect her somehow. "Gideon already knows what I am," Elizabeth reminded her.

"And that's why he won't want you to get involved, so if he doesn't know our plans, he won't try to stop you."

"And we won't have an argument about it," Elizabeth said, completing the thought.

Mrs. Bates smiled at that. "Which was my ultimate goal, yes. You also won't have to lie to him."

"Which is the one thing he can't forgive, I know. I'll never lie to Gideon, but you must accept the fact that means we'll probably have lots of arguments."

"I accept that fully, which is why I'm going to avoid this one by not telling him anything about this just yet."

. . .

Priscilla was with her two little girls when Elizabeth arrived the next morning. They were, Priscilla informed her proudly, aged two and four. They were probably too young to even remember their father. They were both blonde, like their mother, and so very small and defenseless that Elizabeth had to swallow down the surge of rage that bubbled up at the thought of what had been taken from them.

After sending the children back to the nursery with their nanny, Priscilla took Elizabeth upstairs. "This was Endicott's room," she explained, opening one of the doors that led off the hallway. It was a bedroom, although plainly not the master bedroom, containing a double bed, dresser, washstand and wardrobe cabinet, but it also contained a desk and, oddly enough, a safe.

"He used this as his office?" Elizabeth asked. Usually, men had a study of some sort where they smoked and read their newspapers and conducted whatever business men of that social class conducted at home. A house of this size would have such a room and it would ordinarily be downstairs.

"His office and his, uh, bedroom as well."

Elizabeth couldn't help noticing that the room didn't adjoin any other, the way bedrooms of married couples usually did, and Priscilla had said it was *his* room. "I see."

"And to save you from asking, Mr. Knight and I did not share a bedroom," Priscilla said, her pale cheeks pinkening.

"I wasn't going to ask."

"I wanted you to know, though, so you'd understand why . . . Well, why I didn't know very much about him."

"You did say you didn't know him very well."

"As I told you, we'd hardly spoken before the marriage. That night—our wedding night—he told me he would allow me my privacy—that's how he phrased it—and he moved his things into this room. I thought . . . I suppose I assumed it would be temporary. You aren't married, Elizabeth, but I was, and I know how much men enjoy the privileges of the marriage bed."

Now it was Elizabeth's turn to blush, which she did because she thought of Gideon and how very much he would enjoy those privileges. "So I understand."

"I enjoyed them, too. With DeForrest, that is. I was relieved when Mr. Knight didn't demand his rights immediately, though. I couldn't imagine . . . Well, at any rate, I didn't have to. Mr. Knight never mentioned the subject again."

Elizabeth was starting to develop a completely new theory about Endicott Knight, but she'd keep it to herself for now. "Is this where he kept all of his papers?"

"This is where he kept everything that belonged

to him. And he also kept the door locked. I don't think he realized I have duplicate keys to all the rooms, just in case one gets lost. I never used my key while he was alive, of course, but when he died, I opened the room. I needed to get fresh clothes for him to be buried in, but I haven't been in here since."

"Do you know anything about Mr. Knight's business dealings?"

"Nothing at all. He didn't seem to have an office elsewhere or a profession of any kind. He inherited his money, or so I understood, and lived off the interest."

The way most rich people did. "Do you know his friends?"

"Not really. He never invited anyone to the house. In fact, he was hardly ever here himself. He went to his club most days and often took his supper there. Some days I didn't see him at all."

How curious. A man so anxious to marry he allows his minister to practically kidnap a bride for him and then declines to consummate the marriage or even spend any time with his new wife. "Did he seem particularly anxious or worried just before he died?"

Priscilla frowned as she considered the question. "Now that you ask, he did seem anxious, but that wasn't at all unusual."

"What do you mean?"

"I mean he always seemed worried and

distracted. I did try to develop some sort of relationship with him. We were married, after all, no matter how it had come about. But he seemed almost incapable of having a conversation."

"Incapable?"

"I know it sounds odd, but when I did manage to catch him at home and at leisure, I would ask him about his day or whatever, trying to engage him. But he never said anything except to answer a question or two before . . . I'm not sure how to describe it, but I got the feeling he was thinking about something else, something very important, and he couldn't focus his attention on me for more than a moment or two."

"So he didn't ever seem particularly excited or happy about anything, I suppose." Which is how he would have appeared if he were about to fall for a con, thinking he was going to turn his fortune into a much larger fortune.

"Not that I ever saw. He always seemed . . . sad, I guess. Or worried, like I said."

"Do you know what club he belonged to?" Maybe some of his friends there would know more, although she'd need Gideon's help with something like that.

"No, I'm sorry. He never talked about it."

"That's all right. Someone will know, or there's probably a bill from them somewhere in his desk."

"Do you need me to help you sort through

his things?" Priscilla asked with no enthusiasm whatsoever.

"Not at all. Go off and play with your beautiful little girls and leave me to it. I'll let you know if I need anything."

When Priscilla had departed, Elizabeth closed the door in case one of the servants got nosy. Keeping secrets from servants was always difficult, but there was no reason to make it too easy for them.

She sat down in the desk chair and scooted it closer to the desk. The top of the desk was clear, but in the first drawer she opened, she found a stack of recent mail. Only the top envelope had been opened. It bore no return address and had been addressed in neat block printing. She pulled out a piece of stationery that had been folded around a photograph. She unwrapped the photograph and stared at it for a long moment.

The image was so bizarre and unexpected that at first her mind couldn't even comprehend what she was seeing, and when she did, she yelped and tossed it away as if it had burned her.

CHAPTER TWO

Gideon was reviewing some estate documents for a client when his law clerk knocked on his office door.

"A young lady is here to see you, sir. She does not have an appointment."

Plainly, Smith considered anyone foolish enough to arrive at the offices of Devoss and Van Aken without an appointment to be beneath contempt.

"Did she give her name?"

"A Miss Miles, I believe."

Gideon managed to reveal only surprise. No one knew his true relationship with Elizabeth yet, and he certainly did not intend to give anyone in his law firm reason to gossip. "Oh yes. Miss Miles is a friend of my mother's. A fellow suffragist. Please show her in, Smith."

Smith wasn't going to give in easily. "Are you sure, sir?"

"Of course I'm sure. If Miss Miles needs more than a few minutes of my time, I will instruct her to make an appointment to come back later."

That seemed to placate Smith, even though Gideon had no intention of sending Elizabeth away to make an appointment, and he did as Gideon had instructed.

Elizabeth, as usual, looked lovely when Smith escorted her into his office, and for a moment Gideon almost forgot to breathe. She smiled at him but betrayed nothing beyond common courtesy until Smith had closed the door behind himself.

"I don't think he approves of me," she said, her beautiful blue eyes wide with mock concern as she set down the bag she'd been carrying.

"We rarely have such beautiful clients at Devoss and Van Aken," he said, hurrying around his desk to greet her properly. "They tend to be portly and middle-aged at best."

"Ah, that would explain his dismay." She gave him her hands and lifted her face for his kiss. "He must have guessed I'm not here to prepare my last will and testament."

When he'd properly welcomed her, he sat her down in one of the client chairs situated in front of his desk and took the other so he could hold her hand while they talked. "Then why are you here, if I may inquire, or did you just come to apologize for going straight home last evening and leaving me bereft of your company?"

"I came because I need your legal advice, Mr. Bates."

"Then you really are here to make your last will and testament?"

"Of course not, although I'm sure you'd advise me that everyone should have one."

"I certainly would."

To his surprise, her playful smile faded. "I really do need your advice about something, Gideon. It's concerning Priscilla Knight."

"Does it have to do with Knight's estate? Because even if he didn't have a will, she should inherit everything."

"It has to do with Knight, but . . . I don't know what your mother told you about our conversation with Priscilla yesterday . . ."

"She didn't say much of anything."

"Then you don't know the reason Priscilla asked me to call on her. The real reason. She has just learned that Mr. Knight somehow managed to squander both his fortune and her own, and he has left her penniless."

"That's impossible. There must be some mistake," Gideon said instinctively, but he instantly realized it was not impossible at all. Hadn't he and Elizabeth just recently been part of a scheme that had accomplished just such an *impossibility?*

"Priscilla thought it must be a mistake as well, although your mother and I . . . Well, I see you're thinking the same thing we were. We thought Mr. Knight might have been taken advantage of, so your mother suggested—because of my unique experience—that Priscilla allow me to go through Mr. Knight's papers to see if I could figure out what happened to the money."

"And neither of you thought about mentioning this to me?" Gideon said, dismayed he wasn't able to keep the anger from his voice.

"Of course we did, my darling, but Priscilla was too embarrassed to ask anyone . . . or rather to ask any *man* for help. She thought her banker might be lying to her, and she didn't know whom to trust."

"You could have told her to trust me." Now he sounded dangerously close to whiny. He cleared his throat in an effort to get some dignity back. "I mean, you know I would have told her the truth."

"Of course I know that, but at the time your mother and I were fairly certain Mr. Knight had been conned out of his fortune. You couldn't have done anything about that, and your knowing would have just caused Priscilla more humiliation."

That did make sense in a female sort of way, he supposed. Then he realized what she'd said. "But now you don't think he was conned."

"No, I don't, and I want you to know that as soon as I figured it out, I came straight here to see you, although I now realize I should have made an appointment first."

"I'll make sure Smith knows you never need an appointment." He glanced down at the bag she had carried in. He could see now that it appeared to be a man's valise.

She released his hand and reached down to open

the case. She pulled out a ledger. "Mr. Knight was rather good at keeping his accounts, it would seem. I'm not sure why, but thank heaven he was. I think these pages give a very interesting picture of what became of his fortune." She opened the book to a page she'd marked with an envelope and handed it to him.

Gideon wasn't an accountant, but he didn't need to be to read the story told in these pages. This was apparently a record of Knight's household expenditures. Beginning on the page she'd indicated, each month a generous set amount was deposited, probably from the income of his investments, and each expense was recorded and subtracted. All of them seemed to be normal expenditures for a man running his own household. He noted Knight seemed to have belonged to several clubs, including the Manchester Club, where Gideon himself belonged, although he didn't recognize all of the names. The monthly fees for each were paid out accordingly, although one club seemed to have much higher fees than the others, and Knight paid them two or three times a month. Gideon turned the page.

"This is where it starts to get interesting," Elizabeth said, pointing to the new page. The date was approximately three years earlier. The monthly deposit increased substantially, and Knight had paid out five thousand dollars in a lump sum.

"Do you know what these letters stand for?"

Gideon asked, indicating the letters identifying the five thousand dollar expenditure.

"No, and neither does Priscilla. Keep going."

A few months later, Knight made another large deposit and withdrawal, this time for three thousand dollars. The trend continued until a month when the deposit was much smaller than usual and the balance at the end of the month was less than a hundred dollars. The following month, the deposit was even smaller and the ending balance even lower.

"I suspect Knight was running out of money at this point, and that's about when he married Priscilla and got access to her money," Elizabeth said, pointing to a date in the ledger shortly after the lowest monthly balance.

Within a few days of the wedding, Knight had deposited another substantial amount of money into the account and made another large payment to the person or business indicated by the mysterious letters.

"Priscilla told me he sold his house when they got married, or at least he told her he did, so that would account for some of the money he used after they married, but obviously, if she's now penniless, he used her money, too."

"Priscilla should have consulted an attorney before she married Knight. He would have advised her to put some of her first husband's money into a trust for the children," Gideon said, still scanning the ledger entries and seeing the same pattern of huge amounts of money being paid out with no logical explanation.

"I don't think Priscilla ever really intended to marry Knight, though."

"What?" Gideon looked up from the figures in amazement.

"She was devastated when her first husband died, and she said she doesn't remember much from that time. Everything seemed foggy, she said. But Reverend Honesdale and his wife called on her almost daily, and Mrs. Honesdale kept telling her she needed a man to take care of her and the children. Then, even though Priscilla doesn't remember ever agreeing to it, one day they showed up with Knight and a witness and performed the ceremony."

"Just like that?"

"Just like that. She was so embarrassed, because her first husband hadn't even been dead four months. She knew people would talk, but she had no explanation for how she'd ended up remarried so quickly. She doesn't even remember Knight proposing to her."

"And you say Reverend Honesdale performed the ceremony?"

"Yes."

"None of this makes any sense at all."

"Doesn't it?" Elizabeth asked. "What do those large payments suggest to you?"

"Not a con," Gideon said. "Nobody would fall for a con so many times, over several years, again and again."

"You might be surprised, but in this case, I think you're right. So why would someone be making large payments like that over and over?"

"Debts, maybe. Gambling debts, but I've never heard a hint of scandal about Endicott Knight. If anything, he was always somewhat of a mama's boy."

"He was? What's his mother like?"

"A real harridan, but she's dead."

"When did she die?"

"I don't know. Several years ago, I think."

"Maybe he started sowing some wild oats after she died."

"If he did, he was very discreet. And he was an elder in the church, which is quite an honor for someone so young. He wouldn't have been named elder if he was a known gambler."

"What else could it be, then?"

He wasn't fooled by her wide-eyed innocence. "I think you already have an opinion."

"Of course I do. I just wanted to see if you agreed."

Gideon sighed wearily. "Even though I can't imagine why, I think he was being blackmailed."

"That does explain the payments. Which is the problem with blackmail. It never ends."

"Which is why no one should ever pay in the

first place. But what could someone like Knight have done to attract a blackmailer?"

He should not have been surprised when Elizabeth reached into the valise again and pulled out an envelope. It was addressed to Knight and had been opened. He pulled out a photograph and peered at it for a long moment before he comprehended what he was seeing. Then he gasped and instantly turned the photograph over and slapped it onto his desk. "Did you see this?"

"Yes, unfortunately, which is why I was pretty certain he was being blackmailed. There's a letter, too." She nodded at the envelope he still held.

He pulled the letter out and read it. In simple block letters it said, "Just a reminder."

"I assume the man in the photograph is Knight," Elizabeth said. "I never met him, and I didn't want to ask Priscilla."

"Good heavens, no. She must never see this. But yes, it's Knight." He rubbed his eyes in a vain effort to erase the image of the photograph.

"And the, uh, woman?"

"I have no idea, but I'm guessing the photograph was taken in a brothel."

"Really? Is that what goes on at brothels?" she asked with far too much interest.

He gave her what he hoped was a disapproving frown. "I couldn't say. I have no personal experience."

"But I'm sure you've heard rumors."

"Of course I have, but *you* don't need to hear them."

She looked as if she wanted to disagree but thought better of it. "All right. So Mr. Knight was being blackmailed, and he used up his entire fortune and then married Priscilla practically against her will and used up hers as well."

"The man was a cad," Gideon said, not bothering to hide his anger now. How could anyone do something so despicable?

"And he got the Honesdales to help him."

Gideon had been thinking of all the things he'd like to do to Knight but would never have the opportunity, and he almost missed what she'd said. "What?"

"I said, the Honesdales helped him."

"I doubt that. He's a minister."

"But Mrs. Honesdale convinced Priscilla she needed to remarry."

"Because Priscilla was . . ."

"Because she was penniless?" Elizabeth guessed when he hesitated. "Because she *wasn't* penniless, as I have just shown you. She said she would have been fine with what her first husband left her, and we now know Knight was the one who was penniless. So who told you she married Knight for his money?"

"I'm trying to remember. I think I heard it from more than one source. There was a lot of talk when she remarried so quickly."

"Could it have been from the Honesdales?"

"I don't believe I've ever heard either of them gossip. That would be fatal for a minister, I think. If people thought he couldn't be trusted, they'd never confide in him."

"And your mother tells me people confess everything to ministers."

"Probably not everything, but a lot, I'm sure."

"Do you think Mr. Knight would have confessed *that?*" She gestured toward the photograph still lying facedown on his desk. Gideon hoped it wouldn't leave a scorch mark.

"If he did, I can't imagine why Honesdale would allow a decent woman to marry him."

"Are you sure of that?"

Gideon's first instinct was to defend Honesdale, but he caught himself. "What makes you think the Reverend Honesdale would be involved in something as sordid as blackmail?"

"Nothing in particular, but it is suspicious that he and his wife played such a big role in getting Mr. Knight married to a rich widow before she'd even had a chance to mourn her dead husband. Why do you think he *wasn't* involved?"

"Because he's a man of God."

"I see."

"What does that mean?" Gideon asked uneasily.

"It just means I see your logic."

"It's more than just logic. If I heard the rumor about Priscilla being penniless, maybe

44

the Honesdales did, too. Obviously, everyone believed it, so that would explain why they encouraged Priscilla to remarry so quickly. They had her best interests at heart."

"I suppose you could be right."

"But you don't think so?"

"It doesn't matter if I do or not, and I don't really know enough about the man to judge one way or the other. In any event, none of this helps poor Priscilla in the least. If Knight squandered her fortune and his own in blackmail payments, she has little hope of recovering it."

"But we could at least find out who the blackmailer was and turn him over to the police."

"What good would that do?"

"He'd be arrested and tried and punished," Gideon said. "And he'd never be able to do this to anyone else again."

"Would he really be arrested?"

Gideon opened his mouth to assure her that he would but caught himself when he saw her skepticism. And she was right, unfortunately. He closed his mouth with a snap.

"Just as I thought," she said. "A blackmailer would think nothing of bribing the police to keep from being arrested. And even if he really was arrested and brought to trial and even found guilty, how would that help Priscilla? Would it get her money back?"

"That's . . . unlikely." The police often

confiscated money from criminals, but it rarely found its way back to the original victims.

"And imagine how the newspapers would report on a blackmail trial. They create scandals even when they don't exist. This is a real scandal, and when people find out why Mr. Knight was being blackmailed . . ." Elizabeth shuddered delicately.

Gideon winced at the thought of how the press would swarm on a story like this, like a school of hungry sharks. "But Knight is dead. Scandal won't hurt him."

"You're right, he's dead," Elizabeth said, "so Priscilla is the only one left to suffer. The scandal could certainly hurt her and her poor little girls, too. A story like that would follow them for the rest of their lives."

"And it would ruin the rest of their lives," Gideon said.

"So what can we do? How can we help her?"

Gideon could hardly bear to look at her, the woman he loved more than life itself. The woman who had every right to turn to him for help and expect to receive it. The woman he would die to protect. How could he admit that he was powerless here, that he had no answer for her? "I . . . I've never dealt with a case of blackmail before, and criminal law is not my area of expertise. Let me see what I can find out. There must be something . . . some way to help her."

"Yes, there must," she said, although she didn't sound very hopeful.

She reached for the ledger that lay in his lap, but he stopped her. "Leave these things here." He snatched up the photograph and stuck it back into its envelope. "I'll put them in my safe. We wouldn't want them falling into the wrong hands." He also didn't want her to ever see that photograph again.

"Of course." She managed a smile. "Will I see you this evening?"

"At the salon?" He smiled back, although it felt a little strained. "I'll escort Anna as usual, although I think her mother is getting the wrong idea."

"Mothers often do, but don't worry. Anna has promised not to steal you away from me."

He took her hand in his again. "No one could."

"Lizzie, you know I hate these soirées of Cybil's," the Old Man said when she opened the front door to him that evening. He'd come early, as she'd asked, and as usual, he was immaculately dressed. He really was a handsome man, even in his middle years, tall and slender with silver hair and amazingly blue eyes.

Elizabeth's Aunt Cybil and her "close friend" Zelda were busy preparing refreshments for the guests who attended the event they held every Monday evening at their ramshackle home in Chelsea. This left Elizabeth with some free time to discuss her current problem with her mentor, the Old Man.

"You don't have to stay for the salon," she told him. "I just need some advice from you. Let's go upstairs so nobody overhears us."

"This sounds serious," he said, following her up the stairs. "Has your young man proven false?"

She gave him a glare over her shoulder. "Do you really think I'd ask you for romantic advice?"

"You wound me to the quick." He laid a well-manicured hand over his chest, taking care not to dislodge the diamond stickpin he wore.

"I doubt it."

She led him into her bedroom and shut the door. He lowered himself into the stuffed chair in the corner of her well-decorated room while she sat down on the bed.

"How can I help you, my dear? Does your swain demand a larger dowry?"

"You know perfectly well he doesn't even want the one he's getting. No, this isn't about me at all. I have a friend who asked me for help." She quickly explained Priscilla's marital history and the discovery of her financial situation after the death of Mr. Knight.

"So you think someone conned him?"

"No, although that was my first thought. It turns out someone was blackmailing him."

The Old Man raised his eyebrows. "I hope you don't think I know anything about it."

"No. Blackmail is beneath you, I know." Although cons were right up his alley. "I wanted to ask you about brothels."

He shifted uncomfortably in his chair. "Why on earth do you need to know anything about brothels?"

"Because this Mr. Knight was apparently frequenting them and doing things that, well, that most people would consider shocking."

"I have observed that most people are easily shocked."

"I saw a photograph, and believe me, it would shock even you."

He frowned his disapproval, but unlike Gideon, he knew better than to express it. "And you think this is why he was being blackmailed?"

"Yes, that's pretty clear. The question is, who would know about his, uh, activities?"

He gave the matter a few moments' thought. "If his appetites are as strange as you say, I think you're correct in assuming this man would have to indulge them at a brothel. Depending on what those appetites were, he would also have to find one that specializes in his particular tastes."

"They *specialize?*" she asked in amazement.

He smiled a bit sheepishly. "I'm not sure this is an appropriate topic to discuss with a maiden lady."

"No one ever seemed to hesitate to discuss their adventures with ladies of the evening in front of me before."

"Oh dear. I must speak to the boys about being more careful when you're around."

"I won't be around them anymore," Elizabeth reminded him. "I'm a respectable lady now."

"A respectable lady who wants to know how brothels specialize," he added with some amusement.

Elizabeth sighed in frustration. "Are you going to answer my questions or not?"

"I suppose so. There's no telling who you might ask if I don't, and I don't imagine young Gideon would approve."

"Young Gideon doesn't have experience in this area."

He raised his eyebrows again but had the good sense to say nothing.

"So," she continued, "they *specialize?*"

He sighed in defeat. "Some do. Men with, uh, unusual appetites require cooperation from the, uh, bawds they hire. And, sometimes, uh, special skills." He shrugged apologetically. "They also require a certain level of confidentiality. All of this costs money, too. A lot of money."

"Because a man would be ruined if people found out," she mused, "and that would also make the men vulnerable to blackmail."

"As your Mr. Knight apparently was."

"Who would blackmail him, though?"

"I don't know much about blackmail. It's not a crime people talk about, as you can imagine.

But I suppose anyone who found out his secrets could do it, although I'm sure he took great pains to ensure that no one did."

"So it would have to be someone at the brothel."

"Maybe. That seems logical, but he might have confessed to a friend."

"Or a minister," she mused.

"Did you say minister?"

"Yes, he was a church elder."

"Ah, so he had even more reason than most to hide his unusual tastes."

"Unless he was confessing to unburden himself."

"I can't help you there. I've never been tempted to unburden myself, and certainly never to a minister."

She smiled at that. "I'm sure you haven't."

"So, when is the wedding? I thought young Gideon would be quite eager to take you for his bride."

"We have to wait a bit. He can't be seen to be snatching up his best friend's discarded fiancée."

"Why not? If his best friend was foolish enough to let you slip away . . ."

"It's one of those strange rules they have in society."

"They have a lot of them, I assume."

"More than you can imagine. Some woman wrote a whole book about them."

"Dear Lord. But I suppose you think Gideon is worth it all."

"He is."

"Will he be here this evening?"

"Yes."

"Good. I want to have a word with him."

"About what?" she asked in alarm.

"I haven't decided yet."

"Your father keeps glaring at me," Gideon whispered to Elizabeth when he managed to catch her alone in the hallway later that evening. The crowd at the salon tonight was smaller than usual, only about a dozen people, which meant he had at least a chance of having Elizabeth all to himself for a few moments.

"Don't call him that," she scolded him. "Someone might hear you." But she was smiling, so he knew she was teasing.

"What's he doing here anyway? He doesn't seem interested in talking to anyone."

"He said he wanted to talk to *you*."

Gideon managed not to groan aloud. "Why?"

"He didn't confide in me. Go sit with Miss Adams. She's been left all alone on the sofa."

He glanced into the parlor, where the ancient Miss Adams sat in solitary splendor. "All she ever wants to talk about is poetry."

"Good, then you'll be safe from my father with her."

"Don't call him that," Gideon countered with a grin. "Someone might hear you."

He was heading into the parlor, Elizabeth's laughter tinkling behind him, when the Old Man stepped out in front of him and blocked his way.

"Step outside with me a moment, will you? I'd like to smoke," he said.

Gideon could have pointed out that it was freezing outside and, besides, he didn't smoke, but instead he found his overcoat amid the jumble on the coat tree and followed the Old Man out onto the large front porch. He was, after all, Elizabeth's father.

"Elizabeth said you wanted to talk to me," Gideon said as the Old Man pulled out a cigar, cut off the end and lit it, puffing furiously to get it started.

When he had finished with the ritual and the cigar was burning to his satisfaction, he said, "Lizzie asked me about brothels."

Gideon swore under his breath. "I told her I would handle all that."

"She said you don't have much experience in the matter."

"That doesn't mean—"

"I don't either, at least not in the kind of brothels she was interested in."

"She *told* you?" Gideon asked, not sure if he was more angry or horrified.

"Not the details. Her mother raised her to be a lady, in spite of the education she got from me. All she said was the man in question had rather odd tastes."

"Indeed he did."

"She said there was a photograph."

"She didn't describe it, did she?" Gideon asked with renewed horror.

"No, and I'm disappointed that you allowed her to see it," he said mildly.

"I didn't *allow* her to do anything, since I knew nothing about any of this until she brought it to me and started asking *me* about brothels!" Gideon said in a furious whisper.

The Old Man calmly puffed on his cigar. "Yes, of course. Well, there's no remedy for it now. The question is, how do we throw her off the scent?"

"You mean you think you can convince her to forget about helping her friend?"

The Old Man smiled slightly. "You make it sound impossible."

"It is impossible. And what is also impossible is getting her friend's money back from a blackmailer, but that's what she wants to do."

"Is it, now?"

"Yes, it is. After she showed me what she'd found, I talked to some of my partners in the firm. None of them had ever dealt with a blackmailer, either, but they all agreed it was foolhardy to even try, because—as we already determined—the very reason the blackmail took place is because the victim wanted to avoid scandal, and exposing the blackmailer also exposes the scandal."

The Old Man didn't reply for a long moment,

allowing Gideon to think he'd stymied him. But only for a moment. "I wonder if it's possible to blackmail a blackmailer."

"What?"

"You know, beat him at his own game."

"You mean find out a secret about him and threaten to expose it?"

The Old Man puffed on his cigar again. "That's my understanding of how it works."

Gideon considered the concept for a few moments of his own. "If you've got the stomach for it, I suppose it could work, but first you'd have to find out who the blackmailer is."

"Ah, yes, and you don't know, do you?"

"I don't, and Elizabeth doesn't. The widow doesn't, either. She also doesn't know her husband was being blackmailed. She doesn't even know about her husband's, uh, perversions."

"I think I'd like to see this photograph."

"Why?" Gideon asked suspiciously.

"Not to blackmail anyone," the Old Man assured him with a smile. "They've already been bled dry, in any case. No, I'd like to get an idea of what kind of brothel we're looking for."

"*We?*"

"Did I say 'we'? I meant you. You and Lizzie, although I don't like to think of her looking for brothels."

"She won't be."

"That's why I taught her the grift, you know,"

55

he said, staring out into the darkened street. "I didn't want her involved in my business. I hope you believe that. But her mother died, and I did the best I could, but I knew I wouldn't always be around. Life is uncertain for a female alone. She can't be sure she'll find a good man to take care of her. Far too many men are like this fellow we're talking about. Idiots, the lot of them. And a young woman on her own . . . Well, it's hard for a woman to support herself honestly. I wanted to make sure she'd never be taken advantage of, if you know what I mean."

Gideon found himself in the awkward position of feeling obliged to thank this man for turning his fiancée into a con artist. "I'm sure she's very grateful" was as close as he could come, however.

"Oh, I know what you think of me. I sometimes think the same things, but I took care of my wife and my children, and when I'm gone, they'll be provided for. How many men can say that?"

A lot, Gideon hoped, but he didn't say it aloud. "So you think if we could figure out who the blackmailer is . . . ?"

"That we could blackmail him in return? I think it might be the only hope of getting this poor woman's money back."

"So that means we need to figure out where the dead man went for his entertainment."

"Which is why I need to know more about him.

That photograph—I don't suppose you have it with you?"

"Of course not! It's locked up in my office."

"Then tell me about it."

Gideon glanced around to make sure no one was near enough to hear. Then he whispered the awful details to the Old Man.

He whistled. "I don't expect many places cater to things like that."

"Then it should be easy to find them."

"Easy? Do you think they're listed in the city directory?" the Old Man asked, amused.

"Well, no, but . . ."

"And don't look at me. My tastes run to a feather bed and a willing wench. Nothing exotic about that. You're going to have a hard time finding the kind of place you're looking for, because everything about them is a secret that the men who use them pass by word of mouth and only to people they know and trust."

Gideon frowned. The men at his club often joked about various houses of ill repute but he'd never heard anyone mention one that catered to the kind of appetites Endicott Knight had had. Short of ruining his own reputation by inquiring outright about such places, he didn't have the slightest idea of where to start.

Before he could mention this to the Old Man, the front door opened and Elizabeth stepped out.

"It's freezing," she said, instantly wrapping her

arms around herself against the chill. "What are you two doing out here so long?"

"Discussing your little problem," the Old Man said. "We've decided we might be able to blackmail the blackmailer, if we can figure out who he is."

"What a marvelous idea!" she exclaimed.

"Gideon thought of it," the Old Man said, earning a black look from Gideon, which he ignored. "But we need to know more about this fellow. Who his friends were. That sort of thing. They'll know something."

"His widow doesn't know any of his friends, except for the people he knew at church," Elizabeth said.

Gideon sniffed. "I hardly think Reverend Honesdale and the other elders will be of much help with this."

"Who?" the Old Man said in surprise.

"Reverend Honesdale," Elizabeth said. "He's the minister at—"

But the Old Man was laughing.

"What's so funny?" Gideon demanded.

"I think your job just got a lot easier, son. There's a man who owns several brothels in the city, the regular kind you understand, but maybe he also runs some of the more secret kind, and his name happens to be Matthew Honesdale."

CHAPTER THREE

Elizabeth tried not to smile knowingly when she said to Gideon, "Your minister owns a brothel?"

But Gideon's handsome face, which she loved so dearly, was creased into a puzzled frown. "Reverend Honesdale's given name is Peter."

"A relative, perhaps," the Old Man said. "It's not a common name."

"But . . ." Gideon shook his head in silent denial. "The Honesdales are a family of divines. His father is a minister, and his grandfather was before him."

"A black sheep cousin, then. You should ask him."

"I'm not going to ask a minister if his family owns whorehouses," Gideon said, and Elizabeth was very much afraid he was getting truly angry.

"Not Reverend Honesdale," she said quickly. "Ask this Matthew."

"Ask him if he's a blackmailer?" Gideon was incredulous.

She had no answer for that.

"Maybe one of your clients left him a legacy and you need to see him," the Old Man said.

"Who would . . . ? Oh, I see. I should lie to him."

"It's not unheard of," the Old Man said slyly. He knew about Gideon's aversion to lying.

"You don't have to lie," Elizabeth said. "Tell him his name came up when you were settling an estate. That's perfectly true."

"And *then* I ask him if he's a blackmailer?" Gideon asked, not bothering to hide his annoyance.

"Perhaps not at your very first meeting," the Old Man said. He was enjoying Gideon's discomfort far too much for Elizabeth's taste. "But you can get a feel for the man and at least see his reaction when you mention this poor fellow's name. You might even show him the photograph."

"And what? Ask him if he recognizes the people in it?"

"Or see if he flinches. The man owns whorehouses, as you pointed out. He won't be easily shocked, but not many men could look at what you described without reacting."

"I see," Gideon said. "And if he doesn't react, then I'll know he's familiar with such things."

"Getting him to admit it might be difficult, but you'll at least have a clue to how involved he is."

"Good, that's settled," Elizabeth said. "Can we go inside now?"

"Of course." Gideon quickly slipped his arm around her to escort her back into the house. "I'm sorry. I should have given you my coat."

"Yes, you should have."

The Old Man, still puffing on his cigar, made

no move to follow, but he did say, "Give your charming mother my regards, son."

Elizabeth chose not to notice how Gideon stiffened at the sentiment.

"There you are," Anna said, emerging from the parlor to find them in the hallway. "Were you outside canoodling?"

"Hardly," Gideon said grumpily, hanging his coat back on the coat tree.

"Consulting with the Old Man on some business," Elizabeth said. "What have you been doing?"

"Discussing Wordsworth with Miss Adams. She hates Wordsworth."

"Oh dear."

"I hate Wordsworth, too, but that's beside the point. The point is that you two have been up to something and I know nothing about it." Anna pretended to pout.

Elizabeth glanced at Gideon and caught a panicked expression on his face. Plainly, he did not want to explain Endicott Knight and his predicament to his best friend's younger sister. "It's Priscilla Knight," Elizabeth said to rescue him. "She . . . There are some problems with her late husband's estate."

"And you're helping her?" Anna asked Gideon.

"I'm trying to," he hedged.

Anna gave Elizabeth a shrewd look. "And Mr. Miles is helping you."

All of them knew perfectly well no reputable attorney would consult a con artist for assistance in the usual course of things.

"It's a very unusual case," Elizabeth offered.

Anna smiled sweetly. "It must be."

"Is Miss Adams alone? I should go sit with her," Gideon said with a notable air of desperation.

"Yes, do," Anna said. "Just don't mention Wordsworth."

Gideon fled, the coward, leaving the woman he supposedly loved to deal with Anna's curiosity. Elizabeth would enjoy getting her revenge for this.

"You look lovely tonight," Elizabeth said in an effort to distract her friend.

"Everyone says that, and not just tonight. It's become a constant theme. It's flattering, of course, but honestly, if everyone is noticing the improvement, I must have looked like a mud hen before."

"Before what?"

"Before I murdered you, I think. At least, that's about the time people started noticing me and telling me I looked lovely."

Elizabeth sighed. She would always regret involving Anna in faking her own death, but at the time, it had been the only way to make sure the man she was conning wouldn't ever return and really try to kill her. "I suppose committing murder does wonders for one's complexion."

"I don't think it's my complexion. Unless it's true that bathing in the blood of virgins keeps you young or something."

"Where on earth did you hear that?"

"Oh, I read it in a book Zelda lent me."

"Good heavens. But you haven't really been bathing in the blood of virgins, have you?"

"No, and not in any other kind of blood, either. All I did was pretend to murder you. You were the one who had the blood on you, and it was only chicken blood. So why do you think people are suddenly noticing that *I'm* lovely?"

"Because you are. But don't let it go to your head."

"You sound like my mother," Anna complained.

"Pride goes before a fall."

"Which is also what my mother always says. So how would murdering someone make me prettier?"

"It's your confidence, I think. You . . . you're braver. Yes, I'm sure that's it."

"Really? When we were in jail, I told you I wished I could be brave like you."

"And now you are, and people are noticing."

"But don't think for a moment that you're distracting me from my purpose," Anna said. "What are you and Gideon up to?"

"Nothing you can help with, I'm afraid." She glanced around to make sure they were still alone. "Priscilla Knight's late husband was being blackmailed."

"Blackmailed!" Anna exclaimed too loudly, then clapped a hand over her mouth as if to stifle herself.

"Yes, and now he's dead, so there's nothing to be done about it."

Anna considered this for a moment. "Then why were you consulting your father about it?"

Drat. Anna was much too smart for her own good. Or for Elizabeth's good. "He apparently spent all of his and Priscilla's money paying the blackmail, leaving her with nothing."

"Was Mr. Miles the blackmailer?"

"Of course not!" The Old Man was far from perfect, but he wouldn't stoop that low. Or at least Elizabeth hoped he wouldn't.

"Then why—"

"Gideon thought he might know how to deal with a blackmailer, but he doesn't. No more questions, please! This whole situation is very painful for Priscilla." Or at least it would be when she found out. If only she never had to.

"Oh, I'm sorry. Of course it is. How awful, although it's hard to believe Endicott Knight ever did anything he could be blackmailed for."

"Why do you say that?"

"He was so boring. He hardly ever had two words to say to anyone. I could never figure out why Priscilla married him."

"Really? Didn't you hear any gossip about it?"

"Hmmm. Yes, now that you mention it. I think

someone said Mr. Jenks hadn't left her anything and she had to remarry quickly."

"Who told you that?"

"I . . . You know, I can't remember."

"Think hard."

Anna brightened. "Is it important?"

"It could be."

"Well, then, let me see . . ."

"Was it Mrs. Honesdale?"

Anna frowned. "She doesn't gossip."

"What do you mean, she doesn't gossip? Everyone gossips."

"She doesn't approve of it. I suppose being the minister's wife, she has to be above suspicion and all that."

This didn't fit Elizabeth's theory at all, which meant Anna must be mistaken. "She never says anything about anyone? Even for their own good?"

"Oh no. She always says . . ."

"What does she say?" Elizabeth prodded when Anna hesitated.

"How interesting."

"What's interesting?"

"I never realized it until this moment, but . . . You see, she always scolds people for gossiping, but she still . . ."

Elizabeth wanted to shake her. "What does she still do?"

"She still manages to say things. Now that you've forced me to think about it, I realize it *was*

Mrs. Honesdale who told me Priscilla had been left penniless, except she never really said that."

"What did she say?"

"Nothing of consequence. I mean, people were very surprised when Mrs. Knight remarried so quickly and of course they were talking about it."

"I know, expressing their surprise while really expressing their shock and disapproval."

"Exactly. So Mrs. Honesdale scolded them for thinking badly of Mrs. Knight. She said . . . I'm not sure I remember exactly what she said, but something about how difficult it was for a widow left alone with no resources. At least that was the meaning, and we all understood she was chastening us for judging Mrs. Knight so harshly when she really had no other recourse."

"How very clever. I'll have to remember that."

"And it worked beautifully. All the gossip stopped, or at least the disapproval of her hasty remarriage. Everyone was too busy wondering how DeForrest Jenks had managed to run through all his money."

"So Mrs. Honesdale didn't stop the gossip at all. She just redirected it."

"I suppose so, but no one thought badly of Mrs. Knight anymore."

"And it looks like Mrs. Honesdale did Mrs. Knight a good turn, except for one thing."

"What's that?"

"DeForrest Jenks did not run through his

fortune, and he did not leave Priscilla penniless. In fact, she was quite well off."

"Really? Where would Mrs. Honesdale get the idea that she wasn't?"

"I have no idea."

"And now I *really* don't understand why Priscilla married Mr. Knight."

Elizabeth wasn't going to explain it to her. She didn't want Anna mixed up in this sordid mess. "I never met the man, but maybe he was quite charming when you got to know him."

"That's right, he died right before we went to Washington, and we didn't even know you then. Priscilla wanted to go with us, you know, but Mr. Knight died, and, well, a woman in full mourning can't demonstrate outside the White House."

"Is that really a rule? I don't remember reading it in Mrs. Ordway's book."

"I doubt Mrs. Ordway's book has a chapter on the etiquette of demonstrating for women's suffrage, but widows in full mourning are hardly allowed to leave their homes, so I'm sure demonstrating would be frowned upon."

"You're probably right. I'm sure Priscilla wasn't sorry to have missed our subsequent stay at the workhouse, though."

"Or the hunger strike, but you'd be amazed how many women have told me they envied me for my experiences."

"That's only because they didn't share them."

"What are you two doing out here?" Cybil asked, coming into the hallway from the kitchen. Elizabeth's aunt enjoyed dressing exotically, which she could not normally do in her position as a professor at Hunter College but which she always did at her Monday evening salons. Tonight she wore a red silk Japanese kimono and embroidered satin slippers. Her gray-streaked hair was twisted in a knot on top of her head and held in place by long, black lacquered sticks.

"We're gossiping," Anna told her. "Because Elizabeth is trying very hard to distract me from finding out what she and Gideon are up to."

"Do you think they're planning an elopement?" Cybil asked hopefully.

"Nothing so romantic, and Gideon would never elope. He's far too stodgy and traditional."

"But he is quite charming when you get to know him," Elizabeth countered.

"He certainly is," Cybil said loyally. "Do you realize he's in there talking to Miss Adams? He's a saint."

A lily-livered saint, but Elizabeth wasn't going to admit it.

The front door opened and the Old Man stepped inside, bringing a burst of cold air with him.

"Buster, are you still here?" Cybil said.

"Obviously." He frowned at her use of his childhood nickname. She was the only person alive who dared use it.

"I believe this is the longest you've ever stayed at one of my salons."

"A record I will most likely never break. Miss Vanderslice, you are looking lovely this evening."

Anna gave Elizabeth a knowing glance. "Thank you, Mr. Miles. I hope you are well."

"I am. How is your charming mother?"

"As charming as ever. There seems to be an abundance of that lately."

"Are you leaving? I would be happy to escort you home."

"You don't need an excuse to leave, Buster," Cybil said.

"I was thinking Gideon might want to spend more time with Elizabeth this evening."

"More time to plot or more time to canoodle?" Anna asked slyly.

"There will be no canoodling on my watch," Cybil said.

"So plotting it is," Anna said. "I suppose it is getting late, Mr. Miles, and I'm sure my mother would be delighted to offer you some refreshment for delivering me safely."

"Won't she be surprised to see him?" Elizabeth said. "The last she heard of him, he'd been arrested."

"Oh, we never told her any of that. As far as she knows, Mr. Miles is still upstanding General Sterling."

"General Sterling?" Cybil echoed in confusion.

"It was a con," Elizabeth explained, waving away her concern. "The Old Man had to pretend to be a general."

"Did he con Anna's poor mother?" Cybil asked in dismay.

"Oh no!" Elizabeth assured her. "Someone else entirely, but Anna's mother still thinks he's a general, and David thinks General Sterling was arrested."

"What a tangled web we weave . . ." Cybil recited gleefully.

The Old Man sighed dramatically. "I can see I will have to leave you to Gideon's care, then, Miss Vanderslice. Cybil, it has been a pleasure as always." He turned to Elizabeth and gave her a kiss on the cheek. "Keep me posted on your progress." Since he already had his overcoat on, he took his leave.

"Elizabeth, you aren't doing anything you shouldn't, are you?" Cybil asked, concerned again.

"Not at all." At least she hoped not.

The next morning, Elizabeth went to Gideon's office, where they could discuss the blackmail situation without worrying about being overheard. This time Gideon's clerk greeted her warmly and ushered her right into Gideon's office.

"Did I have an appointment?" she asked when Gideon had kissed her thoroughly.

"I told Smith that we are secretly engaged and he is to treat you with every courtesy."

"Can he be trusted?"

"Smith would carry our secret to his grave if necessary."

"Goodness, I hadn't planned on quite that long of an engagement."

"I assure you, it will not be one moment longer than absolutely necessary."

Placated, Elizabeth took one of the client chairs and Gideon took the other. "What are you planning to do about Matthew Honesdale?" she asked.

He took one of her hands in his. "I could hardly sleep last night for thinking about it. I can't think of any way to approach him that he's likely to respond to."

"What about the estate question the Old Man suggested?"

"It might work to get him to my office, but what do I say once he's here? I can hardly accuse him of blackmail the minute he walks in the door. No man would sit still for that."

"No, he wouldn't."

"And he's certainly not mentioned in Endicott Knight's will, or at least I don't think so, and even if he was, I'm not handling Knight's estate. If he wants to see the will, I couldn't show him anything."

"Even if you were willing to lie and claim he's

inheriting half the estate," Elizabeth finished the thought for him. "How about if you don't say anything at all but just introduce him to Mrs. Knight?"

"Are you suggesting I bring poor Priscilla in to meet this . . . this . . . ?"

"Pimp?" she said helpfully.

"Elizabeth, really . . ."

"I'm sorry." And she was. He was blushing furiously. "And no, I'm not suggesting you involve Priscilla at all. Presumably, he's never met her, so any heavily veiled female would do."

"But who . . . ?" he began and caught himself when the truth dawned. "Oh no, I'm not going to bring you in here to meet a . . . a *pimp,* either."

"I'm far less innocent than Priscilla, and nothing he says can hurt me, since I'm not really Knight's widow."

"You have no idea what he might say. I refuse to subject you to that."

"He's probably going to be on his good behavior, since he's in a fancy attorney's office and he's meeting a respectable female."

"You can't possibly know that."

"And he's related to a family of divines—that's what you called them, isn't it?—so presumably he knows how to act in polite company."

"We don't even know for sure he's related to anyone."

"For heaven's sake, he's not going to attack me

72

in front of you and with an office full of other men ready to rush to my defense if I so much as cry out."

"I'm more concerned with what he might say."

"Probably nothing I haven't already heard. I spent a good part of my youth at Dan the Dude's Saloon with a bunch of grifters, Gideon."

Gideon rubbed his free hand over his face. "Why won't you let me protect you?"

"You can protect me all you want from real dangers. This Matthew Honesdale is no threat to me. If he starts insulting me or being disrespectful, I'll simply walk out. That's what Priscilla would do, certainly, and no lady would endure it."

"All right, suppose I agree to this . . . this charade. What are you going to say to him?"

Oh dear, he had her there. "I guess I was thinking we could see how he reacts and then just play along."

"What if he doesn't react at all? What if he's never heard of Priscilla Knight or Endicott Knight?"

"Then we show him the photograph and ask him what he knows about that sort of thing."

"Dear heaven."

"He's bound to know something, even if it's just where people like that go."

"And even if he does, why would he tell us?"

"He might take pity on a poor widow."

"If he has any respect for you at all, he won't say a word!"

"Gideon, I can make him tell us whatever he knows. I know you don't like to think about it, but getting people to trust me and share their deepest secrets is something a grifter is trained to do. It's something I'm trained to do, and I can do it well."

"You're right, I don't like to think about it, and I especially don't like to see it."

"Not even when it's for a good cause?"

"Is this a good cause?"

"Yes, it is." She didn't bother to hide her frustration with him. "Priscilla Knight is the only woman in your church besides Anna and your mother who treats me like an equal. I didn't even meet her until she was in mourning, and I've only seen her at church and when your mother and I make condolence calls on her, but she has been unfailingly kind and welcoming to me. She is my friend, and I will not stand by and see her the victim of some unspeakable injustice if there's something I can do to help."

"I—"

"And furthermore, aren't you required, as a Christian man, to look after widows and orphans? Priscilla has two defenseless daughters who will suffer for the rest of their lives unless we help them."

"You know I want to help Priscilla and her daughters. I also want to keep you safe."

"Then help me. I could probably find Matthew Honesdale on my own, but that hardly seems like a good idea."

"You wouldn't dare!"

Elizabeth smiled. "No, because I won't have to if you help me."

She was sure he was grinding his teeth, but he said, "You'll be heavily veiled."

"Yes."

"And you'll leave the instant he becomes abusive or insulting."

"Of course."

"Are you going to tell Priscilla anything?"

"Nothing at all, at least not until we must, and I hope we never have to, because I'm sure we'll convince the blackmailer to return her money. We just need to figure out a way to do it."

Gideon sighed, not gracious in defeat but at least resigned. "You realize that's probably impossible."

"Yes," she lied. Where money changing hands was concerned, nothing was really impossible.

"All right. I'll send you word when I've heard from this Matthew Honesdale, but don't be disappointed if he completely ignores my request for a meeting."

"How could he when he thinks he might have inherited money unexpectedly? I don't care who you are, that's always good news."

75

"Is anything interesting going on in the world?" Gideon asked his mother that evening when he found her reading the newspaper in the parlor.

"Oh yes," she said with great enthusiasm. "Several members of the National Woman's Party testified before the House Woman Suffrage Committee on Saturday. We're hoping President Wilson will keep his promise to support a constitutional amendment."

"That's good news, but I was thinking about the war." She had been sitting in one of the chairs by the gas fire, and he took the one opposite her, holding out his hands to warm them.

"Nothing much, I'm afraid. It seems like both armies are still just hunkering down and trying not to freeze to death in their trenches. I'm so grateful you were too old for the draft."

"Too old for the *first* draft," he reminded her. "I'm sure there will be others before this is over."

"Don't say that. Now that we've got American boys over there, surely they'll make an end to it quickly."

"We don't have many American boys over there yet."

"It won't be long before we do. We've been in it since last April."

"But we didn't get our first troops over until just before Christmas."

His mother sighed and let the newspaper slide

to the floor. "Let's talk about something more pleasant. Did you enjoy the salon last night?"

"I don't think I could claim that."

His mother smiled at that. "I'm sure you enjoyed seeing Elizabeth."

"Of course, although we never get much opportunity to even speak to each other with so many other people around. Mr. Miles was there last night, too."

His mother brightened instantly. "Was he? He's such a delightful man."

"Delightful" was not a word Gideon would have used to describe his future father-in-law, and he frowned his disapproval. "He . . . he sends his regards."

"We should have him for dinner."

Gideon made no comment at all to that.

He picked up the newspaper she had dropped, and she gave him a few minutes to glance over it before she said, "Did Elizabeth tell you about our visit with Priscilla Knight on Sunday?"

Gideon froze. He and Elizabeth had agreed not to tell Priscilla of their plans, but they hadn't even thought about what to tell his mother. He folded the newspaper up very carefully, and when he was finished, he said, "I know all about it, Mother. Elizabeth came to see me yesterday after she went through Endicott Knight's papers."

"Did she find something then? Something that will help Priscilla?"

He couldn't think of any reason not to tell her. He knew she could keep a confidence, and she'd never hurt one of her friends. He would just have to censor the more salacious details. "She found out that Knight was being blackmailed."

"Blackmailed? What on earth for?"

"Let's just say his behavior wasn't all we have come to expect from a church elder. Someone apparently found out, someone with even fewer scruples than Knight, and was blackmailing him."

"So that's why . . . Oh dear, did he really spend all of Priscilla's money on blackmail?"

"Hers and all of his before he married her. In fact, that seems to be *why* he married her."

"To get access to her funds? How despicable!"

"Exactly."

"How could anyone do such a thing? I mean, I can understand he did something of which he was ashamed. I don't suppose you're going to tell me what it was."

"Absolutely not."

"So it was heinous indeed, and naturally, he'd want to keep it a secret, but to drag an innocent woman into it, and her children, too. Those poor little girls."

"Elizabeth hasn't told Priscilla about the blackmail yet, so don't say anything."

"But she'll have to know eventually, won't she? If only to explain what happened to her money."

Gideon carefully considered his reply. Should he tell her what he and Elizabeth had discussed? It seemed cruel to give her hope when they really had no plan at all for getting Priscilla's money back. No real plan at least, and probably no real hope, either. But if he needed an ally to help keep Elizabeth from putting herself in danger, his mother would be perfect for the task. She couldn't help if she didn't know, though, so he said, "Elizabeth thinks if we can find the blackmailer, we might be able to get at least some of Priscilla's money back."

"Good heavens. I don't know much about blackmail, but it seems unlikely someone like that would be so generous."

"I didn't say they'd *give* it back. I said we'd get it back."

"How?"

"We're, uh, not sure yet."

Unfortunately, he wasn't quite able to meet his mother's eye, which made her suspicious. *"Gideon?"*

"We have no plan." This was perfectly true.

"And were you discussing this with Mr. Miles?"

"He is aware of the situation, but I'm happy to say he is completely ignorant of the crime of blackmail and had no advice to offer."

"I see."

He was very much afraid she did, but he said,

"Elizabeth has more faith in human nature than seems justified, I'm afraid. She seems to think the blackmailer can be persuaded to return some of the money if properly motivated."

"How does one properly motivate a blackmailer?"

"Since I am also completely ignorant of the crime of blackmail, I don't know at this point."

"Poor Priscilla. She will be devastated." Plainly, she had no faith in Gideon's ability to help her. They were agreed on that, at least.

"I'm sure her friends will stand by her," he said weakly.

"I certainly will, although I'm not sure how much comfort that will be. Is there anything I can do in the meantime?"

"Not that I know of, but promise me you will help if I have to convince Elizabeth she's putting herself in danger."

His mother frowned. "I'm not sure your idea of danger and Elizabeth's will agree. Her background is much different from yours, remember."

"That's true, but now she's one of us." He gestured to indicate their house and their world.

"Is she?"

"What does that mean?"

"I'm not sure Elizabeth will ever truly be 'one of us.'"

"Of course she will."

"Gideon, do you hear what you're saying?"

"Of course I do. Elizabeth has put her past behind her."

"Is that what you want her to do?"

"I certainly don't want her to keep cheating people."

"I can't imagine that she will, but that doesn't mean she's going to change completely."

"I don't want her to change completely."

"What do you want, then?"

"I . . ." How had he gotten into this conversation? "I don't want her to change at all."

"Of course you don't. You love her because of who and what she is."

"But I do expect her to behave in a seemly manner and not put herself in danger."

"What, exactly, do you mean by 'seemly'?"

"Well . . ." He knew what he meant. He just wasn't sure how to explain it. "She would conduct herself like a lady, I suppose."

"A lady like me, for instance?"

"Yes, that's it." His mother was a perfect example.

"Gideon, a few short weeks ago your perfect, ladylike mother was in jail."

"Yes, but—"

"And being abused by guards and on a hunger strike. I was in a *lot* of danger."

"That was different."

"In what way?"

"It was for a good cause, for women's suffrage."

"And Elizabeth was with me."

"Yes, but—"

"I'm sure Elizabeth has no intention of putting herself in danger for no reason."

"Of course not."

"She will also have no intention of becoming a simpering, bloodless society matron who spends her energies serving tea and spreading gossip, which I very much fear is what you have in mind for her."

"That . . . that's not true," he tried, although it stung to think how close she was to the mark. But Elizabeth could never be simpering or bloodless, could she? And it was a husband's duty to protect his wife, after all.

"I hope it's not true, for your sake," she said. "Because Elizabeth will never fit into that role, and if you try to force her, you will lose."

CHAPTER FOUR

Elizabeth hadn't slept well the night before. She kept remembering her argument with Gideon in his office over how they could help Priscilla. They hadn't actually been angry, of course, at least not at each other. And the argument had nothing to do with them personally or their relationship, and Gideon had been his usual self the evening before at the salon. He'd even discussed the situation with the Old Man, which she knew would have been difficult for him.

But she still felt unsettled. Part of it was knowing that they really had no idea how to deal with a blackmailer, even if they managed to identify him. The other part was Gideon's reaction to the situation. She appreciated his concern for her, but didn't he know by now that she was no fragile society girl he had to shield from the slightest unpleasantness?

But he certainly did know that. He'd not only seen but participated in a ruthless con that she'd helped organize. He also knew she'd done it to save her very life. She was used to danger. So why was he suddenly treating her as if he didn't know any of that? Only one explanation made sense, but Elizabeth didn't want to believe it, so she went to the only person who might be able to put her mind at ease.

"Elizabeth, how lovely to see you," Mrs. Bates said, greeting her with a welcoming smile and a hug when the maid had escorted her into the parlor. "I was hoping you'd come to tell me what you'd discovered at Priscilla's house yesterday."

"Didn't Gideon tell you?" Surely, he had.

"Gideon told me what he thought was appropriate for me to hear," she said, "but I know there must be much more. Come and sit down. I'll ring for some tea."

When they were settled on a sofa and Mrs. Bates had rung for tea, Elizabeth said, "What did Gideon tell you?"

"That Mr. Knight was being blackmailed. He wouldn't tell me why, though."

"Of course he wouldn't. It's rather shocking."

"So I gathered. I didn't bother to ask Gideon for details. He'd want to protect me from anything untoward, and I knew I'd eventually talk to you and you'd tell me everything."

"Perhaps not *everything,*" Elizabeth said, smiling weakly.

"Good heavens, is it really so bad?"

"I'm afraid so."

"How do you know?"

"I found a photograph."

"Oh dear. Of Mr. Knight, I assume."

"Yes, of Mr. Knight and a . . . a woman. I'm

not going to describe it to you, so don't even ask."

"I wasn't going to."

"All you need to know is that he would probably have done anything to keep his behavior a secret, which is why someone was able to bleed him dry."

"They took his blood?" Mrs. Bates asked, horrified.

"Oh dear, no, that's just an expression," Elizabeth explained quickly. "But they did take all his money, apparently. He didn't have much left when he married Priscilla, and then he started using her money to pay the blackmail."

"That's what Gideon said, but how . . . ? I mean, why . . . ? Oh, I'm not sure what I mean."

"I know. It's astonishing, and it's even more astonishing when you know how Priscilla came to marry Mr. Knight."

"And we know it wasn't because she needed a husband to support her after Mr. Jenks died."

"No, it wasn't. Tell me, how well do you know Reverend and Mrs. Honesdale?"

"The Honesdales? I . . . I don't know. I never thought about it. He's been our pastor for about five years now, I think. His father is very well known in the city. The father's church is enormous, and his parishioners are quite wealthy. They do a lot of good in the city."

"Are the people in your church happy with the son?"

"I suppose. He delivers a decent sermon every week and visits the sick and does a lovely job at weddings and funerals, but . . . Well, now that you ask, he isn't very sociable. Or rather, he isn't with us. I suppose I assumed he has a circle of friends in the church with whom he does socialize and we just weren't among them, but now that I'm thinking about it, I have no idea who that might be."

A tap on the door distracted them, and the maid carried in a tea tray. Mrs. Bates served them both.

When they'd refreshed themselves, Elizabeth said, "And what about Mrs. Honesdale? What do you think of her?"

"She's always pleasant. I don't think I've ever heard anyone criticize her more than the usual pettiness over her clothes and whatever. Every minister's wife has to suffer that."

"But she's not sociable, either."

"No, I don't think she is. Of course, she's new to the church. Newer than he is, at least."

"What do you mean she's new?"

"They haven't been married very long. I'm not sure exactly how long, a year or perhaps two. Time goes so quickly, it's hard to keep track of other people's lives. But he wasn't married when he came; I do know that. We were all surprised when it was announced, because no one had even met her before they married."

"No one at all?"

"No one that I knew of, at any rate. I'm sure his family must have known her. It would be very odd if they didn't, wouldn't it?"

"I'm sure it would. And they didn't get married at your church?"

"No, it was a private ceremony, I believe. His father probably married them, or perhaps they were married in her home. At any rate, there was just a small announcement in the newspapers, and Reverend Honesdale introduced her from the pulpit one Sunday morning and that was that. What does all this have to do with Priscilla?"

"I'm not sure, but remember, Priscilla told us the Honesdales encouraged her to marry Knight."

"Yes, because they thought she was in desperate straits. But she wasn't, and she insists she had no intention of remarrying again so soon, and Mr. Knight made no effort at all to court her. But surely the Honesdales were only trying to help."

"Do you really believe they were trying to help her?"

"I know it sounds strange, but friends often do step in when they see someone in trouble, and sometimes their help isn't very . . . helpful."

Elizabeth wasn't sure she wanted any friends like that. "But forcing her to marry him?"

"I'm sure they didn't think they were forcing her. And Mr. Knight must have cared for her if he was willing to marry her."

"Or else he just saw a vulnerable woman with

her husband's fortune and thought he'd claim it for his own."

Mrs. Bates sighed. "Yes, that's also a possibility."

"At least he didn't force his attentions on her."

"What do you mean?"

"Priscilla said the marriage was never consummated."

"How very strange," Mrs. Bates said. From the look on her face, she thought it even more than strange.

"Priscilla thought so, too, although I gathered she was grateful."

"I'm sure she was if she hadn't wanted to marry him in the first place. But . . . I probably shouldn't be discussing these matters with you."

"Because I'm not married? I may not be experienced myself, but I grew up around a lot of men, so I've heard about, uh, things."

"Then you probably won't be surprised to learn that it would be highly unusual—not to say unnatural—for a man not to consummate his own marriage."

"I do know that, yes, and Priscilla said as much."

Mrs. Bates finished off her tea and poured herself another cup while she considered this information. "I wonder . . ."

"Yes?"

"Are you sure . . . ? I mean, you said the other person in the photograph was a woman."

"Yes, and enough of her was showing to be sure, so it wasn't that Mr. Knight preferred the company of men."

"So you do know that some people do."

"Yes." She'd have to tell Mrs. Bates about her Aunt Cybil and her dear friend Zelda eventually, but this probably wasn't the right time.

"I'm so sorry you had to see that photograph."

"So am I." Which was quite true. None of this, however, was what really had Elizabeth worried. "Gideon and I are trying to figure out how to get some of Priscilla's money back."

"So he said. He also said you don't really have a plan to do that."

"We don't even know who the blackmailer is yet, although . . . I don't suppose Gideon asked you if Reverend Honesdale has a brother."

"No, he didn't. A brother? I really have no idea. Why does that matter?"

"Because someone named Matthew Honesdale owns several brothels in the city."

"Really? What an interesting coincidence."

"If it is a coincidence. What if this Matthew really is Reverend Honesdale's brother or at least some relation?"

"It's not a common name," Mrs. Bates mused.

"No, it is not."

"But what does this have to do with . . . ? Oh! I see. You think Mr. Knight would have frequented brothels."

"The Old Man felt certain he would have, because of his *proclivities,* so that's where we're going to start."

"Elizabeth! You can't mean it. You can't possibly even think about going to a brothel."

Elizabeth bit back a smile at Mrs. Bates's horrified expression. "I have no intention of it. You can't think Gideon would even consider such a thing, either."

"Oh dear, of course not. What was I thinking? You frightened me for a moment. But you said—"

"I said we were going to start there, but I meant with Matthew Honesdale himself. Gideon is going to ask to see him concerning an estate."

"Gideon is going to purposely mislead him?" Mrs. Bates asked in wonder.

"Not really. His name truly has come up concerning Mr. Knight's estate, and that's what we're going to ask him about."

"We?"

At last they had reached Elizabeth's main purpose in coming here. "Yes, we. I convinced Gideon to let me be present when he meets with Honesdale."

Mrs. Bates frowned, and for a moment she looked very like Gideon. "Are you sure that's wise? A man like that . . ."

"Now you sound like Gideon."

"And now I understand what he was talking about last night."

"What do you mean?"

"I mean he asked me to support him if he had to convince you not to put yourself in danger."

Now Elizabeth frowned. "And what did you tell him?"

"I told him his idea of danger and yours would probably be very different."

"You were absolutely right," Elizabeth said wearily.

"I also warned him not to try to turn you into a silly, empty-headed society matron."

"Thank you for that, but do you really think that's what he wants to do?"

"I think he doesn't ever want to see you in danger again. You frightened him very badly the last time."

"And I'll certainly never do that again."

"But you can't blame him for feeling protective, although I suppose I also can't blame you for chafing at it."

"Not when you remember that you and I first met when we were both in jail."

"Exactly. I'm just asking you to be patient with him, and before you object, I also asked him to remember who you are and that your background is very different from ours. He must allow you your freedom."

"I'm trying so very hard to learn all the rules so I won't embarrass you," Elizabeth said in dismay.

Mrs. Bates smiled wanly and took Elizabeth's

hand in both of hers. "Oh, Elizabeth, you can learn all the etiquette rules in the world, but that won't change who you are. Just so you know, I wouldn't change you for the world, and Gideon wouldn't, either, although he may not realize that yet."

"When is he going to realize it?"

"Very soon, I'm sure. He agreed to let you attend the meeting with this Matthew Honesdale, didn't he?"

"Yes, but he's not very happy about it."

"I'm sure he's not, and I must admit, I'm concerned as well. This man could be very uncouth."

Elizabeth almost laughed out loud at the idea of a brothel owner being merely "uncouth." He surely was much, much worse than that, although she wasn't going to admit it to Mrs. Bates. "I'm used to uncouth men, Mrs. Bates, and I've promised Gideon I'll leave if he is offensive."

"If he's satisfied, I suppose I must be as well. But how will he explain your presence? He can hardly pass you off as a law clerk."

Surely, there must be female law clerks somewhere, but probably not at Devoss and Van Aken. "No, I'm going to pretend to be Priscilla."

"Priscilla?"

"Yes, it's logical for her to be there, since it's her husband's estate, but we aren't going to tell her about this meeting until we know more. I'll wear a veil in case he's seen her before, but I doubt they would have ever met."

"I see, but is it really necessary for you to be there at all?"

"I'm probably much better at judging if someone is lying than Gideon. I've at least had more experience at it, and I'm definitely better at lying myself. I want to know if he knew Mr. Knight, and if so, what he knew about him. Gideon and I agree that we can't accuse him outright of being a blackmailer, but we can see his reaction when we ask him about Knight, and that will tell us something."

"And if he claims he never heard of Mr. Knight?"

"Then we ask him where Mr. Knight would have gone to satisfy his unusual desires."

"Oh, Elizabeth, how sordid."

"Nothing about blackmail is wholesome, Mrs. Bates, and we're fighting for Priscilla's future and for her daughters' futures."

"You're right, of course. I just wish . . . Well, I suppose I wish none of this had ever happened."

"But it did happen, and if people like us don't do something, it will keep happening."

"You're absolutely right, and that's why I'm going with you when you meet with this Matthew person."

"I'm not sure that's a good idea."

"Oh, I won't actually meet with him. I

wouldn't have any idea what to say to a man like that, but I won't let you go there alone. You'll come here first, and we'll go to Gideon's office together."

Elizabeth didn't need her support, of course, but the thought that Mrs. Bates cared enough to offer it made Elizabeth want to laugh and cry at the same time. Was this how families were supposed to treat each other? How lovely! "I'm so glad you said that. Would you be willing to go with me to see Priscilla, too?"

"I thought you weren't going to tell her about this meeting."

"We're not, but she doesn't know anything about the blackmail yet. She'll be wanting to know what I found out from Gideon, and I think we at least need to warn her about what might be coming."

Gideon looked up to find their young office boy, Alfred, standing anxiously in his office doorway. His eyes were very large in his freckled face. "I delivered your message, Mr. Bates."

"And did you find Mr. Honesdale at home?" Gideon had been amazed to find Matthew Honesdale listed in the city directory.

"No, sir, but they sent me to . . ." He glanced over his shoulder and lowered his voice to a whisper. "I think it was a house of ill repute."

Gideon should have foreseen that possibility and sent one of the clerks instead. "I'm sorry,

94

Alfred. I hope you don't believe yourself compromised in any way."

"Oh no, sir. It's . . . Well, it was all a bit exciting for me. I've never even been near a place like that before."

That he knew of. Everyone in New York walked past places like that daily without realizing it. No sense in mentioning it to Alfred, though. "And was Mr. Honesdale there?"

"He was. It was all very proper, too. A maid answered the door and asked me what I wanted with Mr. Honesdale. She had me wait in the hall while she went to see if he was receiving. Then she sent me into the parlor, and Mr. Honesdale was there. He took your note and read it. He asked me did I know anything about the estate you mentioned, and I said I didn't because I'm just the office boy. Then he said he'd call on you tomorrow afternoon, like you suggested."

Gideon nodded. "So if it was all very proper, what made you think it was a house of ill repute?"

"I . . ." Alfred blushed scarlet. "The pictures, sir."

"The pictures?"

"Yes, well, there were very improper paintings on the walls. Of ladies without any clothes."

"Don't you see paintings like that in museums?" Gideon asked, biting back a smile.

"Not like these, I don't."

"I see. Well, I apologize for subjecting you to

95

that, Alfred. I'll be more careful in the future."

"Oh," he said, elaborately casual, "I didn't mind, sir."

"Just remember what goes on in houses like that isn't as pleasant as you might think."

"Oh yes, sir. I'll remember."

As Alfred darted away, Gideon sighed. He needed to have a serious talk with Alfred about the dangers of brothels. Maybe he'd just show him the photograph of Endicott Knight instead. That should scare him into a lifetime of chastity.

In the meantime, he'd have to prepare for the meeting with Matthew Honesdale tomorrow. What sort of man made his living from prostitution? Not the sort of man he ever wanted Elizabeth to meet, he was sure. And could he really be related to Peter Honesdale and his illustrious father? Surely, such a scandalous relationship would be public knowledge if he were. The father—what was his name? Nathan, he thought—was a moral crusader, famous for all the good works his church did. Was he so fierce a fighter against depravity because his own son promoted it? Such things did happen. But any relationship was secondary to Gideon's issues. First he had to find out what Matthew Honesdale knew about Endicott Knight, and if he had been blackmailing him.

"Thank you both for coming," Priscilla said that afternoon when she'd welcomed Elizabeth and

Mrs. Bates into her parlor. "You're wearing your pin, Mrs. Bates," she added with obvious delight.

Mrs. Bates touched the rectangular pin on her lapel. It was a small silver replica of a jail door with a tiny chain and a lock in the shape of a heart. "Yes, I'm rather proud of it."

"Elizabeth, I never see you wear yours."

Elizabeth hated the heat that rose in her cheeks. She shouldn't be embarrassed, or at least she shouldn't let anyone know she was. "I just never think to put it on."

"Actually, Elizabeth is too modest to wear her pin," Mrs. Bates said, giving Elizabeth the disapproving look she hated to see.

"What do you have to be modest about?" Priscilla said. "You should be proud to have been jailed for freedom."

Jailed for freedom. That's what they called it when the suffragists were arrested for demonstrating. "I'm just embarrassed that the very first time I demonstrated, I was arrested and jailed for weeks. All the other women had been working for the cause for much longer before they were imprisoned."

"I see. You don't think you earned it, but that's nonsense," Priscilla said. "You were in jail the same as everyone else, and I know you participated in the hunger strike. You have as much right to wear the pin as any of the others. If I'd been able to go with you, it would have been my first demonstration, too, and I wouldn't hesitate to wear my pin."

"There you are, Elizabeth," Mrs. Bates said. "I hope Priscilla has convinced you."

Of course Mrs. Bates knew the real reason Elizabeth had been at the demonstration that day, and it had nothing to do with women's rights. She should be grateful Mrs. Bates still considered her as worthy as the rest of their fellow prisoners. So maybe she *should* wear her pin. She'd have to think about that some more. Meanwhile, she would change the subject.

"I know you must be curious about what I found in Mr. Knight's papers."

Priscilla's expression instantly grew solemn. "I *have* been anxious to know if Gideon was able to tell you anything."

"He was, but I'm afraid the news isn't very good."

"Quite honestly, I didn't expect it to be, so you'd best just tell me and get it over with."

"It appears that Mr. Knight was being blackmailed."

"Blackmailed?" Priscilla frowned in confusion. "Isn't that when someone knows a secret about you and you pay them money not to tell anyone?"

Elizabeth blinked. Imagine not being sure what blackmail was. "Yes, it is."

"But what secret could Mr. Knight have had?"

Mrs. Bates sent Elizabeth a slightly panicked

glance, but Elizabeth never flinched. "We're not sure. We, uh, think he may have had a mistress."

Priscilla considered that for a moment. "Of course, that makes perfect sense, and it explains why he never . . ." She turned to Mrs. Bates. "Did Elizabeth tell you? Mr. Knight and I never shared a bed."

To her credit, Mrs. Bates didn't flinch, either. "A mistress would certainly explain it, then."

Elizabeth was fairly certain at least some men who had mistresses also had marital relations with their wives, but she wasn't going to suggest that.

"But how did you know he was being black-mailed?" Priscilla asked.

This time Elizabeth exchanged a desperate glance with Mrs. Bates. "I found a letter that had recently arrived. It, uh, indicated to me that someone was blackmailing him, and Gideon agreed. You see, I also found a ledger in which Mr. Knight had listed all of his household expenses, going back several years. At some point about three years ago, he started withdrawing large sums of money periodically, but we could find no reason for him to do so."

"And did this continue after we were married?" Priscilla asked.

"I'm afraid so. In fact, it appears that he had spent nearly all of his own fortune by the time he married you."

They waited while Priscilla absorbed that information. "Does that mean . . . ? Of course, you can't know for certain but . . . does it seem to you that he may have chosen me because he knew DeForrest had left me well off?"

"And that when you married him, he would have complete control of your assets? Yes, that is very much what we suspect," Elizabeth said.

As the enormity of Knight's duplicity became clear to Priscilla, color flooded her cheeks and her eyes grew bright with horror. "And he used my money—the money DeForrest had left for our children—to pay some person to keep his filthy secrets?"

"Oh, Priscilla, we're so sorry to have to tell you this," Mrs. Bates said quickly. "It's such an awful betrayal, and you can't even have the satisfaction of seeing him punished for it now."

Tears flooded Priscilla's lovely blue eyes, and she instinctively pulled a black-bordered handkerchief from the sleeve of her black mourning gown and dabbed at them. "I don't think I've ever hated anyone this much in my entire life!"

"You have a right to," Elizabeth said before Mrs. Bates could chime in with some bunkum about Christian forgiveness. Priscilla could think about that later. Right now she needed to be angry. "And you have a right to wish him dead, but since he's already dead, we need to think about something more practical."

"Practical?" Priscilla echoed, thoroughly angry now. "What part of this is the least bit *practical?*"

"We're going to try to find out who the blackmailer is and see if we can get him to return at least some of your money." Elizabeth could feel Mrs. Bates's astonished stare, so Elizabeth didn't dare even glance at her. She kept her focus on Priscilla and her fury.

"Do they do that? Return your money?" Priscilla asked with almost comic astonishment.

"Not voluntarily," Elizabeth said. "But they have done something criminal and probably don't want anyone to know that."

"Are you thinking of blackmailing the blackmailer?" Mrs. Bates asked.

"We're thinking of asking him to do the right thing in his own best interest," Elizabeth explained to Priscilla in answer to Mrs. Bates's question.

"That seems . . . dangerous," Mrs. Bates said.

"Blackmailers aren't dangerous," Elizabeth said with certainty, "unless they know your secrets."

"But Endicott is dead," Priscilla said.

That stopped Elizabeth for a moment. She really hadn't considered Knight's death except as the catalyst that had started their investigation. Now that she thought about it, though, it had come at a particularly significant time, just when Priscilla's money had run out. And how had

Knight died? She realized she didn't really know any details. "Wasn't his death an accident?"

Priscilla pursed her lips as if she'd tasted something unpleasant. "That's what we told people. A terrible accident."

"But you don't think it was an accident?" Mrs. Bates said gently.

"I told myself it must have been. What else could it be? But now . . ."

"What exactly happened?" Elizabeth asked.

"He was hit by a train on Eleventh Avenue."

"Death Avenue," Mrs. Bates murmured.

"Yes, Death Avenue," Priscilla said. "Because so many people have been killed by the train that runs right down the middle of the street."

"But don't they have the cowboy who rides in front of the train to warn people?" Elizabeth said.

"Yes, the West Side Cowboy," Mrs. Bates said, "but somebody on a horse waving a lantern and riding far ahead of the train still doesn't stop people from crossing in front of it if they think they can make it. Most of the people killed are children, who don't know any better. Adults are usually more careful."

"Yes," Priscilla said with a trace of bitterness. "You'd think a grown man would have sense enough to be careful, but it was nearly midnight and they said he'd been drinking."

"Midnight?" Mrs. Bates echoed.

"Midnight in Hell's Kitchen," Elizabeth mused

as she realized in what neighborhood the accident would have taken place.

"And what on earth was he doing there?" Priscilla demanded. "He told me he was going to his club. Of course, that's what he always said when he left every day, and I never questioned him."

Hell's Kitchen was home to any number of saloons and brothels and all manner of vice and depravity, which probably explained exactly what Endicott Knight was doing there, but Elizabeth wasn't going to mention that to Priscilla.

"It could have been an accident, then," Mrs. Bates said. "If he'd been drinking, that is."

"Yes, and I had no reason to doubt it. Now, however, I can't help but wonder . . ."

"Wonder what?" Elizabeth asked, wondering herself if Priscilla had come to the same conclusion she had.

She had not. "If he didn't commit suicide."

"Suicide?" Mrs. Bates said, obviously horrified by the idea.

"If he really had stolen all my money to pay his blackmail," Priscilla said, "and he knew my money was gone and he had no way to get any more, well . . . I'd like to think his conscience bothered him at least a bit, but I imagine he was just in despair that he was going to be ruined."

"So he took his own life," Mrs. Bates said. "It's possible, I suppose, but we'll never know, will we?"

"Not if it was suicide, no," Elizabeth said. But there was a third possibility, although she couldn't imagine why a blackmailer would murder his victim. A dead victim couldn't make any further payments. Knight wasn't able to make more payments, of course, but did the blackmailer know that? And even if he did, why bother to kill his victim and risk discovery?

She really needed to know more about blackmail.

"I do know DeForrest's death was an accident, though," Priscilla hastily explained. "He didn't have a mistress or any other dark secrets, so I know he wasn't being blackmailed, and he certainly had no reason to kill himself."

"No one ever suggested otherwise, did they?" Mrs. Bates asked.

"Of course not. He couldn't possibly have done that to himself." Priscilla dabbed at her eyes again.

"How did Mr. Jenks die?" Elizabeth asked. "If you don't mind telling me, that is."

"I don't like talking about it, of course, but not because I think there's anything suspicious. I just hate remembering that he's gone, and for no reason. It was all so awful."

"It was terribly tragic," Mrs. Bates said. "And undoubtedly an accident."

"A gargoyle, of all things," Priscilla said bitterly.

"A *gargoyle?*" Elizabeth wasn't even sure what that was.

"One of those ugly statues you see on the roofs of buildings," Mrs. Bates said.

"Outside his club," Priscilla said. "He was standing there on the sidewalk, probably waiting for a cab, but it was late and . . ." She had to stop when her voice broke.

"It fell off the building," Mrs. Bates said. "The gargoyle, I mean. A huge thing, made of cement or stone or something."

"If he'd been standing just a few feet away, it would have missed him completely," Priscilla said. "They said he died instantly, which I suppose was a blessing, if anything about it could be called a blessing."

"How awful" was all Elizabeth could think to say. And how convenient for Endicott Knight that a young woman of his acquaintance suddenly became a rich widow just when he was in need of a new fortune.

Was it really one of those freak accidents that happened in a city like New York, or could someone have found a unique way to quickly get rid of poor DeForrest Jenks? Dropping a stone gargoyle on someone's head seemed like a rather risky enterprise, though. How could you be sure he'd be standing in just the right spot? Wouldn't he hear someone prying the thing loose? Surely they were attached rather securely, or people would constantly be dodging them and the city would be littered with smashed gargoyles. Still, Elizabeth couldn't help thinking how fortuitous Mr. Jenks's death had been for Knight.

And she didn't believe in luck.

CHAPTER FIVE

As always, the sight of Elizabeth immediately raised Gideon's spirits when he arrived home and found her sitting in the parlor with his mother that evening. She jumped up and came to him, taking both his hands in hers, her eyes bright with happiness at the sight of him.

"You're freezing," she said when she'd squeezed his hands. "Come over here by the fire so we can tell you about our day."

When she had seated him in her own chair and brought over a footstool for him, and his mother had greeted him, Elizabeth perched on the arm of his chair and rested her hand possessively on his shoulder. She smelled delicious, like violets, and he slipped his arm around her waist, just to keep her from slipping off her perch. He needed to send his mother on an errand or something so he could kiss her.

"We found out some interesting things today, but first tell us if you heard from Matthew Honesdale."

He briefly considered telling them about Albert's experience at the brothel but thought better of it. "Yes, I did. Mr. Honesdale is going to call at my office tomorrow at two o'clock."

"I told you he'd come if he thought he'd

inherited some money," Elizabeth said, smiling smugly.

"I will never underestimate you again, my darling girl," he promised.

"See that you don't. And I told your mother all about it, and she is determined to escort me to your office for safekeeping."

Gideon managed not to wince. "Mother, do you think that's a good idea?"

"I'm not going to see Mr. Honesdale. I'm just going to accompany Elizabeth there and back. She may need my support after this meeting."

He couldn't argue with that reasoning, although having yet another female for whose well-being he felt responsible so near Matthew Honesdale made him more than slightly nauseated. "I'm sure Mr. Devoss will be happy to entertain you, Mother."

"Oh dear, I didn't think of that. I don't suppose we can afford to offend your employer, can we?"

"More importantly, you don't want to break his heart. He asks about you often. We should probably have him for dinner."

"What a wonderful idea. We could invite Mr. Miles, too, and make a party of it."

Elizabeth looked slightly panicked. "I hope you two are joking."

"Mother never jokes about her social obligations, do you, Mother?"

She shook her head in mock despair. "Elizabeth,

108

tell him what we learned from Priscilla today."

"You went to see Mrs. Knight?" he asked in surprise.

"I knew she would be worrying about what you had discovered from the papers I brought you to look at, so I thought we should at least tell her something."

"You didn't tell her about . . ." He caught himself and glanced warily at his mother.

"Your mother knows everything, no thanks to you," Elizabeth said. "She's much more worldly than you give her credit for."

"You didn't show her the photograph," he said in dismay.

"How could I? You have it locked away."

"Oh, that's right. Such a wise move on my part."

"She wouldn't even describe it to me," his mother said, pretending to pout.

"You don't need to be any more worldly than you already are, Mother."

"So your mother knows everything," Elizabeth said. "And no, we did not tell Priscilla about the photograph. I thought she should know Mr. Knight was being blackmailed, though."

"Didn't she want to know why?"

"Of course she did. I told her we thought he had a mistress."

"Didn't she want to know who this mistress was?"

"But we don't know ourselves, just as we don't know who the blackmailer is, so we couldn't tell her anything. But now she knows what happened to her money and why it's unlikely we'll get any of it back."

"Elizabeth did say you were going to try, though," his mother said.

"Was that a good idea?" he asked Elizabeth, knowing full well it was a horrible idea.

"I couldn't leave her without hope, but she knows it's unlikely."

He studied her beautiful face for a long moment. Usually, he was so taken with her beauty that he didn't notice anything else, but this time . . . "You don't really think it's unlikely."

"I need hope, too."

Now he was nauseated again. "You really think you can get her money back, don't you?"

"Oh, Gideon, how could we possibly do that?"

"I don't have the slightest idea, but I have a feeling you do."

"You know I've spent a good portion of my young life studying ways to take money from people."

"Not from blackmailers. They're too dangerous."

"I'm sure you're right. It would be much too dangerous to take money from a blackmailer."

Gideon frowned. She'd agreed much too easily. "Did you just say it would be too dangerous to take money from a blackmailer?"

"Yes, I did. I thought you'd be pleased."

"I am pleased." Then why didn't he feel pleased?

"Isn't that what I should have said? Your mother has been so patient, helping me learn how a respectable lady is supposed to act, and I thought for sure I should agree with you just then. Wasn't that the right thing to do?"

"Of course it was. You should always . . ." Always what? Agree with her husband? He wasn't her husband yet, and even if he were, should she always agree with him? Well, when he was right, surely, and wasn't he always thinking of her best interests?

"I should always what?" she asked.

"I'm just trying to keep you safe," he said lamely.

"And no one can fault you for that, my dear," his mother said so sweetly he had to look at her to make sure she really meant it.

He needed to change the subject. "Does Priscilla know about Matthew Honesdale?"

"Of course not. We agreed not to tell her yet, remember?" Elizabeth said. "I just told her you were investigating."

"Good."

Elizabeth smiled at his praise. Or at something.

"We also found out some interesting things about Mr. Knight's death," his mother said.

"His death?"

"Yes, do you remember how he died?"

"Some sort of accident, I thought."

"He was run over by a train on Death Avenue," Elizabeth said a little too gleefully for Gideon's peace of mind.

"You hardly ever hear of people getting run over there anymore," he said. "Doesn't that cowboy scare them off?"

"He tries, I'm sure, but people in a hurry will take chances," his mother said. "And apparently, Mr. Knight had been drinking."

"And it was midnight, so it was also dark," Elizabeth said. "If you're going to get run over by a train, I think those circumstances would be perfect for it."

"Do you think he *wanted* to get run over by a train?" Gideon asked in amazement.

"Priscilla thinks it's possible," Elizabeth said. "It occurs to me that someone might have pushed him, but I think Priscilla may be right about suicide. Think about it. He had already used up his entire fortune paying blackmail, and he'd managed to save himself once by marrying Priscilla practically against her will. Then he'd used up all of her money. Short of committing bigamy, he had no prospects for refilling his coffers, so he would be unable to continue paying the blackmailer to keep his secrets."

"Most men in that situation would probably choose to end their lives rather than face the scandal and humiliation of exposure," his mother added.

Gideon wanted to refute the claim that *most* men would choose suicide, but since he was unlikely to ever find himself in that situation, he really couldn't judge. "I suppose suicide is more likely than murder, too. A blackmailer isn't likely to kill the goose laying the golden eggs, even if he was temporarily out of gold."

"And the timing is suspicious as well," Elizabeth said. "Just when he'd exhausted Priscilla's fortune, he receives the photograph in the mail with a note reminding him of his indiscretions. He must have been desperate."

"And whom could he turn to for help without revealing the very secret he was trying to keep?" his mother added.

"Poor devil," Gideon said.

Elizabeth gave a very ladylike snort. "The only 'poor' person in this mess is Priscilla."

"You're right, of course. She's the one who deserves our sympathy," Gideon said quickly.

"We also discussed her first husband's death," Elizabeth said, apparently placated. "Did you know he was killed by a gargoyle?"

"Yes, I'd forgotten about that. There was quite a bit of outrage when it happened."

"Why?"

"Because it happened at the club. We belonged to the same club, DeForrest and I. There was an

113

official inquiry about how the building was being maintained. A lot of the members were worried they'd be the next to go if one of the other sculptures fell."

"Did they find that the other *sculptures* were also loose?"

"As a matter of fact, they didn't. They all seemed quite secure, but we had them removed just the same."

"A very good idea," his mother said.

"Didn't anyone think it odd that Mr. Jenks just happened to be standing there when it fell?" Elizabeth asked.

"Everyone thought it odd," Gideon said, remembering. "Especially because he'd stayed so late that night. It wasn't his habit, you see. He also seemed a little drunk, which also wasn't his habit. No one remembered exactly when he left, but he must have been the last one to go that night."

"Why would he have been standing on the sidewalk?"

"Waiting for a cab to go by, probably. That's what everyone said must have happened. There aren't many cabs that late, though, and if he was drunk, he might not have realized how long he'd been waiting or that he should walk down to a busier street or even give up and take a trolley or the El."

"At least we're sure he didn't commit suicide," Elizabeth said, apropos of nothing.

"Did you think he might have?" Gideon asked uneasily.

"Not at all. But doesn't it seem odd that he died just when Mr. Knight needed to marry a rich widow?"

Did she really think Knight purposely dropped a gargoyle on DeForrest Jenks so he could marry his widow? "Most likely Knight only thought of his scheme after Jenks died. He saw a rich widow and took his chance."

"But didn't everyone think Priscilla was penniless when her husband died?"

"You're right, they did," his mother said. "How odd."

But he could see Elizabeth didn't think it odd at all. "What do you think happened?"

She gave him her dazzling smile. "I think Mr. Jenks died and Mr. Knight married Priscilla and squandered all her money, and then he died, too. I also think we should discuss what we're going to ask Mr. Honesdale when he comes to see you tomorrow."

Mercifully, the maid tapped at the door at that moment to tell them supper was ready.

"I can hardly see a thing," Elizabeth complained when Mrs. Bates had adjusted the widow's veil over her face. She had dressed Elizabeth in her severe widow's weeds at the house but allowed her to make the journey to Gideon's office

115

without the veil. Now they'd reached the offices of Devoss and Van Aken, and Mrs. Bates was putting the finishing touches on her ensemble.

"You'll get used to it," Mrs. Bates said. "The best part is that, while you can see out, it's difficult for others to see in. You can stare at someone to your heart's content and they'll never know."

"Which is, of course, my main purpose in being here."

"Good heavens," Gideon said when Alfred escorted her into his office.

"Do I look properly bereaved?" she asked.

"How would I know? I can't see your face at all."

"Which is the purpose of the veil," his mother reminded him. She'd followed Elizabeth in. She glanced around the room. "Move one of the client chairs over there." She pointed to a space between Gideon's desk and the wall. "Elizabeth will need a clear view of Mr. Honesdale, and she shouldn't be seated beside him, in any case. I think the widow would want to remain unobtrusive."

When Alfred and Gideon had made the necessary furniture adjustments, Elizabeth took her seat and Mrs. Bates wished them luck and withdrew. The plan was for her to wait in one of the conference rooms, but Mr. Devoss had seen her come in and insisted on serving her tea in his office. Elizabeth would have to tease her mercilessly later.

When they were alone, Gideon said, "Try not to speak any more than necessary. Priscilla would be much too well-bred and probably too intimidated to ask him a lot of questions."

"How do you know? She might interrogate him thoroughly if she thought he was blackmailing Knight."

"Because that's how ladies behave in attorneys' offices. Their husbands ask the questions."

He would know that better than she, naturally. "But my husband is dead, or at least Priscilla's is. Does not having a husband mean she can't get any information?"

"I'll ask the questions we decided on, so you should get all the information you want."

"What if he says something directly to me?"

"You can answer him, if it's a civil question, but if he says anything crude or insulting—"

"I know, I'll walk out, thoroughly offended. Don't worry. I'm an expert at that."

Gideon rubbed a hand over his face. "I wish you'd let me handle this."

"You are going to handle it. I'm just going to sit here and grieve."

He muttered something that sounded like "Promises, promises," but she didn't ask him to repeat it.

No sooner had Gideon taken his seat behind his

desk than someone knocked on his office door.

"Mr. Honesdale to see you, Mr. Bates," Smith announced.

Elizabeth drew a steadying breath and straightened her shoulders as Smith escorted Matthew Honesdale in.

He was not at all what she had expected. If she hadn't known better, she would have thought he was another of the attorneys in Gideon's firm. He was a tall man of average build with brown hair parted in the middle and pomaded into submission. He wore a conservatively cut wool suit in a muted dark blue plaid with an unadorned gold watch chain stretched across his vest. His well-trimmed mustache gave him a kind of dignity.

Gideon came around his desk to shake Honesdale's hand. "Thank you for coming, Mr. Honesdale. It's good to meet you."

"I must say, you got me curious, although I can guess why you wanted to . . ." He trailed off because he had noticed Elizabeth sitting by the desk.

"Mrs. Knight wanted to sit in at our meeting," Gideon said. It was the truth, or would have been if Priscilla had even known about the meeting, and he hadn't actually said that Elizabeth was Priscilla. In point of fact, as Mrs. Bates had reminded them last night, no one should consider actually introducing a lady like Priscilla to a man

118

who owned houses of ill repute, so this allowed Honesdale to know who Priscilla was without actually making an introduction.

Honesdale seemed mildly surprised but he betrayed no other emotions. He merely nodded politely. "Mrs. Knight."

Elizabeth gave no sign of acknowledgment, which was entirely proper.

"Please, sit down, Mr. Honesdale."

He did, and Gideon took his own seat back behind his desk.

"Did you say you could guess why I asked you to meet with me?" Gideon asked. Honesdale had been looking at Elizabeth, his expression thoughtful, and he turned his attention back to Gideon. "When you said it had to do with an estate, I couldn't think of anyone I knew who had recently died, or at least no one who might leave me any money, and then I remembered the mortgage."

"The mortgage," Gideon echoed. Elizabeth knew he must be as surprised as she, but he somehow managed not to show it.

"Yes." Honesdale reached into his inside jacket pocket and pulled out a packet of documents. "I was holding a mortgage for a man named Endicott Knight, and I'd seen his death notice in the newspaper." His gazed flicked to Elizabeth. "My condolences, ma'am." He turned back to Gideon again. "I thought this might be about him, and since Mrs. Knight is here, I assume I guessed correctly. If she wants to redeem the mortgage from me, I'll have no objection."

He laid the packet on Gideon's desk and slid it toward him. Gideon opened it and unfolded the papers. Elizabeth couldn't read the type through the veil, but she could see the official gold seal and the flourish of signatures at the bottom.

"May I ask how you came to hold a mortgage on Mr. Knight's property?" Gideon asked when he was satisfied everything was in order.

Mr. Honesdale leaned back in his chair and crossed one leg over the other. He was trying to appear relaxed, but Elizabeth could tell he didn't want to answer the question. "Mr. Knight apparently found himself in need of funds, and a friend of mine asked if I would make him a loan in return for a mortgage on his house."

"And may I ask the name of your friend?" Gideon said.

"No, you may not. I can't see that it matters, in any case. All that matters is I own the mortgage, as you can plainly see."

This was not something they'd suspected, so they hadn't planned for it. Gideon glanced at Elizabeth while he reorganized his thoughts. Elizabeth decided she'd give him some time to do so.

"Are you planning to foreclose on the mortgage if I can't pay it, Mr. Honesdale?" she asked. She used the icily formal tone the Old Man had taught her years ago and was pleased to see it had the desired effect on Honesdale.

He blinked in surprise. "I can't say I've given the matter any thought, Mrs. Knight, so I wasn't planning to do anything at all."

"Mrs. Knight finds herself in straitened circumstances at the moment," Gideon said. "I'm sure she would appreciate your forbearance."

"Ah, I sce," Honesdale said, although Elizabeth knew he didn't see anything at all since he had no idea why he was really here. "I'm sorry to hear that, and I can assure you, I have no intention of putting you out in the street."

"That's very benevolent of you, Mr Honesdale," Gideon said before Elizabeth could jump in again.

"Oh yes, an act of true Christian charity," Honesdale said with some amusement. "I've been waiting for you to ask me about my name. People like you usually get around to it sooner or later. Aren't you the least bit curious?"

"As a matter of fact, I am," Gideon admitted. "My own pastor's name is Honesdale."

"Uncle Nathan or Cousin Peter?"

To his credit, Gideon looked only mildly surprised. Elizabeth had only barely managed not to yelp. "Peter. So you're a relative."

"And the black sheep of the family, a fact of which I am very proud."

Gideon, bless him, soldiered on undaunted. "You'll remember that I mentioned your name had come up in regard to Mr. Knight's estate."

"You didn't say it was Knight's, but yes, that's what you said."

"And I mentioned that Mrs. Knight is in straitened circumstances. That is because Mr. Knight had exhausted all their resources paying off a blackmailer."

This time it was Honesdale who straightened. "A blackmailer?" He seemed genuinely surprised, but maybe he was just surprised that they knew. "What do you mean, a blackmailer?"

"I think I made myself clear. Mr. Knight was paying out large sums of money to someone who was threatening to expose his darkest secrets."

Now Honesdale simply looked confused. His glance darted from Gideon to Elizabeth and back again. "So when my name came up because of the mortgage, you naturally thought a man in my line of work would be a blackmailer, too."

Gideon let him wait for a moment before he said, "You must admit that a man in your line of work, as you put it, would have knowledge of a man's darkest secrets."

Elizabeth had expected Honesdale to explode in anger. Instead he just stared at Gideon for a few seconds and then gave a bark of mirthless laughter. "That's the trouble with you straight-arrow types. You make all kinds of assumptions about people like me that couldn't possibly be true."

"But it's certainly true that—"

"That I know a lot of secrets, sure," he said. "And what do you think would happen if I went around telling other people those secrets? Or even worse, blackmailing people by threatening to tell them? I'll tell you what would happen. People would stop visiting my, uh, businesses." He gave Elizabeth an uneasy glance. "I'm sorry, Mrs. Knight, but you must know what my business is or you wouldn't think I blackmailed your husband."

Elizabeth gave him a regal nod of her head to acknowledge the truth of his suspicion.

"My business depends on discretion. In a city like this, there are lots of places men can go for amusement. They go to *my* places because I cater to the carriage trade, and they pay me a pretty penny for the privilege. But those men talk to each other, and they'd leave me in a minute if they caught the slightest whiff of betrayal. Why would I jeopardize a business that has made me a fortune to get a few thousand dollars from a man like Knight?"

They'd expected him to deny being the black-mailer, of course, but they hadn't expected he could prove it. His argument was convincing, though. She could see Gideon thought so, too. Still, they had one more ace up their sleeves.

"I'm glad to know you weren't involved, Mr. Honesdale," Gideon said. The Old Man would thoroughly approve of his nerve. He'd hardly blinked during Honesdale's diatribe. "But my main reason in asking you to meet with me was to ask your expert opinion about something."

"That's rich, a lawyer asking my opinion about something. What is it?"

Gideon moved a folder from the edge of his desk to the middle and turned it around to face Honesdale. "When this lady"—he nodded to Elizabeth—"was going through Mr. Knight's papers, she discovered this photograph."

Gideon lifted the cover of the folder in which he had placed the incriminating photograph. The cover blocked Elizabeth's view of it but allowed Honesdale to see it.

For all his worldly sophistication, even Honesdale could not suppress a grunt of surprise. Then he looked at Elizabeth with obvious dismay. "You saw this?"

Elizabeth gave another regal nod.

"I'm sorry, ma'am, but your husband should never have left something like that for you to find. It isn't right."

Elizabeth managed a sniffle that made him think she was weeping, and his composure nearly broke. He turned back to Gideon, furious now. "Is that Knight?" He pointed to the photograph.

"Yes. I don't suppose you recognize the, uh,

female?" Gideon had let the folder fall closed, but he made to open it again.

"No, I don't," Honesdale said before he could. "No wonder he was paying the blackmail."

"I was hoping that a man *in your line of work* might be able to tell us where in the city someone would go for this kind of *amusement*."

"Not to one of my places, I can tell you that."

"I would never suggest such a thing."

Honesdale glared at Gideon across the polished surface of his desk. "I'd have to give it some thought."

"But there are places that cater to this kind of thing, aren't there?"

Honesdale started to speak, then caught himself. "Let me see that photograph again."

Gideon obligingly lifted the cover of the folder.

This time Honesdale studied the picture more closely. "This isn't a . . ." He cast Elizabeth an apologetic glance. ". . . a brothel."

"What do you mean? Of course it is," Gideon said.

"No, look at that. The painting on the wall."

Elizabeth wanted to jump up and take another look herself, but she forced herself to sit tight and wait.

Gideon turned the folder and looked at it more closely himself. "What's wrong with it?"

"It's a landscape. You can't see it very clearly, but it looks like a hunting scene, maybe. You know, horses and hounds. That's not the kind of pictures we put in whore . . . uh, the places I own. This is somebody's house."

When Honesdale had gone without revealing anything else of interest, Gideon escorted Elizabeth to one of the conference rooms and rescued his grateful mother from Mr. Devoss. When the three of them were settled in the meeting room, his mother turned to Elizabeth. "What was he like?"

"I was surprised. He looked like an ordinary businessman. He acted like one, too."

His mother turned to him. "What did you think of him?"

"If I hadn't known who he was, I would have taken him for a perfectly respectable gentleman."

"I take it he didn't say anything offensive to Elizabeth, either."

"He was very careful to not offend me," Elizabeth mused. "He obviously knows how to conduct himself in polite company."

"Which he may have learned from his Uncle Nathan," Gideon said.

This revelation had the expected effect on his mother.

"He's Nathan Honesdale's nephew?" she exclaimed. "He admitted it?"

"It's more likely *Nathan* would be the one to deny it, I'd think," Elizabeth said. "I suppose being his nephew is less shocking than our original theory, which had him as his son."

"That's true, but it does explain why he knows how to behave properly," his mother said. "I can't imagine how a young man from a good family could become so depraved, though."

"I'm sure he'd be happy to explain it to you, Mother," Gideon said.

"He probably would. Perhaps I'll pay him a visit and ask him," she countered archly.

Gideon decided to change the subject. "Did you think he was telling the truth when he said he didn't know Knight?" he asked Elizabeth.

"I did. He seemed genuinely surprised when you mentioned blackmail, too. Did you think so?"

"Yes. He actually seemed insulted that we'd accuse him. He pointed out that a man in his line of work had to be discreet or his clients would desert him," he explained to his mother.

"I hadn't thought of that, but I suppose it's true," she said. "Honor among thieves and all that, I guess."

"I believe the saying is 'there's *no* honor among thieves,'" Elizabeth pointed out with some amusement.

"Is it? Well, whatever it is, this doesn't sound like you think he's the blackmailer, which is too bad, because it would have made everything simpler. Was he able to tell you where Mr. Knight might have gone for his . . . activities?"

"He claimed he needed to think about it," Gideon said, "but he did point out something we hadn't noticed in the photograph."

"I don't suppose you'll tell me what it was," his mother said, feigning disappointment.

"Actually, we can," Elizabeth said gleefully. "He noticed that there's a painting on the wall of the room where the photograph was taken. It's some sort of landscape."

"Why would that be important?"

"Because," Gideon said before Elizabeth could answer, "apparently, houses of ill repute have much more salacious pictures hanging on their walls."

"And never landscapes," Elizabeth added. "He suggested the photograph was taken in someone's house."

"Someone's house? Good heavens, you don't think it was Priscilla's house, do you?"

"I can't imagine how it could have been done without her knowledge," Elizabeth said. "You'd know if a strange woman and a photographer came to your house and spent time locked away with your husband, wouldn't you?"

"Of course. And the servants would tell me about it if I wasn't home when it happened."

"Where else could it have been, though?" Elizabeth asked. "Who would allow something like that in their home?"

"And speaking of homes," Gideon said in

128

another attempt to change the subject, "did Priscilla mention who held the mortgage to her house?"

"No, just that her banker had told her it was mortgaged," Elizabeth said. "It seems Mr. Honesdale owns the mortgage," she added for his mother's sake.

"What? How on earth . . . ?"

"We don't know," Gideon said, "but we'd certainly like to. He said a friend had asked him to loan Knight some money and he did it out of the goodness of his heart, or so he wanted us to believe."

"But he wouldn't say who the friend was," Elizabeth added. "He thought we already knew about the mortgage, though, and that's why we summoned him. At least he agreed not to foreclose on Priscilla."

"That was the one good thing we accomplished, I think," Gideon said.

"But if he's not the blackmailer, how are you going to find out who is?" his mother asked.

"He may not be the blackmailer," Elizabeth said, "but I think he knows more than he told us. For instance, he wouldn't tell us who asked him to lend Knight the money, remember? I can't imagine why a *friend* of Knight's would put him in debt to someone like Matthew Honesdale, so I think we can conclude that person didn't really have Knight's best interests at heart but was very interested in getting Knight some funds."

"And you think that person is the blackmailer?" his mother asked.

"Or is connected to him in some way. And who do we know who is connected to Knight and Honesdale both?"

"You can't think Reverend Honesdale had anything to do with this," Gideon said.

"Why not?"

Gideon frowned, unable to believe such a thing.

Elizabeth shrugged at his disapproval. "Or maybe the blackmailer used him, too."

His mother was frowning thoughtfully. "How do you suggest we find out? I can't envision going up to him after church on Sunday and saying, 'Nice sermon and oh, by the way, were you blackmailing Endicott Knight?'"

"And how would a minister get ahold of that photograph?" Gideon added, sure he'd come up with the best argument in Reverend Honesdale's favor yet.

"And yet Reverend Honesdale and his wife were the ones who arranged for Knight and Priscilla to marry."

"But only because they thought she was penniless and needed a husband to take care of her," his mother argued.

"Yet we know that wasn't true, so who told them it was? We know they helped Knight marry Priscilla, and we're sure Knight married her so he could get his hands on her money. If the Honesdales acted innocently, the person who told them the lies about Priscilla is probably the blackmailer."

Gideon had to admit she was right. "But how will we find out?"

Elizabeth smiled. "I suppose we could just ask them."

CHAPTER SIX

Elizabeth and Mrs. Bates hardly had time to take off their coats back at the Bateses' home when Anna Vanderslice arrived. Her cheeks were glowing and her eyes sparkling, and not just from the cold.

"Have you seen the newspapers?" she asked before they could even greet her when she entered the parlor.

"Is it the war?" Mrs. Bates asked.

"No, something even more exciting." She opened the newspaper she'd carried in so they could see the headline.

Mrs. Bates snatched it from her to read the story.

"An amendment passed?" Elizabeth asked, having only been able to read the headline. "Is it the Woman Suffrage Amendment?"

"President Wilson made a speech yesterday, urging members of Congress to pass the Woman Suffrage Amendment," Mrs. Bates reported, having read that far.

"And they passed it today!" Anna added.

"But it was just the House of Representatives," Mrs. Bates said as she read further.

Elizabeth knew getting a constitutional amendment passed wasn't that easy. She hadn't known anything at all about how the government worked until she'd been thrown in jail with a bunch of suffragists last fall, but she was becoming somewhat of an expert.

"It will still have to pass in the Senate," Mrs. Bates said, not happily. "That will be much harder."

"I don't know why it should be," Anna said, "if it passed this easily in the House."

"Because it's taken many tries to pass it in the House, and the House of Representatives knows they can pass anything they like without fear that it will become law. They know the Senate will refuse to pass a lot of what they've approved."

"Why doesn't the House just refuse to pass those things in the first place, then?" Anna asked, annoyed.

"Because this way they can please their voters by saying they tried to pass whatever it was and still rest assured that something they consider bad won't ever become a law because the Senate will stop it."

"What a silly way to run a government," Anna said.

"But at least if it passed in the House, that's a start," Elizabeth said. "And now we know that our demonstrations can work. We'll convince the Senate, too."

Mrs. Bates sighed and handed the newspaper to Elizabeth. "I just hope it happens in my lifetime."

Surely, it wouldn't take much longer if President Wilson was finally supporting it, but Elizabeth didn't say so. She knew too much about human nature to be sure of anything.

"Now what have the two of you been up to today?" Anna asked when they'd seated themselves before the fire.

"Mrs. Bates has been flirting with Mr. Devoss, and I have been consulting with a pimp," Elizabeth said. She purposely didn't so much as glance at Mrs. Bates so she wouldn't be distracted by her outrage.

Anna, however, was delighted. "I'm not sure which of those is more shocking."

"While both of them are shocking," Mrs. Bates said sternly, "only one of them is true."

"Poor Mr. Devoss," Anna said, guessing correctly.

"Indeed," Elizabeth said. "Although we only have her word that she wasn't flirting."

"I assure you, I will never encourage poor Roger Devoss. And aren't you even the least bit curious about Elizabeth's activities?"

"Elizabeth did mention last night that she would be meeting with a rather unsavory person today. A pimp, eh? Just how unsavory was he?"

"Not unsavory at all," Elizabeth said. "I had actually practiced my outraged exit just in case, but he turned out to have excellent manners and to know how to conduct himself in polite company."

"How very disappointing," Anna said. "Is he at least the blackmailer?"

"Does Anna know everything?" Mrs. Bates asked in surprise.

"Almost," Elizabeth admitted. "And we don't think he is the blackmailer. What I didn't tell you, though, is that he's Reverend Honesdale's cousin."

"Are you serious? How on earth could that happen?"

"Every family has a black sheep," Mrs. Bates said.

"Yes, at least one. I'm considering becoming the black sheep for my family," Anna said.

"How would you do that?" Elizabeth asked with real interest.

"Cybil is trying to convince me to enroll at Hunter College."

"That sounds like a marvelous idea," Mrs. Bates said. "And it would hardly make you a black sheep."

"You haven't heard my mother on the subject," Anna said. "So this pimp is Reverend Honesdale's cousin?"

"What an ugly word," Mrs. Bates said. "His name is Matthew Honesdale."

"He has the same last name? Why on earth hasn't this become a scandal?"

"Why should it? Reverend Honesdale and his father have no control over what their relations do," Mrs. Bates said.

"That never stops people from gossiping, though," Anna pointed out. "I can't believe the people in the church don't know it."

"I'm sure some of them do, and they are discreet out of respect for Reverend Honesdale," Mrs. Bates said. "It has probably caused the family considerable distress."

"Distress? Is that what they feel, do you think?" Elizabeth asked.

"Probably 'horror' is more accurate," Anna said. "Or 'humiliation.' Or they try not to think of it at all."

"And I'm guessing this Matthew Honesdale is very discreet," Elizabeth said. "His business is illegal, after all."

"But don't all businessmen like publicity? Doesn't it help their business?"

"Not from what he said. He certainly wouldn't want reporters outside his brothels reporting on who goes in."

"Oh, I suppose not," Anna said.

"You girls are incorrigible." Mrs. Bates shook her head.

"You see, Anna, you're already succeeding in your quest to become a black sheep," Elizabeth said.

"The process is far easier than I expected it would be."

"It's remarkably easy for a young lady," Mrs. Bates said solemnly, "as I hope you know. The

136

slightest hint of scandal and your reputation is ruined."

"I certainly hope no one finds out I murdered Elizabeth, then," Anna said.

But Mrs. Bates's comment had set Elizabeth wondering about something she'd read in Mrs. Ordway's book. "If the Honesdales have a relative—a fairly close relative, since he called our Reverend Honesdale's father his uncle—who operates brothels in the same city, wouldn't a young lady think twice about marrying into the family?"

Mrs. Bates and Anna considered her question for a long moment.

"I think my mother and my brother would certainly have something to say about it," Anna said.

"Oh yes," Mrs. Bates said. "The senior Reverend Honesdale is highly respected, of course, and above reproach, but it's certainly something a family would consider before allowing their daughter to marry."

"And who is Mrs. Honesdale's family?"

"Daisy, you mean?" Mrs. Bates asked with a frown. "I told you, no one knew her before she married Reverend Honesdale. I still don't know who her family is."

"Wasn't there an announcement in the news-paper with the names of the bride's parents? Mrs. Ordway strongly recommends that, doesn't she?" Elizabeth said.

"I suppose there must have been," Mrs. Bates said, glancing at Anna. "Do you remember?"

"I don't. It didn't seem important at the time," Anna said. "Where did they say she was from?"

"Some odd place, I think. New Jersey?"

Anna shook her head. "You're right, it was odd, but not . . . Was it Maryland?"

"I think you're right. But if she's from Maryland, wouldn't she have a Southern accent?"

"People in Maryland don't have a Southern accent," Elizabeth informed them. "Don't you remember from when we were in Washington City?"

"I'm not sure we met many people from Maryland on that trip," Mrs. Bates reminded her. "The people in Virginia have a Southern accent, though."

Elizabeth decided not to argue. "At any rate, Daisy Honesdale came from some state nobody can remember where people don't have Southern accents and nobody knows who her family is. Do we even know how Reverend Honesdale met her?"

Mrs. Bates and Anna exchanged another look. Anna shrugged. Mrs. Bates said, "I don't think we ever heard."

"Why are you suddenly so interested in Daisy Honesdale?" Anna asked.

"Because there's something strange about the Honesdale family. The nephew of a well-known minister owns brothels. The son of the well-known minister suddenly marries a woman no one ever heard of before in a private ceremony with none of his parishioners present. That couple encourages a widow in their church to marry a man she barely knows who also happens to need her money because he's being blackmailed."

"When you put it like that, it does sound suspicious," Anna said.

"But it could also be easily and innocently explained," Mrs. Bates said. "This Matthew Honesdale could have rebelled against his religious family. Some boys do. Peter Honesdale could have met a woman from a less socially prominent family and fallen in love. To save her embarrassment, they kept their courtship and wedding private so no one learned of her humble background and thought less of her. I've already mentioned that Daisy and Peter could simply have had Priscilla's best interests at heart when they brought her and Mr. Knight together."

Mrs. Bates was right, of course, but Elizabeth had often observed that people's reasons for doing things were usually selfish and self-serving. Mrs. Bates might be right about one or two of those things being acts of generosity, but not all of them. Human nature was simply too prone to self-interest.

"Mrs. Bates, I think the time has come for me to start paying calls on some of the women I'll need to know when I marry Gideon," Elizabeth said.

Mrs. Bates blinked in surprise at the sudden change of subject, but then her eyes narrowed in suspicion. "I've been trying to get you to do that for weeks. What suddenly changed your mind?"

"I was just thinking that if Daisy Honesdale doesn't have any family or childhood friends in the city, she might get lonely and long for female companionship."

"How kind of you to think of that," Anna said with forced enthusiasm, ever the loyal supporter.

Not fooled, Mrs. Bates gave her a disgusted frown before turning back to Elizabeth. "And exactly what would you hope to accomplish with such a visit?"

"As someone from North Dakota, I also don't have many friends in the city. We could commiserate."

"You're from South Dakota," Anna said.

"South Dakota? Are you sure?"

"Positive."

"Mrs. Bates, do you remember if it's North or South?" Elizabeth asked.

"I'm sure it doesn't matter, since you've never been to either one of them in your life."

She was right, of course, but Elizabeth was sure Mrs. Ordway would say Mrs. Bates was rude to mention it. She'd have to look that up. Meanwhile, she certainly wasn't going to accuse

Gideon's mother of being rude. "I can't believe I forgot. I never forget the tale."

"What tale?" Anna asked.

"The *tale* is the story you tell the mark when you're conning him."

Anna glanced at Mrs. Bates. "Were we marks?"

"Of course not. I never asked you for any money, did I? Although I had to con you a little, because if you thought I was a suffragist, too, you'd look after me."

"And your life was in danger, so you can certainly be excused for lying back then," Mrs. Bates said. "But that's all behind us now, so do you think it's advisable to still claim to be from the Dakotas, whether it be North or South, when you're really from Chelsea?"

The Old Man had always advised telling as much of the truth as you could, since it was always easier to remember. Did Mrs. Ordway know that rule? Perhaps Elizabeth should write an updated etiquette book to cover all these unusual circumstances. "You're probably right. So maybe I'm just trying to get to know her better since I'll be attending her husband's church."

"I think that's perfectly logical," Mrs. Bates said. "You probably shouldn't mention your relationship with Gideon just yet, though."

"Do you think she would gossip?" Elizabeth glanced at Anna, remembering their conversation about the way Daisy Honesdale managed to gossip without seeming to. From her expression, Anna remembered it, too.

"Mrs. Honesdale doesn't approve of gossip," Mrs. Bates said. "I don't believe I've ever heard her say a bad word about anyone."

"How difficult that must be for her," Elizabeth said, earning a scowl from Mrs. Bates. "And you'll go with me?"

"Of course," Mrs. Bates said. "Since you are my protégée, your spiritual well-being is of utmost concern to me, and I want you to meet all the important people in our lives."

Elizabeth couldn't help wondering how much longer the Honesdales would be important if they were guilty of what she suspected.

Mrs. Honesdale's at-home afternoon was on Friday, which happened to be the following day. Anna had begged to go along, but Mrs. Bates convinced her that three would be too many to descend upon the unsuspecting minister's wife, especially if she had additional callers.

Elizabeth was more than prepared for the visit. She'd spent most of the previous evening and that morning studying Mrs. Ordway's chapters on calls and conversation. She didn't want to break any etiquette rules that would expose her as a counterfeit lady, after all. Oddly enough, Mrs. Ordway's rules were remarkably similar to those followed by a good con man: Don't monopolize the conversation. Don't argue. Don't contradict. Don't interrupt. Of course, Mrs. Ordway didn't think it proper to inquire into another person's private affairs, but how else could you find out if a mark was worth fleecing? And how else could Elizabeth find out if Mrs. Honesdale was who she claimed to be? So she'd have to tread carefully.

"Mrs. Bates," Daisy Honesdale said, rising to greet them in her parlor when her maid announced them. "And Miss Miles. How nice to see you." Daisy appeared to be alone, which would make the job much easier.

The minister's house was exactly what Elizabeth had expected, a modest home a mere block from the church and furnished with an eye more for frugality than fashion. The horsehair-upholstered furniture would last a generation, at least, and the tables were obviously family pieces that had been passed down because someone had died, and had been received out of obligation rather than pleasure. The minister's wife wore a gown every bit as modest as her house so far as style was concerned, but Elizabeth noted the fabric was the best quality and her shawl was cashmere. Her shoes were the softest calfskin, and the brooch at her throat appeared to be made of genuine precious stones, if Elizabeth's eyes did not deceive her.

What surprised her the most, however, was that Mrs. Honesdale was older than she'd realized at first. Now that she had the leisure to study the woman in decent light, she realized Mrs. Honesdale was much closer to forty than thirty, which was surprising because Reverend Honesdale surely was much younger.

"Would you care for tea?" Mrs. Honesdale asked. "I have some lovely ladyfingers, too." She rang without waiting for their reply.

"I'm taking Elizabeth around to meet people in our church," Mrs. Bates said. "She's seriously considering joining, you see."

"How nice," Mrs. Honesdale said, although she didn't seem to think it nice at all.

"I think it's important to find a church as soon as possible after moving to a new place," Elizabeth said quickly, before Mrs. Honesdale could ask what church she belonged to now.

"It certainly is. You never know when you'll need the support only a church family can provide."

"Mrs. Knight told me how supportive everyone was when her husband died. Or perhaps I should say 'husbands,' since she lost two of them."

Mrs. Honesdale shook her head. "A very sad situation. I hope she felt that we provided all the comfort she needed during that difficult time."

"I'm sure she does," Mrs. Bates said.

"Are you and Miss Miles related?" Mrs. Honesdale asked Mrs. Bates.

"No, we aren't."

"Why do you ask?" Elizabeth said.

"I was just wondering why Mrs. Bates has taken such an interest in you." Mrs. Honesdale smiled to soften her words, but Elizabeth wasn't fooled. She was dying of curiosity.

"Miss Miles and I met when I was demonstrating for women's suffrage in Washington City in November."

"Oh my, and were you imprisoned as well, Miss Miles?" Mrs. Honesdale seemed amused for some reason.

"Yes, I was." Elizabeth instinctively touched the pin she'd chosen to wear today.

"I could hardly credit it when I heard Mrs. Bates had been arrested. I had no idea demonstrating for women's rights was illegal."

"Our demonstrations were not illegal," Mrs. Bates said with just the slightest trace of annoyance. "They charged us with obstructing traffic, which we weren't doing, but the president was tired of seeing us every day, so any excuse would do."

"Don't you support women's suffrage, Mrs. Honesdale?" Elizabeth asked.

Mrs. Honesdale smiled what she probably intended to be a kind smile. Elizabeth recognized the effort she put into it because she'd done the very same thing many times. A smile could say any number of things, and Elizabeth had practiced her variations in front of a mirror until the average observer couldn't tell she was acting.

145

Mrs. Honesdale could use a bit more practice.

"I believe a woman's place is in the home. The scripture is very clear about that."

"Can't a woman take care of her family and still vote?" Elizabeth asked with wide-eyed innocence she knew looked genuine enough to fool Mrs. Honesdale and probably even Mrs. Bates.

"Why would a woman want to soil herself with the dirt of politics? A woman's duty is to keep herself pure and make her home a refuge from the pollution of the outside world where her husband can restore himself."

That sounded awfully boring to Elizabeth, but she said, "I don't have a husband and neither does Mrs. Bates."

"If you did, he would probably forbid you from putting yourself in a situation where you ended up in jail, Miss Miles. That would be his Christian duty."

Would it? She'd have to make sure Gideon didn't feel it was his Christian duty to keep her chained to the kitchen stove once they were married. She glanced at Mrs. Bates and was amused to see her pressing her lips tightly together as if holding back a scathing reply, which she would probably consider rude to make to her minister's wife. Elizabeth felt sorry for her having to use so much restraint. "Hopefully, women won't have to put themselves in that sort of situation anymore. Did you know the House of Representatives passed the Women's Suffrage Amendment yesterday?"

Mrs. Honesdale actually winced a bit. "I'm afraid I don't read the newspapers, or at least I only read the society section."

Was she really so ignorant? Although Elizabeth had to admit she hadn't used to pay much attention to the workings of government, either. Meanwhile, she'd already counted at least two ways in which Mrs. Honesdale had violated Mrs. Ordway's rules of etiquette. She decided it was time to violate one or two herself.

"I understand you're fairly new to the church as well, Mrs. Honesdale, and to the city, too. Where is your home?"

"I . . . A small town in Maryland. You would never have heard of it."

So small it probably didn't even exist. "How did you meet your husband, then?"

"Friends. Mutual friends introduced us." Her expression was still undisturbed, but Elizabeth noticed her hands had grown a bit restless.

"It must have been difficult to court from so far away."

Her smile was a little crooked this time. "We wrote a lot of heartfelt letters."

"Your family must miss you."

"I . . . I don't have any family left, I'm afraid."

"I'm so sorry," Mrs. Bates said quickly, before Elizabeth could break another rule by asking another question instead of expressing sympathy.

Elizabeth was quite offended, since she knew perfectly well that expressing sympathy was the correct response. She managed not to sigh.

"I've been blessed by finding the Honesdale family. I would feel selfish wishing for more."

"Is it a large family?" Elizabeth asked. "Does Reverend Honesdale have brothers and sisters?"

"No, unfortunately my husband is an only child, but his parents have treated me like the daughter they never had."

"Cousins, then? Sometimes they can be as close as siblings."

Mrs. Honesdale's smile was noticeably strained now. "No cousins that I know of."

Or none she wanted to claim.

Mrs. Honesdale was rescued by the maid, who brought in the tea tray. Mrs. Honesdale served them tea and ladyfingers. She admitted she had gotten them from a bakery, since a minister couldn't afford a cook.

"Do you find New York much different from Baltimore?" Elizabeth asked when they'd had an opportunity to enjoy their refreshments.

"I . . . New York is like no other place on earth, or so I'm told."

Which didn't answer the question but did answer another of Elizabeth's. "I hope you like it, though."

"It can be overwhelming at times. Do you like it?"

"Very much. It's so very different from South

Dakota." She didn't dare glance at Mrs. Bates, and she would point out later that she hadn't actually claimed to be from there. She had to be from somewhere, though, since she'd led Mrs. Honesdale to believe she'd recently arrived. "I'm fortunate that Mrs. Bates has taken me under her wing, because she has given me the opportunity to learn so much about the city."

"And are you planning to stay? Since you are thinking about joining the church, I mean."

"I'm thinking New York is where I belong, and I believe Mrs. Bates agrees." She would have to tell Gideon how good she was getting at misleading people without really lying. She'd never realized it was a skill she'd need.

"Yes, I do think she belongs here," Mrs. Bates said. "Elizabeth is the daughter I never had." Mrs. Bates gave her such a loving look that Elizabeth almost lost her composure. But Mrs. Bates was probably just saying that to explain her interest in Elizabeth's spiritual well-being.

"Mrs. Bates is very kind," Elizabeth said. "I'm so fortunate to have been jailed with her." Did Mrs. Honesdale wince just a bit? Elizabeth hoped so. "Did you know Mrs. Knight had planned to travel to Washington City with Mrs. Bates to demonstrate, too, but she couldn't go because her husband died?"

"I think she may have mentioned it," Mrs. Honesdale said a little grudgingly.

"I'm surprised Mr. Knight would have allowed it," Elizabeth said, "if what you say is true about it being a man's Christian duty to keep his wife at home. Wasn't Mr. Knight an elder in the church?"

"Yes, he was, but I can't speak for him. I don't know his views."

"So he may have disagreed with you? Or with Reverend Honesdale, I mean, since he's the one who decides what you can and cannot do."

This time her annoyance was unmistakable if subtle. "A woman must submit to her husband's will." But Mrs. Honesdale didn't have to like it, and apparently she didn't. How interesting. "And speaking of husbands, you mentioned that you are unmarried, Miss Miles. What does your family think of a single female being off on her own?"

"Like you, I have no family to speak of." Elizabeth usually made a point of not speaking about them. "But I'm hardly on my own. Mrs. Bates is looking after me quite well."

"I'm sure she is, but I meant your trip to Washington City to, uh, demonstrate. I'm sure my family would never have permitted me to do such a thing."

Since she claimed to have no family, how could she be sure? But Mrs. Ordway would say it was rude to ask that. "I can't speak for your family, but mine always encouraged independence."

"Did they? But independence can be difficult

150

for a female to achieve without resources, can't it?"

Aha! Elizabeth would have to alter her opinion of Mrs. Honesdale. She was even more clever than Elizabeth had given her credit for being. Mrs. Honesdale had just opened a door for Elizabeth, so she decided to walk through to see where it led. "Yes, it can, but I'm extremely fortunate to have resources."

"How lucky you are. Too many young women who are orphaned find themselves destitute and at the mercy of circumstances."

By which they all knew she meant "at the mercy of men." The circumstances of which Mrs. Honesdale spoke often forced women to sell the only thing of value they possessed: themselves. "I hope you don't speak from experience," Elizabeth said, schooling her expression to innocent concern.

Mrs. Honesdale's answering smile was sweetly tragic. "I did have to make my own way in the world until I married Mr. Honesdale."

"And now you have a loving husband and a beautiful home."

"I hope you are as fortunate as I someday," Mrs. Honesdale said in a tone she must imagine made her sound wise. "But a young woman with resources who is as lovely as you are should have no trouble at all attracting a husband."

"And you think that should be my life's goal?"

"Most young women would consider it so, but perhaps suffragettes are a different breed."

"*Suffragists.*"

"What?" Mrs. Honesdale asked, confused.

"We call ourselves *suffragists*. The term 'suffragette' is demeaning."

Mrs. Bates had had enough of their sparring. "It's a common mistake. I'm sure Mrs. Honesdale meant no offense."

"Of course I didn't. I had no idea. The newspapers—"

"Are always determined to give offense," Elizabeth said. "You can certainly be excused for not knowing."

"I apologize. But I am curious. Do *suffragists* not aspire to marriage?"

Elizabeth thought of Anna. "Not all of us do, just as not all women who aspire to marriage will achieve their goal. That's why we believe women need equal rights, so they can earn a decent living on their own if they remain single."

"I see." She didn't seem happy about it, though.

"Surely, you can sympathize. You said yourself that you had to make your own way before you married."

"Yes, but that is not God's plan."

"God should have made all females rich and beautiful, then, so men would be clamoring to marry every one of them," Elizabeth said, not daring to glance at Mrs. Bates, who she thought must be nearly choking on her embarrassment at Elizabeth's boldness. "How did you earn your living, if you don't mind my asking?"

Plainly, she did, but she said, "I turned my home into a boardinghouse."

"Oh my," Mrs. Bates said before Elizabeth could express an opinion. "That must be very hard work."

"It was, of course, but I only catered to young ladies, and they weren't any trouble at all."

"Unless they couldn't earn enough to pay their rent," Elizabeth offered.

"I must admit, that was sometimes a problem," Mrs. Honesdale said grudgingly. Because women only earned a pittance compared to men.

"I suppose that explains why you were so concerned about Mrs. Knight when her first husband died," Elizabeth said.

"I'm sorry, I don't . . ." Mrs. Honesdale said, obviously confused.

"When you heard her first husband had left her penniless, I mean," Elizabeth explained. "So you encouraged her to remarry quickly."

"Oh yes, well, I couldn't bear to see Mrs. Knight reduced to . . ." She gestured vaguely.

"Operating a boardinghouse?" Elizabeth said helpfully.

"Not that there's any shame in it," Mrs. Bates added hastily. "It's a perfectly respectable way to make a living."

"But there was no reason Mrs. Knight had to do any such thing," Mrs. Honesdale said, having regained her composure.

"Not when she could simply marry herself off to another man who could support her," Elizabeth said.

Mrs. Honesdale obviously took offense at that. "I'm sure Mrs. Knight was very fond of Mr. Knight and took great comfort in knowing her daughters would be provided for."

Elizabeth pretended to consider that for a moment. "And yet, Mrs. Knight told us that her first husband, Mr. Jenks, had left her very well provided for and she didn't have to remarry at all."

"Really? How odd," Mrs. Honesdale said.

"What do you consider odd?"

Mrs. Honesdale blinked a few times, and Elizabeth figured she was scrambling for an answer. "That I . . . We were sure . . . I mean, we'd heard . . . Reverend Honesdale and I, that is . . ."

"That Mrs. Knight was penniless?"

"Perhaps not penniless, but in reduced circumstances."

"And who told you this?"

"I . . . I don't remember."

"Could you try to remember? It's very important," Elizabeth said.

"I can't think why it would be. In any case, I believe it was general knowledge."

154

"But someone had to start the rumor, and since it wasn't true . . ." Elizabeth shrugged.

"You probably think, as a minister's wife, I shouldn't listen to gossip, and I assure you, I do not do so by choice, but sometimes . . . Well, people don't often speak about their own needs, so we must rely on others to keep us informed. Mr. Honesdale and I always want to be of service whenever we can, and if gossip is the only way we can learn of people's needs, then it is a necessary evil."

"And of course you never spread gossip yourself," Mrs. Bates said loyally.

"Not knowingly, and this is the first I have heard about Mr. Jenks. I'm very glad he didn't leave his family destitute."

"If you had known, would you still have encouraged Priscilla to marry Mr. Knight so soon after Mr. Jenks died?"

"I'm afraid I can't take credit for that. Mr. Honesdale and I suggested Mr. Knight call on her. We were hoping, naturally, but we hardly *encouraged* a romance between them."

Which was a very different story than Priscilla had told.

"And are you sure you don't remember who told you Priscilla was in reduced circumstances?" Elizabeth said.

"I'm sorry, but no. It was so long ago, and . . ."

. . . and that person probably didn't even exist,

because if Mrs. Honesdale would lie about her role in getting Priscilla and Endicott Knight married, she'd lie about everything.

Elizabeth could think of only one reason for the minister's wife to lie at all.

CHAPTER SEVEN

"I'm sorry if I embarrassed you," Elizabeth said to Mrs. Bates as they walked home from their visit.

"I wasn't embarrassed, although I have to admit I was a bit shocked at the way you interrogated Mrs. Honesdale."

"Interrogated? Oh dear, I hope I wasn't that aggressive."

Mrs. Bates smiled kindly. "Let's just say I don't think Mrs. Ordway would have been pleased."

"You're right. She definitely does not approve of disagreements during social calls."

"Which is why I was surprised that Mrs. Honesdale expressed her disapproval of the suffrage movement quite so ardently."

"I was surprised, too. Mrs. Ordway is quite firm on the subject. Do you suppose . . . ?"

"Do I suppose what, my dear?"

Elizabeth feigned dismay. "I wouldn't want to be guilty of gossip, of course, but . . ."

Mrs. Bates chuckled and shook her head. "Out with it!"

"All right, but first let me ask you something. Did you need to read Mrs. Ordway's book or something like it to learn all the rules of society?"

"Heavens, no. I've been going on calls ever since I was a girl, and one simply learns how to behave. My mother instructed me, too, of course."

"And you probably learned even more from watching other women," Elizabeth guessed.

"Yes, and listening to what they criticize in others, which is probably the best lesson of all. Society women always know when someone is, uh, inexperienced."

Elizabeth smiled slyly. "You mean *new money,* don't you?"

"That is such a snobbish term."

"Yes, particularly when so many *old money* families don't have any money at all."

"We still have our pride, dear, and no one can take that but ourselves."

"What does that mean?"

"I have no idea," Mrs. Bates admitted. "At any rate, I think what you're tactfully trying to ask me is whether I think Mrs. Honesdale is old money or new."

"Was I being tactful? It was completely unintentional."

"And quite honestly, you could use more practice at it, but to answer your question, Mrs. Honesdale is definitely new money."

"I knew it!"

"One shouldn't look too pleased when proven right."

Elizabeth made a mental note of it. "This is very interesting."

"Why?"

"Because we know that Reverend Honesdale's cousin operates illegal businesses, and if that fact were known, it might limit his ability to marry a woman from a socially prominent family, and now we know his wife is not from a socially prominent family."

"I'm not sure why it should be significant, though. Many people marry someone from a different social class. Millionaires often marry showgirls, for example."

"Do Knickerbocker scions marry con men's daughters?" Elizabeth asked with feigned innocence.

"Gideon would not like to be called a scion, but I certainly hope they do, which only goes to prove my point."

Elizabeth pretended to consider her argument while they waited at a corner for the traffic cop to stop the motorcars so they could cross. "How old do you think Mrs. Honesdale is?"

"I don't know. I've never given it any thought."

"I think she's close to forty."

"She couldn't be."

"Why not?"

"Because Reverend Honesdale is only thirty-one."

"Why couldn't she be forty, then?"

"I . . . Well, I suppose she could be, but it just seems . . . I mean, men usually marry women younger than they are or at least the same age."

"I suppose they do," Elizabeth said as they ventured out to cross the street, "and a woman her age is unlikely to give him children, which ministers are expected to have, I'd guess."

"No more so than any other man, but children are always an expected outcome of marriage, at least if the couple is young."

"But Mrs. Honesdale is not young, and she's not from a wealthy or socially prominent family. Did you notice her dress?"

"Not particularly."

"I did. It was very expensive."

"I'm sure you're mistaken. I thought it very plain."

"I didn't say it was fancy. I said it was expensive. It fit her perfectly, and did you notice the little pleats? Some dressmaker spent hours on them. That dress cost more than Reverend Honesdale earns in a month."

Mrs. Bates frowned as they parted momentarily to pass on either side of a woman who had stopped on the sidewalk for no apparent reason. "I did notice her shoes were very nice," she admitted when they came together again.

"Handmade. And her shawl was cashmere."

"How could you . . . ?"

"You need to be able to size up a mark to know if he's worth your trouble," Elizabeth said apologetically. "But don't tell me you didn't notice those pleats."

"They were lovely, I'll admit, but I'm sure there's some explanation."

"I'm certain of it."

Daisy had resisted going to find Peter at the church when her visitors had left. The church was always crawling with people who thought it was their duty to observe and report whatever the pastor was doing or not doing, none of which ever completely met with their approval.

No, the church was too dangerous. This house was the only place they could really talk, and then only after the maids had left for the day. Today, she had sent them home early, preferring to fix supper herself rather than delay her discussion with Peter.

"Why are you sitting here in the dark, darling?" he asked when he came into the parlor. He switched on the electric lamp on the table beside her chair.

"Sit down, Peter. We need to talk."

He registered alarm, as she had intended, and took the chair next to hers. "What's wrong?"

"Mrs. Bates brought that Miles girl to visit me today."

"But that's good, isn't it? You said you wanted to know more about her."

"She was remarkably reticent, however, for one who did so much talking."

"Didn't you ask her any questions?"

Ninny. "Of course I did, and she did her best to give me as little information as possible. She claimed she's from South Dakota, of all places, and she has no family, and she intends to make her home in New York and join our church."

"That's a lot," he said.

"That's nothing, and most of it probably isn't even true. Nobody is from South Dakota."

"I'm sure someone is, darling."

"No one we know. No one in New York."

"It is very far away."

Shut up. "She was remarkably insistent about hearing my life story, however."

"You didn't tell her, did you?" he asked in alarm.

"Do you think I'm a fool? No, I told her the Maryland story."

"People have always liked that story."

Because she'd created it for that purpose. "Priscilla has been confiding in her."

"Has Priscilla found out about . . . ?"

"I don't know, but she told Miss Miles that Jenks left her well off. Miss Miles wanted to know if I remembered who had started the rumor that she was penniless."

"I believe we said she was in reduced circumstances."

"It doesn't matter what we said. The important thing is that we are not the ones who said it. Someone else told us, and we had no reason to doubt it."

"And we saw it as our Christian duty to help her find a husband to take care of her," he parroted.

"And of her children. Don't forget the children."

"I won't," he promised. "But who did you say told us?"

"I said I don't remember, and neither do you. It was simply common knowledge."

"Common knowledge. That sounds reasonable."

"And that's all you know."

"Yes, that's all I know. This is so complicated. It didn't seem complicated when we started."

Idiot. "It's not complicated. I warned you the Miles girl was smart, but she's not as smart as we are. She just wants to help her friend. All we have to do is convince her we want that, too."

"Yes, we do. That's why we introduced her to Endicott in the first place."

"Don't say that, Peter. Don't say anything about it."

"All right. But I don't like the idea of this girl snooping around. Can't we just . . ." He gestured helplessly.

"If we must, but it would be a shame to waste her."

Peter smiled. "Yes, it would. It would be a terrible shame."

"So you think Mrs. Honesdale's expensive dress proves she was blackmailing Endicott Knight?"

163

Gideon asked skeptically after Elizabeth and his mother had told him about their visit over dinner. Now they had withdrawn to the parlor, where they could discuss it without being overheard by the servants.

"Don't forget the shoes and the shawl," Elizabeth said.

"And even all of them together don't prove anything," his mother said, "but it does seem a bit extravagant for a minister's wife."

"Maybe she had family money," he said, remembering Elizabeth would have *family money,* too. He should be happy about that, he supposed.

"I don't think so. She told us she had to turn her home into a boardinghouse to support herself," Elizabeth said.

"But she owned a home, so she wasn't exactly destitute."

"He's right," his mother said to Elizabeth. "We didn't think of that."

"So where did she get a house?" Gideon asked.

"We assumed she inherited it, I suppose," his mother said. "She said she doesn't have any family left."

"Or maybe she was married before," Elizabeth said.

"She didn't say anything about a first husband," his mother said.

"We didn't ask her, either," Elizabeth said. "She

164

could have been a widow, which would explain her age."

"Why do you need to explain her age?" Gideon asked. This conversation was proving more confusing than enlightening.

"Elizabeth thinks Daisy is somewhat older than Reverend Honesdale."

"Maybe she just looks older," he suggested. "Some women don't age well."

"I can't believe you said such an ungentlemanly thing," his mother said.

"He's right, though," Elizabeth said, "and I'd guess Mrs. Honesdale has seen some hardship, but no matter what, she's definitely older than thirty-one."

"Thirty-one?" Gideon echoed, having lost the thread again.

"Reverend Honesdale is thirty-one, dear. He's a few months younger than you are."

"Which means he's eligible for the draft," Elizabeth said. "Unless ministers are exempt."

"I imagine they are, unless they want to go as chaplains," Gideon said. "What does all of this have to do with finding our blackmailer, though?"

"As you already surmised, Elizabeth suspects Mrs. Honesdale might have spent some of the blackmail money on her wardrobe," his mother said.

"I'm just saying it's a possibility, but I did think it strange that she couldn't remember who told her Mr. Jenks had died penniless. And Anna told me she heard it from Mrs. Honesdale herself."

"Mrs. Honesdale does not gossip, though," his mother said.

"Not in the usual way, no," Elizabeth said. "She simply told Anna and some others not to judge Priscilla because she'd found herself in need or something like that. She basically shamed them for gossiping while spreading a different story herself."

"That's rather clever," his mother said with way too much admiration.

"I think she's more than clever," Elizabeth said. "And I'd love to find out what she knows about DeForrest Jenks's death."

"You can't possibly think she had anything to do with that," Gideon said.

"Not personally," Elizabeth said and smiled in a way she must know would totally distract him. "But I don't even think she's from Maryland."

"I didn't even know she was," Gideon said.

"What makes you doubt her?" his mother asked.

"She said she was from a small town and refused to name it, but when I asked her if New York was different from Baltimore, she didn't even blink."

"Why would that mean she's not from Maryland?" he asked.

"Because how many towns in Maryland can you name?"

166

"I . . ." He considered. "Baltimore."

"Exactly. If she were from Baltimore, she would have said she was in the first place. But she made up some silly story about the town being so small, we would never have heard of it. When I asked her about Baltimore, she didn't say she wasn't from there, though, so I knew she was lying."

Gideon rubbed his temple. He was now completely lost. "How . . . ?"

"If I asked you how Albany compared to Washington City, what would you say?"

"I'd say I don't know anything about Albany."

"Yes, because you didn't grow up there. When I asked her how Baltimore compared to New York, she should have said she'd never lived in Baltimore. Instead, she said something like no city is like New York, which means she doesn't know anything about Baltimore except that it was a city in Maryland, but she must have thought she'd told me she'd lived there, so she couldn't claim ignorance."

"That doesn't make any sense."

"Oh!" his mother exclaimed suddenly. "Are you saying she forgot the tale? Like you forgot North and South Dakota?"

"What tail?" Gideon asked.

"Yes!" Elizabeth exclaimed right back. "That's it, she forgot the tale, and it wasn't even a very good one to start with."

"What are you talking about? And what does it have to do with North and South Dakota?"

"North and South Dakota don't matter at all. The tale is the story a con man tells a mark to win his confidence," Elizabeth explained, her beautiful blue eyes brightening even more than usual. "Mrs. Honesdale has a story she tells about herself. That's her *tale*. She says she's from Maryland, but she claims she's from a small town and doesn't even tell you the name of it. Details are so important, though, which is why her tale isn't very good."

"Why do you suppose she won't say the name of the town?" his mother asked.

"Because if she did, there's a very small chance that someone she meets will have heard of it. Maybe my aunt Matilda was born and raised there and I spent every summer at her farm. How excited I would be to ask where she lived and who we might know in common."

"And you would soon realize she knew nothing about the town," his mother said. She was far too interested in learning the tricks of a con man.

"What does Baltimore have to do with this?" he asked.

"She could have claimed to be from Baltimore, because it's a large city and she couldn't be expected to know everyone who lives there, but because it's a large city, the chances that she'll meet someone familiar with it would be greater. I'm going to guess that she's never even been there, so she couldn't even reminisce about it."

"Then why did you ask her about it?" Gideon asked.

"As a test, to see if she was paying attention. A casual visitor wouldn't ask her about a city for no reason, so she must have assumed she'd mentioned it. As your mother pointed out, though, she'd forgotten the tale and didn't realize she hadn't mentioned it at all. She's a liar, but she's not very good at it."

"Maybe she just doesn't get much practice," his mother said generously.

"Mother, you don't need to excuse her failure to lie well," Gideon said.

His mother shrugged sheepishly. "I suppose you're right, dear."

Elizabeth gave a suspicious little cough behind her hand before she said, "Anyway, she's not from Maryland. And your mother agrees with me that she's a newcomer to society, so Reverend Honesdale married beneath him."

Finally, something he understood. "Which he might have to do if his cousin owns brothels."

"Yes. The question is, how far beneath him was she?" Elizabeth said.

"What does that mean?" Gideon asked.

"I can't help wondering what really set all of this in motion. I mean, when did it really start?"

"With Mr. Knight's perversions, I should expect," his mother said primly.

"Yes, but who first thought of involving Priscilla?" Elizabeth said. "I keep thinking her first husband's death was awfully convenient for Mr. Knight, coming as it did just when he ran out of money."

"But how could they know Priscilla would be willing to marry Mr. Knight?" his mother said.

"That's just it: she wasn't willing at all. They practically forced her, and she was so grief stricken, she didn't have the strength to resist."

"Elizabeth, really," his mother chided. "That sounds like something from a penny dreadful, and Mr. Honesdale is a minister, after all. I just can't believe he'd be a party to that."

Elizabeth didn't seem the least bit chagrined at the rebuke. "I'd just like to be sure that Mr. Jenks's death was really an accident."

"How could you possibly determine that?" Gideon asked.

"I was hoping you'd look into it for me."

"Good evening, Mr. Bates. We haven't seen you in a while," the manager said as he admitted Gideon to the venerable old building that housed the Manchester Club.

"Thank you, Tom," Gideon said as Tom helped him out of his overcoat. "I've been busy lately." He'd been spending every spare moment with Elizabeth, so going to his club had not seemed appealing. Since Elizabeth had asked him to look

170

into how DeForrest Jenks had died, however, he'd decided to stop in after seeing her home.

"Who's here tonight?" Gideon asked, rubbing the warmth back into his hands.

Tom named a few men in whom Gideon had little interest. "And Mr. Vanderslice. He'll be happy to see you, I'm sure."

Gideon had shamelessly neglected his oldest friend of late, but he couldn't spend time with David and Elizabeth together. Since Elizabeth and David had broken their engagement, things between them had been a bit awkward, or at least they probably would be if they ever saw each other. He found David in the card room, reading a newspaper. Four men were playing cards at one of the tables. Gideon nodded as he walked by and genially turned down their invitation to join them.

At the sound of his voice, David looked up and greeted him warmly. When Gideon had claimed a chair beside him and asked the waiter for some whiskey to take the chill off, David said, "Is old Devoss working you pretty hard lately?"

"No harder than usual. My mother has been keeping me busy, though." By continuing to invite Elizabeth to their home, but he didn't say that.

"She spends a lot of time with Elizabeth, doesn't she?"

Did he sound bitter? Jealous? No, just curious.

"Yes, she does. I think she enjoys having a protégée."

"Anna used to fill that role, but lately, she's been occupying her time with literary salons."

"You sound like you disapprove."

David frowned and was saved from having to reply by the arrival of the waiter with their drinks.

When the waiter had gone, David said, "She wants to go to college."

Since when? "Anna? Really?"

"She thinks she'll have to make her own way in the world, and she wants to have a profession."

Had Anna told her family of her intention to remain single? "That seems very sensible of her."

"Sensible? She's barely twenty. She'll probably be married before the year is out."

So she hadn't told them, and it certainly wasn't his place to explain Anna's reasons to her family. "Not with all the eligible young men being sent to Europe."

"I suppose that might slow her down a bit, but the war won't last much longer once our boys get over there."

They could only hope. "What kind of profession does Anna want to train for?"

"Teaching, I think. Or maybe social work. She changes her mind daily."

"Maybe you should let her go. She's a smart girl. She'd be a good teacher."

"My sister will never have to earn her own living."

Gideon raised his eyebrows in mock surprise. "Have you suddenly come into a fortune and didn't bother to mention it to me?"

David looked suitably humbled. "Of course not, but you can't think I'd make her get a job, even if she never marries. I'll always take care of her."

"Maybe she wants to do something worthwhile with her life."

"You sound like a suffragist."

"And Anna is one."

David sighed. "Maybe you're right. It can't hurt, can it?"

"No, it can't." Gideon decided to change the subject. "I've been thinking about poor Jenks lately."

"Jenks?" David echoed with a wince. "Poor devil. And to think it could have been any one of us."

"Do you think so?"

"Don't you? That concrete beast could have fallen at any time."

"Maybe so, but how often have you stood outside the club in that particular spot?"

David opened his mouth to reply and then closed it with a snap. "What are you getting at?"

"Answer my question first."

David rubbed his chin thoughtfully. "I don't

think I've ever stood outside the club in that particular spot or in any other particular spot, come to think of it."

"We all thought he must have been waiting for a cab, but that isn't where you'd stand if you were watching for one, is it?"

"No, it isn't, now that you say it. The driver would never see you so close to the building in the dark. You'd have to stand out by the curb."

"And if he'd been standing by the curb, the gargoyle wouldn't have hit him. So why was he standing where he was standing?"

"You might as well ask why the gargoyle fell when he was standing there. It was just a horrible coincidence."

"Were you here that night?"

David nodded. "I left before it happened, though."

"Everyone left before it happened, from what they said. Did you speak to Jenks that night?"

"Just to say hello."

"How did he seem?"

"I don't know. I didn't pay any attention. If I'd known what was going to happen, I might have, I guess, but I didn't."

"Did you notice him drinking more than usual?"

"I don't pay attention to how much people drink, but he shouldn't have been overindulging. Honesdale was with him, after all."

Every one of Gideon's nerves sprang to life. "Honesdale? *Peter* Honesdale?"

"Do we know any other Honesdale?"

Gideon did, of course. "I'd forgotten he's a member."

"He hardly ever comes," David said, finishing his drink and signaling for another. "Ministers have all sorts of responsibilities in the evenings, I'm told."

"Was anyone else with Jenks?"

"Not that I saw, but I wasn't here all evening. And what does it matter? Tom told everyone Jenks was the last to leave."

"And that he was drunk," Gideon added thoughtfully. Maybe Tom was the one he should be questioning.

"Yes, it was a sad business, but there's nothing to be done except take down the other gargoyles, which we already did. Say, I've been wondering . . ."

"Wondering what?" Gideon asked when David hesitated.

David glanced around to see if anyone was paying attention. No one was. Then he leaned forward and lowered his voice. "General Sterling sent me a bank draft."

"General Sterling?" Gideon echoed in amazement, since General Sterling did not really exist. He was just someone Elizabeth's father had pretended to be so they could cheat a very evil

175

man out of his fortune. David didn't know that, though. "Are you sure it was he?"

"I assume so. It was for the same amount as my commission would have been on the, uh, transaction. I was wondering if you'd received your payment as well."

"You were supposed to pay my fee," Gideon reminded him with just a trace of sarcasm and David had the grace to flush.

"Oh yes, right you are. I'd forgotten. I'll take care of that at once."

"But you got paid. How interesting." More than interesting. Did Elizabeth know? Or perhaps a better question was, did General Sterling know?

"I thought Sterling would go to jail for his part in the scheme, and surely, he didn't see any profit after the government confiscated the, uh . . ." He glanced around again. ". . . merchandise."

"I suppose you should just be grateful and not ask too many questions." Which was as close as Gideon wanted to come to explaining anything.

"I suppose you're right. I never saw anything in the newspapers about it, so I imagine the army kept everything quiet."

That would have been easy, since the army knew nothing about it.

The waiter brought David a fresh drink and Gideon refused a second one. He needed to talk to Tom, and he wanted to be sober when he did.

· · ·

"Oh, Mr. Bates, I didn't realize you were still here," Tom said later. He'd obviously come into the card room with the intention of tidying up.

"I hope I haven't kept you later than usual."

"Oh no, sir, and don't let me hurry you off."

"Actually, I was waiting to talk to you."

"Me, sir? I hope you haven't found the service unsatisfactory."

"Not at all. I've just been thinking about poor DeForrest Jenks, and I realized I didn't know exactly how his accident happened."

Tom shifted his weight uneasily from one foot to the other. "There wasn't much to it, sir. I mean, except for him dying, which was a tragedy, sure enough. He was waiting outside for a cab and the cursed gargoyle fell off the side of the building."

"Did you have any reason to suspect it might be loose?"

"Not at all, sir, and a lot of people asked us that. We inspected all the others, too, after it happened, and they were still bolted on tight as you please. Of course, the board had them removed just the same. They said nobody would come near the building again until we did."

"Did you see Mr. Jenks out that night?"

He frowned, uncomfortable with this question as he had not been with the others. "I . . . Not exactly, sir."

"What does that mean?"

Tom glanced over his shoulder, as if afraid someone might be lurking there, listening. "I saw him when I came around to check the rooms just after midnight. He was right over there." He indicated the chair in which David had been sitting. "He was asleep, and I didn't want to embarrass him, so I just left him. I figured he'd wake up before long, and if he didn't, I'd give him a shake when I was finished with my work."

"And did you have to wake him?"

"No, sir. I made sure to make some loud noises when I was cleaning up the other rooms, to give him a chance, you know, and when I came back here, he was gone."

"You're sure? He left on his own, then?"

"He must have. Like I said, he was the last one here. The cook and the waiters had gone. We were the only two here."

"Did you see him outside when you left?"

"I always go out the back, after I've locked all the doors, so I wouldn't have seen him."

"And I suppose the gargoyle fell after you'd left."

"Oh yes. They said it was after one o'clock. Some people in the area heard it fall, but they didn't know where the noise came from and it was dark, so nobody found him until the beat cop came by an hour or more later. It was a terrible thing, sir."

"Yes, it was. When they removed the other gargoyles, did you supervise them, Tom?"

"Me? Oh no, sir. Mr. Knight did that."

Gideon's nerves began to tingle again. "Mr. Knight? You mean Endicott Knight?"

"Yes, sir. He was the club president then, so it was his responsibility."

"I see. Do you know the name of the company who removed them?"

"No, sir, but I'm sure I can find out for you."

"I'd appreciate that, Tom. Thank you for your help." He slipped Tom a generous tip and waved away his gratitude.

"Oh, one more thing," Gideon said when they had moved to the foyer and Tom had helped him into his overcoat and opened the front door for him. "Do you remember if Mr. Jenks had been drinking heavily that night?"

"A lot of people asked me that, too, but I really couldn't say. I don't serve the drinks, you see. He had seven or eight drinks charged to his bill that night, but he could've been treating his friends. Our members do that, and Mr. Jenks wasn't one to overindulge."

"Did you ask the waiters?"

"They just keep count of how many drinks to charge to each member. They don't keep track of who drinks them, though."

"I don't suppose they do. Thanks again for your help, Tom."

• • •

"Oh, Elizabeth," Priscilla said when the maid announced her. "I'm afraid I'm going to go insane sitting in this house day after day."

Mrs. Ordway would probably think Elizabeth was visiting the widow too often, but Priscilla obviously thought she'd done the right thing on this wintry morning. "I would have come sooner, but I wanted to have something to tell you first."

"And do you?" Priscilla asked hopefully.

"I'm not sure how important it is, but yes, I do."

Priscilla asked her maid to bring them tea, and they sat by the fire so Elizabeth could warm herself.

Elizabeth had thought long and hard about how much to tell Priscilla. There was no need to tell her all the gruesome details about Endicott Knight, or at least not yet. Still, Priscilla might have known more than she realized about Knight's activities, and Elizabeth was determined to find out if she did. "We haven't made much progress in discovering who was blackmailing Mr. Knight, but Gideon Bates did learn who owns the mortgage on your house."

Priscilla frowned. "Isn't it the bank?"

"No, it's an individual. He said a friend asked him to help out Mr. Knight by taking the mortgage."

"Is it someone I know? Someone from church,

perhaps? Maybe we could convince them to allow us to stay, at least for a while."

"The man who owns your mortgage is Matthew Honesdale."

"Honesdale? Don't you mean *Peter* Honesdale? And that would be so kind of him, to help Endicott that way. But how would he have the funds to mortgage our house?"

"No, not Peter. It's definitely Matthew. It seems he's Reverend Honesdale's cousin."

"His cousin? Oh, I see. Reverend Honesdale must have asked his cousin to help Endicott."

"Did you know Reverend Honesdale had a cousin?"

Priscilla considered the question. "I believe there was some talk about it. Reverend Honesdale's parents took in an orphaned relative and raised him, I believe."

Elizabeth nodded. Ah yes, the typical poor relation who can never express enough gratitude to his benefactors and is therefore always considered unworthy of their generosity. That would explain Matthew Honesdale's magnificent rebellion against his religious upbringing. "This Matthew may well be that child, then. At any rate, he holds the mortgage, and he has assured Mr. Bates that he has no intention of calling in the mortgage at this time."

"That's a great relief, although I suppose it's only a temporary one. I can't expect him to be patient forever."

"No, but at least we have some time to figure out what happened."

"This Matthew Honesdale must be a wealthy man if he can afford to mortgage properties," Priscilla said thoughtfully. "I suppose he isn't a minister."

"No, he isn't," was all Elizabeth could safely say. She decided to change the subject. "Mrs. Bates and I visited Mrs. Honesdale yesterday."

"That's . . . nice," Priscilla said, obviously uncertain how she should react to this information.

"I know you're angry with her," Elizabeth hastily explained, "so I wanted to get to know her a little better to see what I thought of her myself."

"I'm not angry exactly, but I do feel that she abused our friendship."

"I think you have every right to feel that way. May I ask you something in confidence? I don't want you to think I'm a gossip or snobbish or anything like that, but have you ever noticed Mrs. Honesdale isn't exactly . . . ? I mean, she seems to lack some of the social skills one expects of a lady in her position."

"Oh, Elizabeth, how diplomatic you are. If you mean, do I think she's new money, then yes, I have noticed that."

"Actually, I don't think she's new money at all, unless marrying Reverend Honesdale made her so. She actually admitted to me that she operated a boardinghouse to support herself before she married."

"She did?" Priscilla was clearly flabbergasted. "I can't imagine she would say so even if it were true."

Elizabeth couldn't imagine it, either, now that she'd seen Priscilla's reaction. "Why not?"

"Because she's much too proud to admit to having humble beginnings."

Unless, of course, her beginnings were even more humble than operating a boardinghouse. "Did she ever tell you where she's from?"

"Somewhere in Maryland, I believe. She was always very vague. I thought she might go with us to Washington City to protest since she's from that area."

"But she's an Anti." The women who opposed the movement called themselves Antis.

"Yes. I had no idea until I suggested she go with us and she expressed her feelings on the subject. Then, of course, Endicott died and I couldn't go myself."

"Priscilla, you said you thought Mrs. Honesdale had abused your friendship. What did you mean exactly?"

"I mean she used her influence to pressure me into marrying Mr. Knight when I had no intention of doing so."

"Do you think that was her intent? To pressure you, I mean, or could she have just been encouraging you because she thought you were a penniless widow and needed a rich husband?"

Priscilla met her gaze with resolution. "I believe I told you before that my memories of that time aren't really clear. I was so upset by DeForrest's death that I could hardly think straight, and I blamed my distraction on my grief. But since your last visit, I've been going over and over that time in my mind, and I can't believe that grief alone would have made me so malleable."

"I'm sure Mrs. Honesdale can be very persuasive."

"True, but surely my grief would have made me *less* likely to remarry in haste. Even now, the thought of giving myself to another man is abhorrent. No, I can only come up with one explanation for why I was so helpless to resist Daisy's efforts to marry me off to Endicott. I think she must have drugged me."

CHAPTER EIGHT

"Mr. Bates?"

Gideon looked up from the documents he'd been studying to find Alfred standing in his office doorway. "Yes?"

"I think I know why you couldn't find a telephone number for Mr. Knight's house, sir."

Alfred was still clutching the note Gideon had charged him with delivering to Priscilla Knight because Endicott Knight did not appear to have been on the telephone exchange. "And why is that, Alfred?"

"Because nobody lives in his house."

Gideon needed a minute to fully comprehend this information, and even then he was sure he'd misunderstood. "Do you mean no one was home when you knocked on the door?"

"No, sir, although that was what I thought at first. But a house like that usually has a maid, at least, and she'd answer the door even if nobody was home, wouldn't she?"

"Usually, yes." And Priscilla and her children would probably be there, too.

"So I went around to the back door and tried again, but nobody answered there, either. That was when I noticed all the curtains were closed up tight and there wasn't any smoke coming from the chimneys and the backyard was all covered with dried-up weeds. Then the maid from next door called out to ask me what I thought I was doing. I guess she saw me at the back door and decided I was up to no good."

"And did you ask her about the house?"

"Yes. I had to tell her what my business was, so she didn't accuse me of trying to break in, and she told me nobody's lived in the house for months."

"Did you tell her who you were looking for? Maybe I gave you the wrong address."

"I told her I was looking for Mrs. Endicott Knight, and she said there wasn't no such person, as far as she knew. She said *Mr.* Endicott Knight's mother was long dead, and Mr. Knight himself had moved out almost a year ago."

Gideon resisted an urge to smack himself in the head, because Alfred would think him crazy, but suddenly, everything made sense. "Alfred, see if you can connect me with Mrs. DeForrest Jenks. I'm guessing the telephone is listed in her late husband's name."

"Drugged?" Elizabeth echoed, managing to sound suitably horrified, even though she'd suspected something of the kind. "What makes you think Mrs. Honesdale drugged you?"

"I think I told you that I couldn't remember much from that time, and I seemed to see

186

everything through a fog. I'd never felt like that before, and I haven't felt like that since, just for that one period."

"But you said yourself, you were grieving for Mr. Jenks. I think a lot of widows probably don't remember much of what happened after their husbands died, especially in your case, when it was sudden and he was so young."

"That was part of it, I'm sure, but . . . I didn't mention this before, because I hadn't realized the significance of it, but whenever I became the least bit upset, Daisy would make me a cup of tea. She said it was chamomile, but it had a funny aftertaste, and after I drank it, I always felt strange and lethargic. Ordinary chamomile tea doesn't make me feel like that."

What could Daisy Honesdale have used? A few drops of laudanum, perhaps, or some other opiate would have that effect, especially on someone who didn't use it regularly. Many women did, of course. Laudanum didn't cure female complaints, but it did make them easier to bear. The new narcotics law had made obtaining the drug more difficult, but most doctors would prescribe it if asked. "That's a very serious accusation," Elizabeth said gently, thinking how outraged Mrs. Bates and Gideon would be to hear Mrs. Honesdale accused of such a thing.

"And one not very likely to be believed,"

Priscilla said with more than a trace of bitterness. "I shouldn't have told you."

"Oh, I believe you," Elizabeth assured her.

"You do?"

"Of course. It makes perfect sense. Why else would you have married a man you hardly knew while you were still mourning the love of your life?"

"Did I tell you I hardly remember the ceremony? I felt like I dreamed it. Daisy was holding my arm and she would squeeze it and whisper the vows to me when it was time to say them. I didn't want to do it, but I just couldn't find the words to refuse. It was the most horrible feeling in the world."

"Yes, feeling helpless really is the most horrible feeling in the world. I wish we could go back and change what happened, but we can't, especially now that Mr. Knight is dead."

"And thanks to him I'm a penniless widow living in a house that doesn't belong to me at the mercy of a man I've never met. What is going to become of us, Elizabeth? How will I take care of my girls?"

Priscilla's eyes had filled with tears, and she pulled a black-bordered handkerchief from her sleeve and began to weep into it. Before Elizabeth could even begin to think of something to say that might offer comfort, a telephone rang shrilly from the hallway just outside the parlor.

By the sound of her footsteps, the maid fairly ran to answer it, and after a few moments, she tapped on the parlor door and stuck her head into the room.

"Excuse me, Mrs. Knight, but Mr. Gideon Bates would like to speak to you on the telephone."

The maid showed Gideon into the parlor and announced him. Mrs. Knight rose to greet him and so did another lady, whom Gideon was surprised to see was Elizabeth.

"I was visiting Priscilla when you telephoned, and she asked me to stay," Elizabeth explained when he'd greeted them both.

"I see," he said, although he didn't.

"I already told her that Matthew Honesdale owns her mortgage," she added, "if that's why you've come."

She should have told him she was going to do that, but no harm done, he supposed. "That *is* why I've come, but I've also discovered something else of interest."

Priscilla quickly invited him to sit down, and when they were all settled and Gideon had declined her offer of refreshment, he said, "Mrs. Knight, did your late husband own any other homes?"

"Mr. Knight, you mean?" He nodded. "He had inherited his parents' home, but he sold it after we married."

"Did he tell you that?"

"I . . ." She glanced at Elizabeth as if for assistance.

"Priscilla was just telling me that she doesn't clearly remember everything that happened during the time after Mr. Jenks died and she married Mr. Knight," Elizabeth said.

"That's perfectly understandable," he said as kindly as he could. Priscilla had obviously been crying before he arrived, and he didn't want to set her off again.

"What do you remember him telling you about his house?" Elizabeth asked her.

"We . . . I was concerned that he would expect us—the girls and me—to move into his family's home. I simply couldn't bear the thought of any more upheaval in our lives, but Mr. Knight assured me we could remain here, and . . . I don't remember exactly what he said, but whatever it was, I got the impression he was going to sell that house."

Elizabeth turned to him. "Why are you so interested in that house?"

"You remember when Mr. Honesdale showed me the mortgage documents?"

Elizabeth nodded.

"I made note of the address and jotted it down. Today, I decided I should tell Mrs. Knight that we'd learned who owned the mortgage, but I couldn't find a telephone number for Knight. I sent our office boy with a message, asking Mrs. Knight to set a time when I could call on her, and he discovered the house was empty."

"But the house isn't empty," Mrs. Knight said.

"This house isn't, but Knight's old house is. You see, that's the address that was on the mortgage documents. Mr. Honesdale has a mortgage on that house, not this one."

"How strange," Priscilla said. "If he needed funds, why didn't he just sell that house?"

"I'm not sure we'll ever know for certain," Gideon said, "but perhaps he didn't want to lose his family home, so a mortgage seemed a good compromise."

"Who owns the mortgage on this house then?" Mrs. Knight asked.

"Did someone actually tell you this house is mortgaged?"

Mrs. Knight frowned. "I'm trying to remember. I was speaking with Mr. Renfroe. He was from the bank, and he called on me after Endicott died to warn me about my precarious financial situation."

"Do bankers normally do that?" Elizabeth asked him.

"Not in my experience, but—"

"Mr. Renfroe is an old family friend," Priscilla said. "He said he was concerned because Endicott had withdrawn all of my funds from his bank, and he wanted me to be aware of that. He seemed to be hoping Endicott had simply moved them to a different bank, but that is obviously not the case."

"And Mr. Renfroe told you about the mortgage?"

"He said Endicott had mortgaged the house. I guess I just assumed it was this one, since I thought he'd sold the other one."

"I'll speak with Mr. Renfroe myself and find out for sure," Gideon said.

"That would be such a relief if we can at least remain in our home," Mrs. Knight said.

Gideon didn't remind her that she wouldn't be able to maintain the house without any income, or that he might yet discover another mortgage. Let her enjoy this sense of relief for a few days at least.

"Mr. Bates," Elizabeth said, being artificially formal for Priscilla's benefit. "Did you say this other house is empty? No one lives there?"

"That seems to be the case. Alfred said no one answered the door, and the place looked deserted."

"Is it possible . . . ? You and I were wondering where that photograph might have been taken."

"What photograph?" Mrs. Knight asked.

Gideon winced. Surely, she wasn't going to choose this moment to tell Mrs. Knight about that horrible picture.

"Priscilla, we found a photograph of Mr. Knight and his . . . mistress."

Mistress? Gideon had to give her credit for discretion.

"Oh," Mrs. Knight said, nonplussed. "Is she . . . someone I would know?"

"Not at all, but the photograph seems to have been taken in someone's home, and we were wondering where that might have been."

"I . . . Do you think it was taken *here?*" she asked, horrified.

"No, but we were just . . ."

Gideon held his breath. How would she explain their interest in the photograph?

"Since the photograph was used to blackmail him, we were wondering where Mr. Knight might have met with this woman. That might give us a clue as to who the blackmailer was."

"Could it have been *her* home?"

"We don't think so."

Gideon silently begged Priscilla not to ask how they could be sure. "There was a painting hanging on the wall, one of those hunting scenes that a man might hang in his study," he said quickly.

"I know the kind you mean. We don't have anything like that here. DeForrest abhorred hunting."

"Would Mr. Knight have had a painting like that in his house?" Elizabeth asked.

Mrs. Knight's eyes widened with sudden understanding. "Oh, I see. You think he could have been meeting this woman in the other house."

"It's possible." And that would be another reason he hadn't sold it, but Gideon wasn't going to mention that to her.

"Have you ever been to that house?" Elizabeth asked.

"No, never. And how disappointing if the photograph was taken in his own house, because that won't help you find the blackmailer."

Gideon would reserve judgment on that, and in the meantime . . . "Would you by any chance have the keys to that house?"

"Not that I know of, but I haven't been able to bring myself to go through Endicott's belongings yet. Surely, he must have had them."

"I didn't find them, either," Elizabeth said, "but I didn't go through his personal belongings, just his desk."

"Would you mind if I looked?" Gideon asked.

"Not at all," Mrs. Knight said with relief.

"Shall we go straight over to Knight's house?" Elizabeth asked when she and Gideon had left Priscilla after Gideon had located Endicott Knight's keys.

"No, because you aren't ever going inside Knight's house," Gideon said.

Elizabeth gave him her most outraged look. "Why not?"

"Because heaven knows what we might find there. You saw that photograph."

Unfortunately, she had, but, "Surely, you don't think those things are still going on there."

"No, but we don't know what might have been left behind. Besides, if Knight has been bringing women like that to his house, I don't want you to be seen going inside."

Elizabeth hated to lose an argument, but he had a point. "Are you going, then?"

"Of course."

"Alone?"

"Who would I ask to go with me?"

"I don't know. Maybe Matthew Honesdale would like to see the house."

"I'm thinking he may have been there before."

"So you're going alone?"

He smiled the teasing smile that always set loose a swarm of butterflies in her stomach. "Are you worried about me?"

"Of course I'm worried about you. Matthew Honesdale might know how to act like a gentleman, but that doesn't mean he is one, and as for his cousin . . ."

"I know you've taken a dislike to Reverend and Mrs. Honesdale, but I can't imagine they're hiding out in Endicott Knight's house waiting to attack intruders."

"Someone else might be, though. And I haven't taken a dislike to anyone. I'm just concerned because the Honesdales seem to be much more involved in this than a minister and his wife should be."

To her surprise, he frowned. "I'm afraid you're right."

A lady didn't gape at people, particularly on a public street, but Elizabeth needed all her self-control to curtail the impulse. "You found out something else besides which house Matthew Honesdale has mortgaged, didn't you?"

"I went to my club last night and talked to some people about the night DeForrest Jenks died."

"Oh dear." Elizabeth looked around for a place they could discuss this privately and saw nothing. "Should we get a cab so we can talk?"

"I suppose so. I'll take you home before I go to Knight's house."

"You don't have to go back to your office first?"

"No, Devoss only works us half a day on Saturday."

Gideon flagged down a cab, and when they were settled and the motorcar was nudging its way through the busy streets, Elizabeth said, "Tell me."

"Jenks was with Reverend Honesdale the night he died."

Elizabeth managed not to yelp in delight. Mrs. Ordway would not approve of showing that much emotion. "At the club, you mean?"

196

"Yes. Honesdale doesn't spend much time at the club ordinarily. He's usually busy in the evenings, I gather."

Could that be true? "With church work?"

"I suppose. At any rate, David was surprised to see him that night."

"David? You saw him? How is he?"

Gideon gave her a mockingly fierce glare. "I hope you're not expressing inappropriate concern for the man you jilted."

"Would it be inappropriate for me to hope he isn't suffering a fatal decline from a broken heart?"

"It certainly would. In any case, he's holding up just fine."

"I'm crushed. Did he at least ask about me?"

"In a roundabout way, yes, but more importantly, he told me he'd received a payment from General Sterling."

Elizabeth tried to look more surprised than she was. "Did he?"

"He did. He didn't know for certain that it came from the general, but he assumed it did. He was mystified, since he thought the general was in jail for war profiteering."

"As well he should be," she said as righteously as she could manage.

"Yes, if he'd really been a general and if he'd really been profiteering."

"Was David grateful, at least?"

"Immensely. He's even going to pay me my fee, now that I reminded him of it."

"How responsible of him."

"I must admit, I'm surprised. I didn't expect the Old Man to be so generous."

Elizabeth smiled sweetly. "You underestimate him."

"Or perhaps he isn't the one who sent the payment."

"Who else could have done it?" she asked as innocently as she could. Luckily, it was an expression she executed well. "Only those involved in the con get a cut of the score." And as the roper on that one, she'd received forty-five percent. The Old Man might cheat a little on the amount, but he always paid everyone. A con man who didn't pay his partners quickly went out of business. "Now finish telling me what you found out, and I have something to tell you, too. You said Reverend Honesdale was with Mr. Jenks the night he died."

Gideon sighed in defeat. "Yes, and Jenks paid for seven or eight drinks that evening, but no one knows how many of those he drank himself."

"So he could have been quite drunk or not. Did anyone notice?"

"Not particularly. Tom, the manager, said Jenks was the last member to leave that night."

"So Honesdale wasn't still there with him?"

"Tom didn't see him if he was, and Jenks was

dozing alone in the card room when Tom made his rounds."

"So that suggests he was drunk. Did Tom try to wake him?"

"He says not, and when he came back later, Jenks was gone. Tom leaves from the back door, so he didn't see Jenks standing out front."

"If Jenks woke up and walked out by himself, he couldn't have been too drunk."

But Gideon didn't agree. He didn't say anything at all.

"There's more," she guessed.

"I also asked Tom about the gargoyle that fell. We removed all the others after Jenks was killed, but Tom confirmed that none of them were loose."

"Would it be unusual for just one to have come loose?"

"Probably not, but that's not what bothered me. What bothered me was that Endicott Knight was the president of the club then, and he oversaw removing the others."

"If I told you this, you'd probably say it was a coincidence," she tried.

"Yes, I would, but I'm starting to see too many coincidences in all of this."

He was right, of course, and she'd already seen them.

"You said you had something to tell me, too," he said.

"Yes, I do." And maybe this time he'd share her

suspicions. "Remember Priscilla said she doesn't recall much of what happened after Mr. Jenks died?"

"Yes."

"She said she's been thinking about it a lot lately, and she recalls that Mrs. Honesdale often made her some tea when she came to visit. Priscilla thinks the tea was drugged."

After the cab driver dropped him off in front of Endicott Knight's old home, Gideon stood on the sidewalk for a long moment studying the house. He couldn't stop thinking about Elizabeth's theory that Daisy Honesdale had drugged Priscilla Knight in order to make her more compliant. The very thought was inconceivable, or rather it should have been and would have been a mere week earlier. Today, however, nothing seemed beyond the realm of possibility.

Maybe Elizabeth was right and he should have brought someone with him to go through the house, but he still couldn't think of whom he could have asked in good conscience. Of course, he might not find anything at all, which was his fondest hope.

With a weary sigh, he climbed the front steps and found the correct key and opened the front door.

"Hello?" he called, just in case. "Anybody home?"

But as Alfred had described, the house was cold and empty, the rooms dim behind their drawn curtains. Dust covers draped most of the furniture so it looked like a dwelling for large, blocky ghosts.

Gideon went systematically from room to room. The image from the photograph was burned into his memory, so he recognized the painting the instant he found it in the largest bedroom upstairs. The masculine furnishings of the room told him this was the master's bedchamber. The beds in the other bedrooms had been stripped and the mattresses rolled up, but here the bed was made, as if waiting for the master to return at any moment.

The other rooms were dusty, and this one was, too, but here the dust had been disturbed. Not swept or cleaned, but shifted and dragged and probably even caught up by the equipment pictured in the photograph. Mercifully, that equipment had been removed, or at least moved from this room. Gideon had no intention of searching the attics for it. All that remained from the photograph was the ordinary painting hanging on the wall of men on horseback hunting foxes.

What things had happened here? And now that Priscilla had raised the possibility that she had been drugged to make her more compliant, he had to wonder about Endicott as well. Had he willingly posed for that photograph? Because a photograph like that, taken indoors in poor light, would have required a camera, a photographer, and a flash lamp that produced a blinding explosion of light.

No one had snuck up on him and caught him by surprise. Either he had knowingly cooperated or he'd been under the influence of something stronger than alcohol and hadn't known what was happening. Since the photograph had been used to blackmail him, Gideon couldn't imagine Knight had participated willingly. He might have regularly indulged his appetites in unusual ways, but no man in his right mind would allow someone to obtain proof of it that could ruin him.

No dust covers protected the furniture in this room, so Gideon took a few minutes to check the drawers in the dresser and nightstand. Finding them empty, he went into the bathroom to check there. The cabinets were empty, but he did see a small brown glass bottle that had rolled into a corner.

It was empty now, too, but it had once contained laudanum.

Gideon climbed out of the cab that evening and took the steps two at a time up the front porch of the ramshackle old house where Elizabeth lived. Even though he'd seen her earlier today, he couldn't wait to see her again, and he twisted the doorbell with a little more enthusiasm than was necessary. The door opened and there she was, wearing a bright red dress with lots of straps crisscrossing on the top that still left her silky white arms and shoulders bare, and a long skirt that clung to her curves, making his breath lodge sharply somewhere behind his breast bone.

"Hello," he managed.

"Is that all you can say?" she asked, twirling completely around so he could appreciate her from all sides.

"Just let me catch my breath."

Her laugh rang like fine crystal. "Come inside and kiss me so I can put on my lip rouge."

He happily obeyed.

"Won't you be cold?" he asked while she used the hallway mirror to paint her lips.

"Oh, please," she said, laying her free hand over her heart. "I don't think I can stand all this romantic talk."

"I'm only thinking of your welfare."

"Women never think of their welfare where fashion is concerned, but don't worry, I have a coat."

She did indeed, an amazing thing with a cape-like collar made of some kind of fur. "Is this new?"

"Most of my clothes are new. You made me return all those beautiful things I got in Washington City."

The beautiful things she'd *stolen* in Washington

City, but he wouldn't mention that. It was a lifetime ago, in any case. Or almost two months, which was practically the same thing with Elizabeth. "Well, it's beautiful, and the dress is . . ."

"Breathtaking?" she offered with a grin when he couldn't come up with a word to describe her magnificence.

"Completely. Come on. Anna will be freezing out there in the cab."

"I hope *she* has a coat," Elizabeth said with a laugh.

Anna was tucked up under a lap robe of dubious origins, since it came with the cab, but she did indeed have a coat over her gown. "I hope you appreciate the sacrifices I make for you both," she said when Elizabeth had climbed into the cab and greeted her.

Gideon climbed in behind her and instructed the cab driver to take them to the theater, where the three of them were going to see a very funny comedy, according to the reviews.

"Sacrifices?" Elizabeth scoffed. "We're taking you to the theater."

"Gideon has paid me so much attention lately that David is convinced he's going to marry me."

"No, he's not," Gideon said. "He told me last night that he's thinking of sending you to college."

"Really? Did he say that?"

"Yes, he did, after I convinced him it would keep you out of trouble."

"Oh, Gideon, I could kiss you!"

"No, you couldn't. It would spoil your lip rouge."

"Oh, Anna, that's such good news," Elizabeth said. "How soon could you start?"

"I don't know. I'll have to ask Cybil. Probably not until the fall term. The spring term starts in just a few weeks. Did David say he would pay my tuition?"

"I assumed that would be his responsibility," Gideon said, surprised that she would ask. "He just received a commission from General Sterling, so now would be a good time to ask him."

"General Sterling?" Anna cried in delight. "Are you serious?"

"He's very generous," Elizabeth said primly.

"I'll have to thank him next time we meet," Anna said.

"That's not really necessary, and it would just embarrass him," Elizabeth said, confirming Gideon's suspicion that her father knew nothing of the payment. "So did you find anything at the house today, my darling?" she added before he could comment on General Sterling's generosity.

"What house?" Anna asked. Elizabeth briefly told her about the mortgage situation and the painting. "So did you find anything?" Anna echoed when she had been brought up to date.

"Nothing that was in the photograph except the painting, I'm happy to say."

"What else was in the photograph?" Anna asked eagerly.

"The less you know about it, the better," Gideon said sternly. "I didn't search the attics or the cellars, so something might be hidden there, but the only thing in the house itself was a . . ."

"A what?" Elizabeth prodded when he hesitated.

"An empty bottle of laudanum."

"Laudanum?" Anna echoed. "How Victorian."

"Lots of people still use it," Elizabeth reminded her. "They just have to get it from their doctors now."

"That's true, and I'm sure we have a bottle of it somewhere in the house. Probably everyone in New York does."

"You may be right," Gideon said, "but Knight's house didn't have anything else like that, or at least his bedroom and bathroom didn't. He'd taken all his personal belongings to Priscilla's house when they married, I guess. In any case, the bottle was on the floor in a corner, like someone had dropped it and not bothered to go pick it up."

"Maybe he dropped it himself when he was packing," Anna said.

"But you don't think so, do you?" Elizabeth said.

"An empty bottle? No, I don't think so. I was trying to imagine what happened the day—or night—that photograph was taken. Someone had to set up a camera and use a flash lamp. Knight had to know someone was taking a photograph."

"Oh, I see," Elizabeth said. "It doesn't seem logical that he would allow such a thing."

"My goodness, no," Anna said. "How awful if it fell into the wrong hands."

"Which it did, since someone was blackmailing him," Elizabeth said.

"So unless he'd lost his mind, I think Knight was somehow tricked into having the photograph made," he said.

"Just as Priscilla was somehow tricked into marrying Mr. Knight," Elizabeth said.

"Did Knight drug her, do you think?" Anna asked. "That would certainly explain why she married him."

"We think someone drugged her," Elizabeth said before Gideon could reply. "Knight must have been desperate by that time."

Anna sighed. "What a horrible situation, and poor Priscilla was an innocent victim."

Fortunately, they had arrived at the theater, or at least to the queue of cabs lined up to drop people at the theater, so all discussion of Endicott Knight's tragedies had to end. Gideon assisted his two ladies from the cab and counted his blessings. He would be the envy of every man who saw him tonight, and he intended to enjoy it. Knight and his troubles could wait for another day.

• • •

In spite of her late evening, Elizabeth was up early on Sunday morning. She had to attend church with Gideon and Mrs. Bates, and not just because she was planning to marry Gideon someday. Now she should probably cultivate her friendship with Mrs. Honesdale and figure out a way to win the Reverend Mr. Honesdale's confidence as well. Before she did that, however, she needed to set something else in motion.

Cybil and Zelda were still sound asleep when Elizabeth crept downstairs and placed a telephone call to the Old Man.

"Lizzie, what in God's name is the matter? And it better be life or death if you woke me up at the crack of dawn."

"It's only the crack of dawn because it's wintertime and the sun comes up late," she informed him. "And it *is* life and death, although not *my* life or death, I'm happy to say. I need to have some people followed."

"What people?"

"Just some people," she said, ever mindful of eavesdropping operators.

The Old Man muttered something that was probably not a phrase usually heard in church. "Why on earth do you need to have people followed?"

"You know why."

"Oh," he said, probably only now coming fully

awake. "And did the man I told you about prove to be, uh, helpful?"

"Yes, he did, and now I just need a recommendation, someone who can tell me where certain people go and who they see."

"I'll tell Jake."

"Jake?" Jake would hate being given such a menial task. He was the Old Man's son, after all, and destined for great things.

"Yes, Jake. He's not good for anything else anymore. He's lost his nerve."

"What?" she cried, outraged.

"It's true. He'll tell you himself. I'll send him over."

"Have him come to Cybil's for supper tonight."

When they'd finished their conversation, Elizabeth replaced the earpiece on the candlestick phone and sighed. She shouldn't feel guilty. It was Jake's fault their last con together had curdled and things had gone so badly for both of them. But even if it wasn't her fault, she might at least be able to set things right again.

The trick would be doing so without Gideon finding out any of this.

CHAPTER NINE

Elizabeth had a difficult time concentrating on the sermon that morning. She kept imagining Reverend Honesdale as the man in the infamous photograph instead of Endicott Knight. Would she ever get that image out of her mind?

Only if she could figure out who had taken the photograph in the first place.

After the service, she left Mrs. Bates and Gideon chatting with some of their neighbors to find Priscilla, who was enduring some sympathetic ramblings from two elderly ladies when Elizabeth rescued her.

"Just get me out of here before I have to speak to Daisy," she whispered to Elizabeth, who did try her hardest, but she was no match for a professional churchwoman. Neither of them even saw her coming.

"Miss Miles, Priscilla, how lovely to see you both," Daisy said, cutting them off by stepping out of a row of pews to block their progress down the center aisle. They couldn't proceed without literally shoving her out of the way. Elizabeth might have risked it if Gideon and Mrs. Bates weren't standing so near.

"Mrs. Honesdale," Elizabeth said brightly. "How are you this fine morning?"

"I'm so glad to see you are continuing to attend services, Miss Miles. Perhaps you'd like to make an appointment to meet with my husband to discuss joining the church."

An appointment with Reverend Honesdale was exactly what she wanted, but she needed to discuss it with Gideon first. "I think I *would* like to speak with him. Should I telephone him at the church office?"

"That would be best, I think. I'll tell him to expect to hear from you." She turned her attention to Priscilla, who actually stiffened in response. "Priscilla, I hope you're doing well. It seems like an age since we last visited."

"I'm not really receiving right now." Priscilla's face had gone pale. "I'm sure you understand."

"Friends can help allay the loneliness at a time like this," Mrs. Honesdale said.

"Yes, they can. If you'll excuse me, I'm not feeling well." She stepped forward, giving Mrs. Honesdale no choice but to step aside if she didn't want to get run over.

"If you need anything, please let me know," Mrs. Honesdale called after them as Elizabeth took Priscilla's arm and led her down the aisle.

Gideon had been watching and quickly joined them. He took Priscilla's other arm. They even managed to slip by Reverend Honesdale, who was greeting worshippers as they left the church.

"I'm sorry," Elizabeth said when they reached the sidewalk. "I didn't see her coming."

"Neither did I," Priscilla said. She thanked Gideon.

"We could find a cab for you," Elizabeth said.

"No, I'm fine. I just said I didn't feel well to get away from her. I can walk home. The fresh air will do me good."

"May I visit you tomorrow morning?" Elizabeth asked.

"Oh, please do!"

Priscilla took her leave, and Mrs. Bates joined Elizabeth and Gideon on the sidewalk. They explained what they had learned about what had happened to Priscilla as they walked the few blocks to the Bateses' house.

"How terrible that Priscilla blames the Honesdales," Mrs. Bates said as they removed their coats in the foyer.

"Not if they really are to blame," Elizabeth said.

"They seem to have been involved at least in some way," Gideon said.

"I can't believe they knew about Mr. Knight's secret life, though. He was an elder in the church, for heaven's sake. How could Reverend Honesdale tolerate that? I know that things are starting to look bad for them, but what if they really are innocent victims?"

"We certainly will give them the benefit of

every doubt," Elizabeth said, earning a sharp glance and a frown from Gideon.

He didn't have an opportunity to ask her what she'd meant until later that afternoon, though, since Mrs. Bates insisted on discussing more pleasant topics over Sunday dinner. When Mrs. Bates withdrew to her room to rest, Elizabeth and Gideon were finally able to speak freely.

"You're planning something," he said when they were snuggled up on the sofa in the parlor.

"That sounds more like an accusation than an observation."

"Just tell me what it is so I won't be surprised. I'm not going to have to watch Anna shoot you again, am I?"

"I told you how sorry I was about that."

"I know, and I wasn't even supposed to be there when it happened. I just don't ever want to do that again."

"I'm not planning any shooting."

"But you are planning something."

"I just can't help thinking your mother might be right," she said, trying out her innocent face to see how Gideon would react.

He wasn't impressed in the slightest. "You don't need to pretend to agree with her."

"But I do feel sorry for her. She's going to be terribly disappointed when she finds out how mistaken she has been about the Honesdales."

"I don't like being wrong about people, either, so it's even difficult for me to accept."

"How would you like some irrefutable proof, then?"

He muttered a curse she pretended not to hear. "Why do I have a feeling I don't want to know how you'll get this proof?"

"I already promised you, no shooting. Actually, it's all perfectly safe, and you can even be there when it happens if you like. Of course you'd have to hide, but you could be there."

He groaned but he said, "All right. Just tell me your plan."

"I ask Priscilla to invite Reverend Honesdale to visit her."

"Is that a good idea?"

"Let me finish. I'll be there when he arrives, and we'll tell him what happened, how I was helping Priscilla go through Mr. Knight's papers and I found the photograph."

"Oh dear Lord."

"And we'll pretend to be very upset, just like we really were, so naturally, Priscilla sent for her minister, because she didn't have any idea what it meant or what she should do."

"Is that what a woman in Priscilla's situation would do? Send for a minister?"

"How should I know? And more importantly, how should Honesdale know? This is not a situation many widows find themselves in."

"I should hope not."

"So we ask him for his advice because he's someone people go to for advice and he's always been so helpful, and then we see what he says."

Gideon considered her plan for a long moment. "And then what?" he said finally.

"And then we'll know if he's involved or not."

"How?"

"First of all, by how he reacts when he sees the photograph."

Gideon winced. "You're going to show it to him?"

"Of course. If he's innocent, he'll be horrified, just as you were."

"What if he just pretends to be horrified?"

She gave him a pitying look. "I'll be able to tell if he's pretending. And then we'll see what advice he gives Priscilla. That should tell us everything we need to know."

"This is not a good idea."

"Why not? You can't think Priscilla and I would be in any danger from a minister."

"Not if I'm there with you."

"You can't be there with us, though."

"Why not?"

"Because he'll wonder why an important man like you would need advice from him on something like this. Why any man would, for that matter. I'm afraid you just aren't helpless enough to suit the purpose."

"And you are?"

"Don't be ridiculous, but he doesn't know that. He sees me as an ordinary female, which is to say unworldly and helpless and not quite bright, and he'll feel very confident of having the upper hand. He'll either become protective and chivalrous and supportive—if he's truly innocent and concerned for our welfare—or he'll brush off our concerns and assure us that he can handle the situation for us and we are not to think of it again—if he's guilty."

He stared at her in amazement. "How do you know he'll do this?"

"Because that's how men treat women. I know it because every woman knows it."

"Is that how I treat you?"

She gave him a reassuring smile. "You're getting much better."

He sighed in defeat. "But you did say I could be there. *Hidden,*" he added as if the word left a bad taste in his mouth.

"Just in case, because I know how you'll worry. But also to be a witness. Because people never take a woman's word over a man's, and we may need you to verify what happened."

"But surely—"

"Don't even bother arguing the point. Men only believe other men, and you'll realize it's true if you think about it. So are you willing to hide and eavesdrop or not?"

"I . . . I don't suppose I have any choice."

"Good. And I'll need the photograph."

"The photograph? But—"

"How will I show it to him if I don't have it? You can put it into an envelope. I don't want Priscilla to see it and I don't want to see it myself ever again, so an envelope would be perfect."

"I . . . all right. When will this happen?"

"I don't know yet, but soon, I hope. I have to go see Priscilla tomorrow and make sure she's willing to do it."

"Do you think she won't be?"

"She'll be thrilled to do it. I wouldn't have come up with the idea if I didn't think so. But we'll have to plan and rehearse because she's new at this sort of thing. I'll telephone your office and let you know when Honesdale is coming."

"Do you think he'll come tomorrow?"

"Probably. If he's involved, as we think he is, he'll want to know why Priscilla needs to see him, and I doubt he'll waste any time in finding out."

Gideon hadn't wanted to take her home so early, but he agreed when she explained Jake was coming for supper. The two men had not yet met, and Elizabeth was in no hurry to arrange it. Meeting the Old Man was trial enough for someone as honest as Gideon Bates, and she knew Jake wouldn't be nearly as circumspect as the Old Man had been with the person Jake gleefully called "Lizzie's fellow."

Jake arrived early and proceeded to charm his Aunt Cybil and her partner, Zelda. His flattery was carefully specific so they understood it was genuine, and his charm was respectfully polished so they saw him as a harmless yet adored pet.

He didn't bother to use either skill on Elizabeth, who knew him far too well to be taken in by anything he did.

The meal was pleasant enough, with Jake keeping them entertained with stories and quips and feigned interest in the activities of the two older women. Throughout it all, Elizabeth watched for any sign that the Old Man was right about Jake losing his nerve. Dealing with his doting aunts and his tolerant half sister was hardly a test, however, and she saw nothing alarming.

After supper, Cybil and Zelda withdrew to their private rooms so Elizabeth and Jake could discuss the reason she'd invited him there in the first place. Cybil had long since decided to know nothing of her brother's family business.

Elizabeth poured Jake a snifter of the brandy Cybil kept for male visitors and took a seat beside him on the sofa.

"The Old Man said you have a job for me." He didn't quite meet her eye. It was the first sign something wasn't quite right.

"I told him I needed someone followed. It's not much of a job, so I was surprised when he said he'd send you. Did you do something to make him mad?" she teased, the way she'd done a thousand times.

She'd expected a fierce frown and the feigned anger her teasing usually provoked. Instead he smiled sadly and took a swallow of his brandy. "Did he tell you?"

"Tell me what?"

"I've lost my nerve."

Guilt swelled in her chest, but she managed a lighthearted "That's not funny."

"It's not a joke. When I came back from Washington City, I was . . . not myself. I thought it would pass."

"You're recovered now, aren't you? From the beating, I mean?"

"Physically, yes." He flexed the fingers of his left hand absently. That arm had been broken. "But I can't work. Not really, anyway. I can be a lookout or a shill, but if I try roping . . ." He shrugged.

"You are the best roper I know." This wasn't true, of course, but Jake had always thought it was.

He took another sip of brandy. "I freeze up when I talk to a mark. I'm afraid the Old Man is going to decide I'm excess baggage and cut me loose."

"He'd never do that."

Jake just looked at her, his eyes so sad she could hardly stand it.

"He didn't cut *me* loose when my mother died," Elizabeth said.

"He always did like you the best." He'd made that claim before, but never with such resignation.

"That's not true. You're the one he trained. I had to force him to teach me the grift."

"Because you're a girl and he wanted you to be a lady, like your mother. You were special."

This time she heard the bitterness, because his mother hadn't been a lady. "And you're his *son,*" she said with bitterness of her own. "You're the one he spent his time with."

"We've had this argument before, Lizzie, and neither of us ever wins. None of it matters now, anyway. Just tell me about this job. I need some work."

She wasn't finished with him, not by a long shot, but that would have to wait. In the meantime, she really did have a job for him. "I need you to follow some people."

"I can't follow more than one at a time," he said with a small grin that hinted at the old Jake.

"It's a married couple. He's a minister, so he doesn't get around a lot, or at least I don't think he does."

"And the woman?"

"I don't know about her. She might be the one to watch. If you want to get someone to help you, that's all right. I'll pay for both of you."

"When do you want me to start?"

"Probably tomorrow." She told him the whole story, beginning with the death of DeForrest Jenks and ending with her plan to test Reverend Honesdale's reaction tomorrow. "You can pick him up at Priscilla's house and see where he goes after that."

"How did you get mixed up in this, Lizzie?" he asked with a trace of admiration.

"I have no idea. I thought being on the grift was exciting, but not compared to these folks in society."

"I was afraid you'd get bored if you married your Mr. Bates."

"Oh, Jake, were you worried about me?" she asked sweetly.

"A little," he said more solemnly than she expected, "but this is serious. Blackmailers are a nasty lot."

"Some would say it's just another form of the grift."

"They'd be wrong, then. When we cheat a man, it's because he thinks he's cheating somebody else to get the best of it. A blackmailer, though, he's playing off somebody else's misery, and that's a lot more dangerous. You already think these people might've killed the Jenks fellow."

221

"I'm not taking any chances, and why would they care about me? I'm just a friend of the widow's."

"Who's nosing around where she shouldn't be. I hope Bates is going to keep an eye on you."

"Of course he is, but I haven't told him you'll be keeping an eye on the Honesdales, so don't mention it to him."

"I don't even know the man," Jake reminded her. Did he sound put out about that?

"You will soon enough. I've been protecting you from him."

"What? I thought you were protecting *him* from *me*."

Finally, a hint of the old Jake! "Jake, he's an honest man."

Jake actually laughed at that. Grifters always said you can't cheat an honest man, but that's never a problem because there's no such thing as an honest man. "We'll see about that."

"Yes, you will. Meanwhile, keep track of the Honesdales for me."

"How do you think of these things, Elizabeth?" Priscilla asked in wonder the next morning when Elizabeth had explained her idea.

"I don't know," she lied. "You are convinced the Honesdales are involved, but we don't have any real proof, so I was just trying to figure out how to test Reverend Honesdale's intentions."

"But what if he lies? If he's involved in blackmailing Endicott, he won't be above trying to trick us, too."

"Don't worry. You're probably very good at judging when someone is telling the truth or not. You're a mother, and I know my mother always knew if I was fibbing about something."

"You're right. I never thought of that."

"And I'm a pretty good judge of character, too."

"And Mr. Bates will be nearby as well," Priscilla said. "How shall we arrange it so he can hear what we're saying?"

In the end, they determined that Gideon would have to simply listen at the parlor door and duck into the study if Reverend Honesdale left the room unexpectedly. Elizabeth felt certain she could stop him if he tried to do so, or at least slow him down enough to give Gideon a chance to hide. And they'd have to instruct the maid to simply ignore all this ducking and hiding.

Elizabeth helped Priscilla practice the story she was going to tell Honesdale. Then they composed a note begging Honesdale to visit Priscilla that very afternoon and sent it off with a maid. Elizabeth then telephoned Gideon and Jake, and they waited.

Honesdale's reply was everything Elizabeth could have hoped for. He assured Priscilla he would arrive promptly at the appointed hour to comfort her in her time of sorrow. Priscilla was too nervous to eat lunch, but Elizabeth enjoyed her meal. She finally felt as if she were going to accomplish something that would help Priscilla.

Gideon arrived in good time. He'd placed the photograph in an envelope, as she had suggested, and luckily, Priscilla expressed no desire to see it after Gideon explained that it showed Mr. Knight in a rather compromising position. They went over the arrangements for his eavesdropping. He wasn't pleased at the thought of listening outside the door but accepted his assignment with grace. Jake, Elizabeth had to assume, would station himself outside the house at the appointed time and wait.

By the time Honesdale rang Priscilla's door-bell, even Elizabeth could feel the tremors of excitement. Conning people was exhilarating, no matter what the reason.

"Mrs. Knight, I'm so glad you sent for me," Honesdale said when the maid had escorted him inside and Priscilla had stepped forward to greet him. He was tall and slender with the pale face and soft hands of a man who preferred books to action. He wore his blond hair brushed back from his face, and his gray eyes seemed to be trying to take in the entire room at once instead of settling on anything or anyone in particular.

He took Priscilla's offered hand in both of his. "I hope you aren't too distressed." Only then did he notice Elizabeth standing slightly behind Priscilla. "Miss Miles, is it?"

"That's right," Priscilla said quickly. "Elizabeth and I have become close friends and she . . . Well, you'll understand when we tell you what happened. Please, won't you have a seat? Can I get you something? Coffee or tea, perhaps? The wind must be icy today."

"Some coffee would be welcome," he said, taking the seat near the fireplace that she indicated. Priscilla and Elizabeth sat back down on the sofa.

Priscilla instructed the maid to bring them some coffee. When she was gone, Priscilla gave him a sad little smile and twisted her hands nervously in her lap. "You must be wondering why I sent for you."

"Your note was rather urgent, so I canceled my appointments for this afternoon."

"Oh dear, I didn't mean to be such a bother," Priscilla lied. They had carefully worded the note so that he would do just as he claimed to have done.

"That's perfectly all right. I didn't have anything really pressing on my schedule. Now, tell me what I can do for you."

"This is so embarrassing, I hardly know where to begin," Priscilla said, pulling out her handkerchief and puckering up as if she were going to weep.

"Let me tell it," Elizabeth said, reaching over to pat her arm. "This has been distressing to both of us, but I'm sure Priscilla feels it much more than I."

"Now I'm truly concerned," Honesdale said, although he merely looked curious. "What has happened to upset you both?"

Priscilla nodded to indicate Elizabeth should begin. "As Mrs. Knight said, she and I have become good friends," she began, hesitantly at first, as one would expect. "After her husband died, she was rather overwhelmed, as you can imagine, and she asked me to help her go through her husband's things."

Honesdale nodded sagely to encourage her.

"So I was looking through his papers, trying to sort out what was important and determine if Mr. Knight had left any unpaid bills that should be brought to Priscilla's attention, and I found something very disturbing."

"Disturbing?" he echoed expectantly.

"More than disturbing. Quite frankly, I was shocked."

"By what, Miss Miles? There's no need to be mysterious, I'm sure."

"It was a photograph."

Some emotion flickered across Reverend Honesdale's scholarly face, but it was too brief for Elizabeth to identify it. "A disturbing photograph?"

"A *shocking* photograph."

His pale gaze flicked to Priscilla and back again. "It's difficult for me to help you if I don't know what it was a photograph of."

"It's of Mr. Knight," Elizabeth said primly.

"I haven't seen it," Priscilla said quickly. "Elizabeth wouldn't let me look at it, but she told me . . . Well, I know it's a compromising photograph, and there was a note, too."

"A note? What did it say?"

"That the photograph was just a reminder."

"A reminder of what?"

"That's just it," Priscilla said. "We have no idea. I've been through all of Endicott's things, and I didn't find anything else that would explain it."

Honesdale let that lie for a long moment, then said, "I'm not sure what it is you want me to do."

"We aren't sure, either, Reverend Honesdale," Elizabeth said. "Neither of us has any experience in such things, of course, and we hoped you could advise us."

"I'm honored that you felt you could rely on me, but without having seen the photograph in question, I'm afraid I can't offer you any counsel. Without knowing what has disturbed you—"

"Shocked us," Elizabeth corrected him.

"*Shocked* you, then I can't even judge the nature of the problem. What gently bred ladies like yourselves consider shocking might in reality be nothing serious at all."

Elizabeth wanted to ask him for an example, but she didn't dare distract him now. "Would you like to see the photograph?"

"I'm sure I wouldn't *like* to, but I think I must."

Elizabeth exchanged an uneasy glance with Priscilla, just as they'd practiced, and she picked up the envelope that had been lying on the table beside the sofa and handed it across to Reverend Honesdale.

With steady hands, he opened the flap and pulled out the photograph. Once again, some emotion flickered across his face but only for an instant. Then he slid the photograph back into the envelope. "That is indeed shocking."

"So you see why we're concerned," Elizabeth said.

"And yet there is no reason. While this is . . . *unfortunate*—and I must confess, I am disappointed in Mr. Knight for having left such a thing behind where his wife might stumble across it—I don't think it should cause you any further concern."

"No concern? Why not?" Priscilla asked.

"Because whatever his"—Honesdale glanced down at the envelope, which he still held—"sins, Mr. Knight is dead. He is beyond shame or scandal and even retribution. God will judge him, certainly, but nothing in this world can hurt him now. The only person this photograph can hurt now is you, Mrs. Knight."

"Me? But how could it hurt me?"

"Scandal, Mrs. Knight. Scandal and gossip. Although you are completely innocent, people won't particularly care about that when they spread their rumors."

"Oh dear!" Priscilla said, suitably horrified.

They all looked up in surprise when the maid tapped on the door and brought in the coffee. She set the tray down on the table nearest Priscilla's seat and slipped quietly out. No one spoke until she had gone.

"So what do you advise Mrs. Knight to do, Reverend Honesdale?" Elizabeth asked.

"Nothing. Absolutely nothing. Forget this photograph ever existed. In fact, I will take it myself and see it destroyed, so you'll never even be tempted to look at it." He tucked the envelope into his jacket pocket.

"Are you sure?" Priscilla asked. "I mean, shouldn't we inform someone? The authorities, perhaps?"

"The police, you mean? To what end?"

"I don't know. It just seems very bad of someone to have tormented him so."

"Judging from the contents of the photograph, Mr. Knight deserved to be tormented. Wouldn't you agree, Miss Miles?"

Elizabeth widened her eyes at the shock of being asked her opinion. "Yes, indeed." She turned to Priscilla. "I think Reverend Honesdale is right, and he's only thinking of your best interest."

"Well, if you agree, I . . . I suppose I'd be just as happy to never think of it again."

"That's very wise of you, Mrs. Knight. Now, if you'll excuse me, I must be going." Honesdale rose abruptly.

"Must you? Don't you want some coffee before you go?"

"Thank you, but no. I'm afraid I'm late for a pressing engagement," he said, giving the lie to his claim of having canceled all his appointments for the afternoon.

Elizabeth jumped to her feet. "I'll see Reverend Honesdale out."

She followed their guest out into the mercifully empty hall—Gideon had managed to make himself scarce—and to the front door and found his overcoat hanging on the coat tree.

"I hope we can trust your discretion, Reverend Honesdale. Priscilla would be mortified if anyone knew about this."

"I have no intention of telling anyone, and as soon as I get home, I will destroy the photograph. You need have no concern about this, Miss Miles."

"Thank you for your help," she said as she opened the door for him.

"My pleasure."

Elizabeth wondered exactly what part of this encounter he had found pleasurable.

She waited for a long moment, her hand still on the door from pushing it closed, to make sure he was truly gone.

"What were you thinking?" Gideon demanded in a furious whisper as he came out of the study where he'd retreated during Honesdale's exit. He was obviously conscious of the fact that Honesdale might still be nearby and managed to convey his anger while also keeping his voice low. "You let him take the photograph. Without it, we don't have any proof that—"

She held up the envelope so he could see Honesdale had not, in fact, taken the photograph.

His amazement was almost comical. "Where did you get that?"

She merely smiled and gave it to him and returned to the parlor, where Priscilla was pouring coffee for the three of them.

"He was lying," Priscilla announced triumphantly as they came into the room. "He knew exactly what photograph we were talking about. In fact, he knew it was a photograph before we even told him. I'm sure of it."

"So am I." Elizabeth turned to Gideon. "Mothers always know when someone is lying."

"You aren't a mother. And how did you get this from him?" he added, holding up the envelope.

"He dropped it when he was putting on his overcoat."

"That was convenient."

"You don't sound as if you believe me," she chided, taking her seat and accepting a cup of coffee from Priscilla. "Were you able to hear everything he said?"

"Most of it," Gideon said, taking the chair Honesdale had vacated and accepting some coffee from Priscilla. "And Mrs. Knight is right; he already knew what you'd found."

"You should have seen his face when he saw the photograph," Elizabeth said. "He wasn't shocked at all. He actually looked more annoyed than anything."

"You may be right, but why would he have been annoyed?" Priscilla asked.

"Probably because it had been found," Gideon said. "Without it, we would have had no idea what happened to all of the money."

"But we did find it and we do know," Priscilla said. "What do we do now?"

Elizabeth looked at Gideon but he didn't meet her eye. "We'll need some more proof," he said. "We know Knight was being blackmailed and why, and we believe the Honesdales were involved, but we don't have anything to actually prove the money went to them."

"How can you prove that?" Priscilla asked.

Gideon still wouldn't meet Elizabeth's eye. "I need to speak to your banker, to see if he has any idea where the money went."

"And surely, he'll know," Priscilla said.

"Yes, surely," Gideon agreed.

But Elizabeth knew he was simply humoring her. The banker would most likely have no idea. Blackmailers didn't take checks. Knight had probably withdrawn the blackmail payments in cash, and after that, the money would be untraceable. She wasn't going to tell Priscilla that, however, especially because Elizabeth wasn't depending on some banker to help retrieve money paid in blackmail.

CHAPTER TEN

Would Elizabeth keep attending these Monday night salons after they were married and she no longer lived with her aunt? Gideon wondered as he helped Anna out of the cab that had delivered them to the big house in Chelsea. At least he would no longer be expected to escort Anna every week.

Cybil greeted them warmly, kissing Anna on both cheeks. "Elizabeth hasn't come down yet," she said.

Anna looked up at the imposing staircase and said, "Here she is."

Gideon instantly moved to the stairs to meet her and was shocked to see an attractive young man following her down the stairs. The only rooms upstairs were bedrooms, and no young men had any business upstairs in this house.

The young man said something to Elizabeth, and she looked back up at him and smiled the way he'd thought she only smiled at him. Then she turned back and held out her hand to Gideon. He took it in both of his, and when she reached the bottom step, he pulled her in and kissed her soundly, staking his claim for the young man's benefit.

"Oh my," she said with obvious delight when

he was done, and Gideon couldn't resist a glance at the young man to gauge his reaction.

Oddly enough, he merely seemed amused. "So, Lizzie, this must be your fella, because if he's not, your fella better be worried."

"And who are you?" Gideon asked more defensively than he'd intended.

"Gideon, this is Jake," she said.

Jake? For a moment he couldn't remember who Jake was. "Your brother."

"Half brother," he said. "Pleased to meet you, Mr. Bates." He offered his hand, and Gideon had to release Elizabeth's to take it. For a moment, he thought Jake would engage in a little friendly competition to see which of them could out-squeeze the other, but then he released Gideon's hand before he could react.

Jake didn't look much like Elizabeth. His hair was dark and his eyes were brown. Only his smile hinted at the relationship.

"I've never seen you at the salon before," Gideon said.

"I've never been here before, and I'll probably never be back. Oh, hello," he added with interest, having caught sight of Anna.

"Anna, this is my brother, Jake Miles. Jake, my best friend, Anna Vanderslice," Elizabeth said.

"Miss Vanderslice, it's an honor to meet you," Jake said. "I had no idea Lizzie even had friends."

This surprised a laugh out of Anna and brought

235

color to her cheeks. So Jake Miles had a bit of his father's charm and a bit of his sister's wit.

"I'm sure Elizabeth has many friends, Mr. Miles," Anna said. "Come with me. I'll see to it you make some new ones as well."

Gideon watched in amazement as Anna took charge of Jake Miles and ushered him into the parlor, where Cybil's intellectual friends and students were gathering. He smiled as he heard her say, "Let me introduce you to Miss Adams."

"Poor Jake," he said to Elizabeth.

"Were you jealous?" She seemed intrigued by the prospect.

"Of course I was jealous. How do you expect me to feel when I see my fiancée leaving her boudoir with another man? Which begs the question of why you were in your boudoir with another man even if he is your brother."

"Jake had some information for me, and he thought I'd want it right away."

Before he could ask about the information, the front door opened and more guests arrived in a burst of cold air and high spirits. Gideon couldn't imagine why people enjoyed these gatherings so much, but obviously some did.

"Come out to the kitchen," she said, taking him by the hand.

The kitchen was filled with people helping Zelda arrange hors d'oeuvres on plates, but Lizzie pulled him into the butler's pantry, which was, for the moment at least, deserted. He tried to take her in his arms when she'd closed the door, but she held him off.

"Don't you want to know what news Jake had?"

"Not particularly." He reached for her again.

"I hired him to follow Honesdale."

That erased all thoughts of romance from his mind, at least momentarily. "Matthew Honesdale?" was all he could think.

"No, the Reverend Mr. Peter Honesdale. And his wife as well."

"Why? And why didn't you tell me you were going to do this?"

"Because I wanted to know if Honesdale needed to tell anyone else that we'd found the photograph, and I was afraid you'd object to having your minister followed."

Since he probably would have objected, he couldn't argue with that. "But who would he need to tell?"

"His partners, if he has any. I wanted to know if the Honesdales did this alone or if they had help."

"And why would you think they'd need help?"

"Because how much experience would a minister and his wife have with blackmail? And even more importantly, how much experience would they have with the kinds of activities for which Endicott Knight was being blackmailed?"

"You have a point. So did Jake follow Honesdale?"

"He did. He followed him from Priscilla's house."

"And where did he go?"

"Home."

"Probably to tell his wife what happened."

"Probably, since we're pretty sure she's involved."

"Then where did he go?"

"Nowhere. He stayed home."

"That doesn't sound like very important news to me."

"Remember, I also told Jake to follow Daisy Honesdale."

Gideon nodded, finally understanding. "And Daisy went somewhere."

"She did. She left her distraught husband—because he must have been a bit rattled when he found out we had the photograph, and then he calmed down when he took it from us, but when he discovered he no longer had it—"

"You never did explain how you really got it back."

"Every grifter knows how to pick a pocket. You never know when you'll need to do that."

"Good heavens."

"Yes, good heavens."

"And does every grifter know how to follow someone?"

"Some do, because when you put a mark on the send—"

"What?"

She sighed. "When a mark is ready to give you his money, he usually has to return home to get it, or at least have it transferred to another bank in another city. Someone follows him to make sure he doesn't get distracted, and when he gets the money, you follow him to make sure he doesn't get robbed."

"Oh." That made sense in a twisted kind of way, he supposed.

"So imagine how upset Reverend Honesdale must have been when he realized he no longer had the photograph. Daisy must have been livid."

"And where did she go with all her anger?"

"She went to see Matthew Honesdale."

Gideon hadn't slept well. He'd kept thinking about Elizabeth's news that Daisy Honesdale had visited her husband's cousin, who also happened to operate a string of brothels. Why would a respectable minister's wife visit such a man? Alone and, according to Jake, veiled.

Well, the veil was easy enough to figure out. She didn't want anyone to recognize her. But what business could she have had with such a man? And why hadn't Peter gone instead?

Elizabeth thought it indicated Matthew was a partner in the blackmail scheme, regardless of

239

how innocent they had thought him when they met him. That did seem to be the only logical answer, and the man was a pimp, so he could hardly sink lower morally. Blackmail might even be a step up for him.

Gideon had reached that conclusion about the time he'd finished breakfast this morning, and now he was sitting in his office, thinking through it all again and wondering how he could have so misjudged the man on their first meeting.

Smith interrupted him. "You have a visitor, Mr. Bates. He does not have an appointment." His expression reminded Gideon of what Smith thought of visitors with no appointment.

Gideon didn't care. He needed a distraction. "Who is it?"

"Mr. Matthew Honesdale."

Gideon managed not to react, or at least he thought he had. Smith's frown indicated he wasn't completely successful. "Show him in."

By the time Honesdale came into his office, Gideon had control of his emotions again, and hopefully of his face as well. He shook Honesdale's hand and offered him a seat.

"What can I do for you, Mr. Honesdale?"

He hadn't smiled when Gideon greeted him, and now he stared across the expanse of Gideon's desk solemnly. "I wanted to clarify some things you told me at our last meeting, Mr. Bates."

"Of course."

"You asked if I was planning to foreclose on Mrs. Knight's house, and I assured her that I had no intention of doing so. Is that also your recollection?"

"Yes, it is." What did this have to do with the blackmail, and more importantly, with Daisy Honesdale's visit to him last evening?

Honesdale reached into his pocket, pulled out a key and slapped it on Gideon's desk.

"What's that?" Gideon asked.

"A key to Mrs. Knight's house."

Gideon stared at the key for a moment, trying to make sense of this. "Did you receive a key when you made the loan to Mr. Knight?" And if he had a key, that meant he had access to the house, so maybe he was the one who had taken the photograph and . . .

"No, I did not. I only received it yesterday."

Gideon's nerve endings twitched to life. "From whom did you receive it?"

Matthew Honesdale frowned. "From a friend."

"The same friend who asked you to take the mortgage on Mr. Knight's house in the first place?"

Gideon could almost see the inner struggle as Honesdale silently considered his answer. He must have decided that revealing this small detail could do no harm. "Yes, the same friend."

"Why did this friend have a key to the house?" Which was a question Gideon very much wanted answered.

"I . . . I don't know."

But Gideon knew. Peter and Daisy Honesdale had had a key to Endicott Knight's house, the house where Knight had indulged his appetites and the Honesdales had tricked him into betraying himself.

How much of this did Matthew Honesdale know, though? And should Gideon reveal his own knowledge?

"Why have you brought the key here, Mr. Honesdale?" he tried.

Honesdale shifted uneasily in his comfortable chair. "I don't feel it's proper for me to have a key to Mrs. Knight's house."

Which was true, of course, even if he did own the mortgage on it. But more importantly, could Matthew Honesdale be as confused as Gideon had been about the houses? "I'm glad you are willing to respect Mrs. Knight's privacy."

"I certainly wouldn't have used the key, even if I hadn't promised her she could continue to live in the house," Honesdale said, a bit affronted.

Which answered Gideon's unspoken question. "Mr. Honesdale, are you under the impression that Mrs. Knight lives in the house for which you own the mortgage?"

"Of course I am. You were here when we discussed it, and you saw the mortgage documents."

"Yes, I did, but I have subsequently discovered

that Mr. and Mrs. Knight actually owned two houses."

"Two?"

"Yes, Mr. Knight's family home and the home Mrs. Knight inherited from her first husband."

Honesdale was obviously beginning to understand. "And which one does Mrs. Knight live in?"

"The one she inherited from her first husband."

"And let me guess: I own the mortgage on Knight's family home."

"That is correct."

"Did you know this when we met?"

"No, I did not. Mrs. Knight believed Mr. Knight had sold his family's home when they married, so she believed the house she lives in was the only one they owned. When she was told her home was mortgaged, she believed it was the one in which she lives. I only discovered the misunderstanding by accident on Saturday. I had made note of the address on the mortgage documents you showed me, and when I went to call on Mrs. Knight at that address, I found the house sitting empty."

Matthew Honesdale was not stupid, and he must also have been cunning, so he could easily suspect others of cunning as well. He was obviously doing just that as he stared at the key still lying on Gideon's desk. Gideon would have to be careful now, because he very much wanted

Matthew Honesdale as an ally. If he were truly innocent of blackmailing Knight, he could be invaluable.

"Mr. Honesdale, I'm wondering why your friend gave you this key."

"I'm wondering that myself."

"And I'm also wondering why your friend gave you the key at this particular time, when you have owned the mortgage for a number of months. Can you think of any reason?"

This time Honesdale sat back in his chair and gave Gideon a considering look. "No, I can't, but I'm guessing you have an idea."

"I do have an idea, based on information I have learned since our last meeting."

"What information is that?"

Where to start? "You were very helpful when you pointed out that the photograph I showed you of Mr. Knight had been taken in someone's home."

Honesdale muttered a curse as a red flush rose up his neck. "It was Knight's house, wasn't it?"

"The painting you pointed out to me is still hanging in Mr. Knight's bedroom in the house to which you hold the mortgage."

His whole face was scarlet now, and his hands had closed into fists. "So they gave me the key because . . ." He raised his gaze to meet Gideon's, his eyes fairly blazing with fury. ". . . because they wanted to implicate me in the blackmail."

244

"You'd be an easy target, Mr. Honesdale, because of your, uh, business interests."

"But how did they know you'd figured it out about the house?"

"Mrs. Knight showed her minister the photograph. Her minister is Peter Honesdale."

His smile held no mirth. "I see." He considered this information and what it meant for a long moment. "And did she tell him you knew where it had been taken?"

"No. She pretended she didn't know anything about it at all, just to see what he would say."

"Ah, so the key was merely some kind of insurance, in case you figured it out." He shook his head. "You thought I was the one behind it, didn't you? The photograph and the blackmail, I mean. In spite of my very logical reasons for not being involved."

"We already suspected Reverend Honesdale, and you're his close relative."

"And I'm a whoremonger, so naturally, I'm the one who led him astray."

"Whoremonger?" Gideon echoed. "I don't think I've ever heard that word outside of church."

"That's where I first heard it, too," Honesdale said with undisguised bitterness. "I spent a lot of time in church when I was young."

"Was your father also a minister?"

"My father was dead," he said baldly and with no trace of regret. "My mother, too, and Uncle

Nathan took me in. The poor little orphan boy given shelter by the saintly minister and raised with his own son."

"Were they unkind to you?" Gideon asked just to give Honesdale an excuse to tell him the awful details.

"If making you express gratitude for every morsel of food and stitch of clothing is unkind, I suppose they were. I don't even count the beatings, because Peter got them, too. He had to beat the Devil out of us, you see. Uncle Nathan, I mean. He has very strict ideas of how boys should behave. Unfortunately, they change from time to time, so simply learning his rules was never enough. Sometimes he just beat us because he wanted to, I think."

"So you rebelled as drastically as you could."

"And Peter conformed as drastically as he could, or so it seemed."

Gideon's nerves were tingling again, but he merely waited, understanding the human urge to fill a silence with words would encourage Honesdale to continue his tale.

Honesdale smiled, this time for real. "He was jealous of me. Can you imagine? Peter was. I ran away when I was fifteen, or rather I left home. Their home; it was never mine. I had a way with the ladies even then, and I became a cadet because it was easy work."

Gideon couldn't hide his reaction. Cadets were

246

young men who seduced young women and lured them into prostitution. But Honesdale merely lifted his chin in silent defiance.

"You think I tricked girls into becoming whores?" he asked. "Most of them were already selling themselves. I just helped them find a protector so they'd be safe. They were glad to be off the streets. It's not like they had any choice, either, not unless they wanted to starve."

Gideon had the uncomfortable feeling Honesdale was at least partially right, but he wasn't going to excuse a man whose life's work was turning women into prostitutes. "And Peter was jealous of you?"

"Of my freedom from his father. When I started my own place, he became one of my best customers."

Gideon had been expecting something like this. "And you rekindled your friendship."

Honesdale gave a bark of mirthless laughter. "Hardly. I would always be the poor relation and he the chosen son. But I let him think we were friends so I could have my revenge."

"So you told his father about his vices," Gideon guessed.

"No, I didn't."

Suddenly, a new possibility occurred to him. "You were blackmailing him."

"Not at all, although I did enjoy reminding Peter from time to time that I could do so."

"Then what was your revenge?"

"Daisy."

"Daisy?"

Honesdale's smile was predatory this time. "Did you not suspect she isn't what she appears?"

Elizabeth and his mother had suspected. "She does lack a certain polish."

"I'll be sure and tell her that was noticed. She'll be mortified."

"How was she your revenge?"

"Can't you guess?"

Perhaps he could. "You passed her off as a member of society when she's actually from a poor family."

"You have no imagination, Bates," Honesdale scoffed. "I wanted to humiliate Uncle Nathan. It would take more than a poor but honest female to do that."

"Are you saying she was a . . . one of your recruits?"

"Now you're accusing *me* of having no imagination. No, Daisy started out as a procurer, like me."

"In Baltimore?"

"What gave you that idea? No, right here in the city. She was a widow running a boardinghouse, but she didn't like honest work. It didn't pay well enough, you see, and it was too much like work. I recruited one of her lodgers, and she realized

248

she could do the same thing. Brothel owners pay well for fresh girls."

"Because they go through them so quickly," Gideon said, not bothering to hide his disgust.

Honesdale shrugged off his disapproval. "In any event, Daisy proved very efficient at her new profession. She found that if she drugged the girls, she got much quicker results and no refusals."

"Good God."

"Good God indeed. Even I found her techniques shocking. I don't think I have ever met a female quite so ruthless. And someone with Daisy's imagination and ambition was bound to rise. I eventually made her the madam at one of my houses, and we were . . . close. She proved to be an astute businesswoman, but she eventually grew weary of the responsibilities. Running a whorehouse is hard work, too, even harder than a boardinghouse. That was when I saw my opportunity, and I told her about Peter."

"You introduced her to him?" Gideon marveled.

"Oh no. He would have suspected my motives. But I did arrange for them to meet in a very respectable way."

"But you couldn't imagine he'd fall in love with her."

Honesdale's grin was almost feral. "You forget, he was my customer for years. I knew his . . . tastes. And Daisy was perfectly willing to cater to them."

Gideon could hardly believe it. "And he was willing to marry her in return?"

"Oh yes. He found her sexually exciting, of course, but her disreputable past meant that he could disgrace his family anytime he wanted."

"And did he want to disgrace them?"

"His father? I'm sure he'd like nothing better, but not if it ruined him, too. I think it was enough just presenting a former madam as his bride to his father, even though his father didn't know it then. They had to elope, because Uncle Nathan would never have countenanced a match with a social nobody, and once the deed was done, my uncle also couldn't countenance a divorce."

"I still don't see how this got you any revenge. No one but you knows what you did."

"My uncle knows Daisy was a madam now. I made sure of it, and seeing his reaction was priceless. He can't exactly disown Peter, but he refuses to see them or invite them to his home. Peter doesn't miss seeing his father, and Daisy makes a presentable preacher's wife in public, and in private, she . . . does other things."

"Like blackmailing people in their congregation."

Honesdale let the accusation lie for a long moment. "Yes, well, that wasn't part of the plan."

"And what was your plan? The rest of it, I mean? After you told your uncle his son had married a madam?"

Honesdale winced. "I suppose I was just going

to wait around for someone to recognize her, and if it didn't happen, I'd arrange for it to happen."

"But how did you convince her to go along with this in the first place? I can't imagine a woman like that would enjoy being a minister's wife."

"I told you, she was tired of running the brothel. It's hard work keeping the girls in line and the customers happy, and Daisy is lazy by nature. She had also started to miss being respectable. So I may have misled her about how much family money the Honesdales have when I suggested she consider seducing Peter into marriage."

"And when she found out Peter didn't have any money, she started blackmailing Knight."

"I told you, blackmail wasn't part of the plan."

"Of *your* plan, perhaps, but obviously Daisy had a plan of her own."

"I probably should have foreseen that. She'd saved a little nest egg when she was working for me, but as I said, she was ambitious."

"And she was probably getting bored. If being a madam was too taxing, being a preacher's wife must have been irksome, to say the least."

Honesdale's handsome face twisted. "Money was always important to her, too, as it always is when you've been poor."

"I wonder how she came to choose Endicott Knight as a victim."

"She may have recognized him from her previous life. Or maybe he confessed his sins to

Peter. However he came to her attention, you can rest assured the blackmail was her idea."

"You're sure of that?"

"Peter isn't . . . clever enough to have come up with this."

"So what does this do to your plan for revenge?"

"Actually, it creates a brand new need for revenge, this time against Daisy."

"Because she tried to implicate you in the blackmail scheme."

"Yes, and after I'd gone to all the trouble to make her respectable."

"What are you going to do?"

"I haven't had time to figure that out yet. I had to verify my suspicions first, and you have done that for me now, so . . ."

"May I ask you to wait? You see, Endicott Knight had used his entire fortune to pay blackmail, and then it appears Peter and Daisy pressured a young widow in their congregation to marry him so he could use her fortune as well."

"Yes, Mrs. Knight. Do you think they'll give it all back to her?" he asked with great amusement.

"Not willingly, but perhaps we can bring some pressure to bear. They're welcome to keep Knight's money, but not his widow's."

"What kind of pressure are you considering?"

Now Gideon smiled mirthlessly. "I don't know yet."

"Because if you're considering going to the police, you might want to reconsider."

"Why do you say that?" Gideon asked, wanting to know Honesdale's reservations.

"Because the *authorities* will never prosecute a Honesdale. I already pay a king's ransom each month to ensure that no one notices I'm breaking the law. I could shoot a man in the middle of Fifth Avenue and not be prosecuted. Oh, they'd have to arrest me for show, but I'd pay my bail and never hear about it again."

"Are you suggesting Reverend Honesdale pays protection money to the police as well?"

"Uncle Nathan? Hardly. But he has influence and powerful friends, which can protect him and his kin even better than bribery. He might not want to speak to Peter, but he'd never allow his son to be investigated, much less tried, for blackmail. The scandal would destroy them both."

"What about murder?"

"What about it?"

"Both Mr. Knight and his widow's first husband died under suspicious circumstances."

"And you think Peter had the nerve to actually kill someone?" Honesdale scoffed.

"Perhaps Daisy did."

That gave him pause. "People get away with murder all the time."

"Would your uncle protect Daisy, too?"

"He might, since it's his family name he cares about."

"Is that why you've gone to such lengths to blacken it?"

"I haven't blackened it. Only Peter can really do that."

"Peter or Daisy," Gideon said. "And in the meantime, Peter and Daisy have tried to frame you for their crimes, regardless of whether you'll ever be prosecuted for them or not."

"You don't need to remind me."

"I'm curious: why did Daisy tell you she was giving you the key?"

"She said Mrs. Knight would be moving out soon, and I would need the key to claim the property."

"And you didn't wonder why she had it?"

"I figured Mrs. Knight had given it to her to pass along. Mrs. Knight doesn't seem like the kind of lady who would come to my house herself."

"And yet you were suspicious."

"After I had time to think about it, yes. Daisy has a way of making a man forget to do that. And when I got suspicious, I came to you."

Gideon should probably be gratified. "You haven't answered my question. Will you wait to extract your revenge?"

"Wait for how long?"

"At least until you hear our plan."

Honesdale leaned back in his chair and considered Gideon's request for a long moment. "Yes, I'll wait, but only because I'm curious to see how you intend to outwit them."

"You don't think we can?"

"I don't think you're used to getting your hands dirty, Mr. Bates, and that's what it will take to beat them at their own game."

Gideon was very much afraid he was right.

Zelda Goodnight answered the door when Gideon arrived at the house in Chelsea. "Mr. Bates, what a surprise. Was Elizabeth expecting you?"

"No, she wasn't. I hope she's home, though."

She ushered him inside, quickly shutting the door on the wintry cold. "She's here, but I'm sure she'll want a minute to primp before she shows herself." A tiny, fragile female almost a foot shorter than he, she smiled up at him fondly. He was always amazed at how easily Zelda and Cybil had accepted him.

"She doesn't need to primp for me."

"I'm sure she doesn't, but she will anyway. Please hang your coat up and have a seat in the parlor while I warn her you're here."

He'd managed to warm himself by the time Elizabeth appeared. "Gideon, what a lovely surprise."

He allowed himself only one kiss because they had important things to discuss. "Matthew

Honesdale came to my office today," he told her when they were seated on the sofa.

Her beautiful blue eyes grew wide. "Why?"

He quickly told her about the key and Matthew's plan for revenge and how it had gone wrong.

"He's right, you know," she said. "The authorities won't have any interest at all in prosecuting Peter and Daisy for blackmail, and I doubt Priscilla will have much stomach for it, even if they did."

"But we might be able to prove they murdered DeForrest Jenks and maybe even Endicott Knight."

"Gideon, we don't even know whether they were murdered or not, so how can we prove it?"

"But if we can—"

"*If* we can, and *if* we can convince the authorities to bring them to trial, and *if* they are convicted, will that help Priscilla?"

"It will give her justice."

"You can't eat justice, Gideon. You can't put a roof over your head with justice."

"And then we could sue them. It would take some time, but—"

"And how would Priscilla support herself until then, assuming they're convicted of murder, assuming they even committed murder and we were able to find the proof, and assuming she could sue them and win?"

"I . . . She could sell Knight's house and—"

"And pay off Matthew Honesdale's mortgage."

She was right, of course, but they had few options. "Are you saying we shouldn't at least try to bring them to justice?"

"How often do people really get justice in this world, Gideon?"

"The courts are filled with cases in which—"

"In which murderers are hanged and thieves are locked away, but do the victims get their money returned or their loved ones brought back to life?"

"Well, no, but—"

"Of course not, because that's not how justice works. An eye for an eye just leaves both parties half-blind. Priscilla doesn't need justice. She needs retribution."

"Retribution? How is she supposed to get that?"

"I think you know. We've already discussed it. She needs her money back so she can live her life and raise her children."

"Are you proposing we blackmail the blackmailers?" Which, as he recalled, was what they had once discussed.

"No, because we don't have any proof to blackmail them with. I'm proposing we run a con on them."

CHAPTER ELEVEN

Elizabeth couldn't believe Gideon was still naïve enough to think the law could bring Peter and Daisy Honesdale to account. Hadn't they already decided that was impossible?

But she also couldn't believe the way he was looking at her. "Run a con? You can't be serious."

"Why not? They stole Knight's money and then they stole Priscilla's money. They deserve to have it stolen back from them."

"Elizabeth, two wrongs don't make a right."

"What?"

"A wrongful action is not a morally appropriate way to correct a previous wrongful action."

"Even if it's the *only way* to correct the previous wrongful action?"

At least he had to think about that. "But it's not the only way. Honorable men created the rule of law to give us another option. If men were left to their own devices, they'd just keep killing and stealing from each other in an attempt to get revenge. We'd live in a constant state of chaos and danger. The law provides an orderly way to settle grievances and punish crime."

"I'm entirely in favor of avoiding chaos and danger," she said, "and what I'm proposing would cause neither. You've already admitted your precious rule of law has no hope of settling this grievance or punishing this crime, so why shouldn't we take matters into our own hands?"

"Because it's wrong."

"And two wrongs don't make a right."

"Exactly." He looked triumphant, like he thought he'd won the argument.

"What's more important, Gideon, following the rules or saving innocent people?"

"I think you'll find that following the rules is always best for the majority."

"But not for everyone."

"What?"

"Not everyone. Just the majority."

"There are always exceptions, but if we want to live in a civilized world, we have to have rules."

"And you think it's more important to follow these rules than to bend them to help someone in trouble."

He frowned. "You're talking about doing more than just bending some rules, Elizabeth."

"Yes, I am. I'm talking about cheating some blackmailers out of their ill-gotten gains."

"Don't you see how wrong that is?"

She supposed she could. She'd always known how the world viewed her family's way of life. But everyone they cheated thought they were going to profit by cheating someone else. They were betting on a fixed horse race or buying counterfeit money or beating the stock market by getting an inside tip. None of them were innocent victims, not like Priscilla and her children. "Cheating a cheater doesn't seem so very wrong to me."

"But don't you see, that makes you a cheater, too. A thief. No better than they are."

Elizabeth's heart had begun to ache. "Is that so very important? Being better than they are?"

"Someone must be, if civilization is to survive."

But she didn't want civilization to survive if people like the Honesdales profited and people like Priscilla and her children were ruined in the process. "So you don't think we should try to get Priscilla's money back?"

"By legal means, yes."

"Legal means won't work."

"But we can't break the law."

"We?" she asked.

"I can't, and I can't allow you to do that, either."

"What do you mean you can't *allow* me to?"

"I know what you're used to, but . . . you're living in my world now, Elizabeth."

"I don't think I can live in your world, Gideon."

He was obviously confused. "What do you mean?"

"I mean I can't meet your standards." Now her heart was breaking, but she would just have to bear the pain somehow, because she had no other choice.

"I don't understand. Of course you meet my standards."

"No, I don't. I think your rule of law is ridiculous and horrible. I know you think you're right and maybe you are, but we're human beings, Gideon. We're not perfect, and sometimes the rules don't fit us."

"I know your background is different from mine, but that doesn't mean . . ."

"It doesn't mean what? That I can't be changed to become *morally appropriate?*"

"I didn't mean that!"

"Yes, you did. Your life is the law, and you want everything to follow your rules. But not everything can. I can't. I don't even want to." Had someone warned her about this? Someone should have. Someone older and wiser who should have known a man like Gideon Bates could never accept her for who she really was. She blinked back the tears that threatened. "I think you should leave."

"Leave? Why? We need to talk about this."

"We just did talk about it, and now I know I made a terrible mistake." She rose and walked to the parlor door.

"What mistake? What do you mean?" Desperate now, he followed her.

"You thought you could save me."

"Save you from what?" he asked, exasperated.

"From my life of crime, I suppose."

261

"I don't want to save you from anything. I love you just the way you are."

"Then why are you trying to change me?"

He had no answer for that.

She pulled the door open. "You need to go, Gideon, and don't come back."

"What do you mean, 'don't come back'?" he cried.

"I don't think we should see each other again. It would be too hard."

"You can't just send me away. We're going to be married."

But she shook her head, fighting the tears that burned to be shed. "No, we aren't."

In the end, Cybil and Zelda had come running at the sound of Elizabeth and Gideon shouting at each other because Gideon refused to believe her and Elizabeth insisted she was serious.

Zelda had finally convinced Gideon to give Elizabeth time to calm down and sent him home while Cybil had taken Elizabeth back to the parlor, where she could weep in privacy.

"It's only natural," Cybil assured Elizabeth when she'd stopped sobbing. "All couples argue."

"You two don't," Elizabeth said, still dabbing her eyes.

Cybil and Zelda exchanged a glance. "Of course we do, dear," Zelda said. "Not as much as we did in the beginning, of course. But in the beginning, it takes time and a bit of shouting before two people can work out their differences."

"This is far more serious than just a difference of opinion," Elizabeth assured them.

"It always is, Lizzie," Cybil said wryly.

"But this *really* is," Elizabeth wailed. "He's perfect. He's *honest!* He never even tells a lie. And he wants me to be just like him!"

"Oh my, that is serious," Zelda said.

"Perhaps you misunderstood him," Cybil said.

"I don't think so. He was perfectly clear. He even thinks it's wrong to cheat a pair of blackmailers."

"Blackmailers?" Zelda echoed in dismay.

"Where on earth did you encounter black-mailers, Lizzie?" Cybil asked.

"In church."

After that, Elizabeth had to explain everything. She gave them as brief a summary of Priscilla's misfortunes as she could manage. "I don't know exactly how we'd do it, but I'm sure the Old Man can figure out some way to get her money back."

"And to keep some himself for his trouble, I'm sure," Cybil said.

"Everyone has to make a living," Zelda pointed out.

"But the important thing is that Priscilla wouldn't be penniless, and she and her children would be safe," Elizabeth said. "Do you think it would be wrong to help her?"

"Of course it isn't wrong, dear. Women have a difficult enough time in this world without having someone actually steal from them," Cybil said.

"And females must look after each other because, heaven knows, no one else will," Zelda added. "I think you're very noble to care so much for your friend."

"You know how I feel about Buster's vocation," Cybil said, "but this would almost be a vindication."

"Like Robin Hood," Zelda said. She taught romance literature.

"Yes, like Robin Hood," Elizabeth agreed. "Although I'm sure Gideon disapproves of poor Robin, too. He was a thief, after all."

"Really? Poor Gideon," Zelda said.

"Poor Gideon?" Elizabeth cried.

"Yes, he has a heavy burden if his standards are so very high," Zelda said. "If you could help him bring them down a notch or two, you'd be doing him a favor."

"I'm not going to be doing anything for him from now on. I told him I couldn't marry him and sent him away."

"Oh, that won't discourage him," Zelda said.

"Indeed," Cybil said. "Any man put off by such a paltry refusal isn't worth the powder it would take to blow his brains out." Cybil taught history.

"But I meant it! I can't marry a man who thinks I'm evil for wanting to help someone!"

264

"Of course you can't, but you don't need to worry about that now," Cybil said. "Your first concern is helping your friend, and I'm sure Buster will be happy to help you."

Gideon walked the entire way home, hoping to wear off some of his anger. It didn't work. He was half-frozen but still furious when he arrived at home. He'd been hoping his mother was at a meeting, but she wasn't, and as soon as she saw his face, she knew something was wrong.

"It's nothing, Mother," he insisted, trying to warm himself by the fire.

"It's Elizabeth, isn't it?"

"What makes you say that?"

"I can't think of anything else that would make you so angry."

"I'm not angry!" He was far beyond that.

She merely smiled. "It's natural for couples to argue."

"We didn't argue."

"Then why are you so angry?"

"She told me we aren't getting married." Saying the words sent a stabbing pain through his chest, but he ignored it.

"What did you do?"

"I didn't do anything!" And he hadn't. Nothing to deserve that, at least. He was sure of it.

"You must have done something. Why else would she say that?"

He supposed he had said something to upset Elizabeth. In fact, he knew he had, although he still couldn't figure out why she'd taken exception to it. He was right, and he knew it. Why couldn't she see that?

"Well?" his mother said.

"We disagreed about . . . the rule of law."

"Gideon, that's ridiculous. Courting couples do not argue about the rule of law."

"We did."

"Maybe if you told me exactly what the issue was . . ."

"She wants to ask her father to run a con on Reverend and Mrs. Honesdale to steal back Priscilla Knight's money."

"Good heavens!"

"Yes, it's outrageous."

"I . . . Can I assume you have discovered more information since we last spoke that at least makes you certain Reverend and Mrs. Honesdale are the blackmailers?"

"Oh, I'm sorry. Yes, we have. Elizabeth and Priscilla met with Reverend Honesdale yesterday and showed him the photograph."

"Why on earth did they do that?"

"Because Elizabeth thought we'd be able to tell if he already knew about it."

"And were you?"

"Yes. He did not express the least surprise. He wasn't even shocked. He merely told them he would take the photograph and destroy it for them."

"And did he?"

"He, uh . . . He took it, but Elizabeth got it back."

"How did she do that?"

Gideon had to concentrate so he didn't grind his teeth. "Apparently, she knows how to pick someone's pocket."

"Really? What a useful skill that must be."

"It was in this case," he admitted sourly. "But that isn't all. Honesdale went straight home and a short time later, Daisy Honesdale left the house and visited Matthew Honesdale."

"Matthew? He's the cousin who owns the brothels, isn't he?"

"Yes."

"Why would Daisy go to visit a man like that?"

"She gave him the key to Endicott Knight's house, the one he has mortgaged."

"Why would she do that? And why did she have a key to that house at all? And most importantly, how do you know all this?"

"Because Elizabeth had her brother follow Daisy."

"Did he follow her inside Matthew Honesdale's house?"

"Of course not."

"Then how do you know—?"

"Because Matthew came to my office this

morning. We'd told him about the blackmail, and he realized when Daisy gave him the key that she had originally asked him to take the mortgage on Knight's house in order to implicate him in the blackmail, in case it ever came to light. His having the key would be another implication that he was involved. He was rather angry, and he ended up telling me that he was orphaned and Reverend Nathan Honesdale took him in. Nathan was a rather cruel disciplinarian who never felt Matthew was suitably grateful for all Nathan had done for him. Matthew left home when he was fifteen to escape."

"And ended up owning brothels."

"He apparently wanted to embarrass his foster father."

"That doesn't really explain why you think Reverend Honesdale and his wife are blackmailers."

Gideon sighed. How on earth to explain this to his mother? "Matthew claims that Peter became one of his customers."

"At his brothels? How very shocking." She didn't look terribly shocked, though.

"And Daisy, it seems, was a procuress and a madam for Matthew."

"What does a procuress do?"

Gideon rubbed his temples in a vain attempt to ward off a looming headache. "She procures young women for the brothels, sometimes against their will."

Now she did look shocked. "Did you believe him?"

"Yes, I did. Didn't she tell you she ran a boardinghouse for young ladies?"

"She did, but—"

"She used it to lure young ladies into prostitution."

He instantly regretted his bluntness when she went pale.

"I'm sorry, Mother. I shouldn't have told you."

"Don't apologize. It's not your fault, and you had to tell me. So I assume Elizabeth knows all of this."

"Yes, I went to her right after I left the office to tell her about Matthew's visit."

"And she suggested *running a con*—is that the correct phrase?"

"Yes," he said tightly.

"Running a con on the Honesdales in order to get Priscilla's money back. Can't you simply turn them over to the police?"

"I wish it were that simple, but we'd have to prove they were responsible for the blackmail, and while we're sure they were, we don't have any proof that would impress the police."

"So the law can't touch them."

"No," he said through clenched teeth.

"And that's why Elizabeth came up with an alternate plan."

"It's not an alternate plan. It's an illegal plan."

"So was what they did to Priscilla."

He couldn't believe she'd take Elizabeth's side. "Do you think we should ask Mr. Miles to steal money from them?"

His mother simply stared at him for a long moment. Then she said, "I see it now. The rule of law."

"It's all that separates us from the beasts."

"Well, perhaps not *all* that separates us."

"Without it, civilization would crumble."

"Is this what you said to Elizabeth?"

He didn't like that gleam in her eye. "More or less."

"No wonder she said she wouldn't marry you."

"Mother, how can you say that?"

"Easily. I warned you, Gideon. I told you Elizabeth will never become a simpering, blood-less matron."

"I'm not asking her to do that! I'm just asking her not to break the law." Which seemed a perfectly reasonable request!

"You make it sound very black and white."

"It is very black and white."

"To you, perhaps. But you are not a mother with two young children facing a life of poverty."

"I'm not planning to abandon Priscilla to her fate."

"Are you planning to support her for the rest of her life?"

"Mother—"

"Because that's what she needs. If it were possible for her to get a job that would support her and her children, that would be different, but as far as I know, she has no training or education to make that possible. She could get a job in a factory, perhaps, and leave her children alone and unattended in a tenement, I suppose. Or, if she were very lucky, she could find a third man willing to marry her and support her and her children, except she isn't likely to meet such a man in a tenement or a factory."

"All right, I surrender. Priscilla needs more help than I can give her."

"She needs more help than your *laws* can give her, Gideon. The real solution is to change the laws or at least the unwritten rules so women like Priscilla can find employment and they aren't at the mercy of men who behave as Mr. Knight has done."

"I'm afraid that's beyond my power, Mother."

"Yes, it is, so you need to decide what you can do that is within your power."

"I didn't say I wasn't going to help. I intend to do everything I can."

"As long as it is within the law."

"Most mothers would be proud of a son who wants to obey the law," he said in exasperation.

"I am proud of you, Gideon, but . . ."

"But what?"

"The law isn't always fair, especially to women."

"I know that."

"I hope so."

The next morning, before she went out, Elizabeth had to put cold compresses on her eyes to reduce the swelling caused by her weeping. Even then, she looked as if she hadn't slept for a week. She settled for a veil, although she knew it wouldn't fool the Old Man. At least people wouldn't be staring at her in the street.

She had to appreciate the irony of going to Dan the Dude's Saloon in a veil, though. If she were engaged to Gideon—or married to him!—she wouldn't dare be seen entering such a place. Now that it no longer mattered, she was discreetly covered.

Of course, she didn't go through the front door. She slipped down the alley to a door few even knew existed and tapped out a code on the weathered wood. After a minute or two, someone slid open a small spy panel and peered out at her. She flipped up her veil to show her face, and the door flew open.

"Lizzie!" Spuds grinned broadly, every wrinkle in his withered face deepening with the effort. "What brings you here?"

"I need to talk to the Old Man. Is he here?"

"He sure is. Come on inside." He led her down the hall, and as they entered the large room where the Old Man's mob gathered, he called out, "The Contessa's here!"

Only about half a dozen men were there, but they all jumped up from their card games to greet her. When they'd finished, she turned to see the Old Man waiting his turn.

He was as well groomed as ever, with not a hair out of place and his tailored suit looking as fresh as the carnation in his lapel. "What brings you all the way down here, Lizzie?"

"I have a job for you."

He smiled at that. "Does your young man know?"

"I don't have a young man."

His eyebrows rose and his smile vanished. "Maybe you should come into my office."

His office was a sparsely furnished room where little actual business was discussed but where he could conduct private conversations when necessary. "I feel like I should offer you a shot of whiskey," he remarked when he'd seated her on a threadbare sofa and sat down beside her.

"I don't need a shot of whiskey. I'm fine."

He frowned his silent disapproval of her lie. "What happened?"

"I realized Gideon and I will never suit. That's all. You shouldn't be surprised."

"No, I shouldn't, but . . ."

"As I said, I have a job for you."

"Does it have something to do with Matthew Honesdale?"

"As a matter of fact, it does, although it turns out Matthew Honesdale was an innocent victim."

"Innocent?"

"Well, not guilty of these crimes, at least." She told him everything they'd learned about the Honesdales and their blackmail scheme.

"I never had much use for churches, but this story is making me question my judgment, Lizzie," he said when she was finished. "I never dreamed there was so much potential for grifting there."

"Don't get any ideas. Besides, blackmail is a long way from grifting."

"I'm sure many people would disagree, but I believe you are correct. So what is the job you have for me?"

"I'd like to get Priscilla's money back from the Honesdales. They were blackmailing Knight long before he married her, so presumably they have his money as well. You're welcome to keep that."

"Unless they've spent it all."

"I don't see any evidence of it at their house. I'm guessing they're going to use it to run off somewhere and start some kind of new life, away from the constraints of being a minister."

"Or maybe they just want to keep blackmailing people and getting richer and richer."

"Not many people have that kind of discipline, and if they started spending a lot of money, the people in their church would notice and begin wondering where it came from."

"Ah yes, you're reminding me of why I don't like churches."

"Too many prying eyes. So if you find out they have a lot more money than I think, you're welcome to that as well. I just want to see Priscilla safely settled again."

"Do you have any suggestions for how to approach them?"

She smiled at that, the first time she'd smiled since last night. "I wouldn't dream of telling you how to conduct your business."

"I was just wondering if you knew Reverend Honesdale's vices. If he likes the horses or he speculates in the stock market."

"I doubt he does either one, although his cousin Matthew hinted he might have some blackmail-worthy appetites. The key might be the house that Knight mortgaged to Matthew Honesdale. Maybe you decide you want to buy it and approach them because of some mix-up in the names."

"Could Peter Honesdale be jealous of his cousin's financial success?"

"I wouldn't be surprised, and probably of his freedom from Peter's father, too. If he hasn't actually thought of it yet, you could plant the seed."

"I might be able to come up with something from that."

"And maybe . . ."

"Maybe what?" he said when she hesitated.

"Maybe you could find something for Jake to do."

The Old Man frowned. "Did you talk to him?"

"Yes, and he did tell me he's lost his nerve, but it could be temporary."

"And if it isn't, I don't want to find out when I need him most."

"I didn't say he had to play a big part."

He sat back and studied her for a moment. "Why all this sudden concern about Jake? I thought you two hated each other."

"We don't hate each other!" she protested.

"Well, you never got along."

"Few siblings do. Didn't you fight with Cybil?"

"All the time. But the two of you didn't grow up together."

"Which made it worse. Did you know Jake thinks you like me the best?"

He smiled at that. "Maybe I do."

"But I always thought you liked him the best, because he's a boy and you taught him everything you know."

"I taught you, too."

"Only after I begged and pleaded and threw tantrums."

"You're a girl."

"And he's jealous because you married my mother, but you didn't marry his."

"I couldn't marry his mother. I was already married to yours," he said indignantly.

"And that makes it even worse," she told him sternly.

"I suppose you're right. Is that why you feel sorry for Jake?"

"I feel sorry for Jake because he can't do the only thing he knows how to do well."

"Becoming respectable has really softened your heart, Lizzie."

"Becoming respectable has nothing to do with it and my heart isn't soft. Being in jail is what made me realize that life isn't fair for other people, too, and that I can do something about it."

"So you want to change the world?" he asked skeptically.

"I want to change the part of it I live in. That's ambitious enough. So will you help me? And if you need some incentive, Knight had a tidy little fortune before the Honesdales got ahold of him, and there's the house, too."

"The house, yes, and Mrs. Honesdale was a madam."

"What are you thinking?" she asked.

When he told her, she laughed out loud.

Gideon considered staying home from the office after a sleepless night during which he thought of

277

every argument he should have used to convince Elizabeth he was right. In the light of day, none of them seemed any more convincing than the ones he'd used, however, and if he stayed home, he'd have to listen to his mother giving him more advice on how to win Elizabeth back. So, bleary-eyed, he made his way to Devoss and Van Aken.

Smith must have thought he was hungover and wordlessly brought him some coffee with a splash of whiskey. Gideon drank it gratefully before picking up the stack of mail Alfred had left on his desk. He disposed of most of it quickly, and then he came to an envelope from the Manchester Club. The bills for his club membership usually went to his house, and it took him a moment to realize what this must be.

Remembering Tom's promise to find the name of the company that had removed the gargoyles from the building, Gideon tore open the envelope and found a single sheet of paper with Tom's best wishes and the name of a masonry company.

From the depths of his memory, which was still fuzzy from lack of sleep, came his promise to Elizabeth to investigate DeForrest Jenks's death. If he could prove it had not been an accident, perhaps he could at least get justice for Priscilla. She couldn't eat justice, as Elizabeth had pointed out, but it would be something.

He checked the address of the company and decided to walk over. The cold and the exercise were just what he needed to clear his head.

Wilson Brothers Masonry was on the west side of the city in a large building near the river. The wind whistled down the streets and alleys, making Gideon sorry he had decided to walk, but at least he was completely awake when he arrived.

The front part of the building seemed to be devoted to offices where, presumably, the Wilson brothers conducted the business portion of masonry, while the rest appeared to be a warehouse where the actual work took place.

A paunchy middle-aged man greeted him from behind a counter and asked him his business.

Gideon gave the man his card. "I'd like to speak to someone about the gargoyle that fell off the Manchester Club a little over a year ago. I'd just like some more information about why it fell," he added hastily when he saw the fellow's alarmed expression.

That didn't seem to allay the fellow's suspicions, but he told Gideon to wait and disappeared into one of the offices, closing the door behind him. A few minutes later, someone emerged from a door that apparently led to the warehouse portion of the building. He wore work clothes and was wiping his hands on a rag as he came. He stopped short when he saw Gideon waiting, then moved more cautiously to the office the other fellow had entered. The door opened instantly at his knock and closed just as instantly behind him.

After a few more minutes, the office door opened and the first fellow came out. "Mr. Wilson would like to see you." He escorted Gideon into the office, where an older man in a suit sat behind a desk and the man in work clothes stood beside him. Neither of them looked happy to see Gideon.

The man in the suit held Gideon's card. He glanced down at it as if double-checking the name. "Mr. Bates, I'm Ezra Wilson. How can I help you?"

He hadn't offered Gideon a seat, so he remained standing. He'd had some time to think while he waited, and he'd realized they probably thought that, since he was an attorney, he was going to sue them or something. "I'm a member of the Manchester Club, and I wanted to find out exactly how and why the gargoyle fell off the building and if the club is in any way responsible."

"The *club?*" Wilson echoed suspiciously.

"Yes. You'll remember that one of our members was killed in the incident, and his widow has found herself in reduced circumstances since his death. If the club was responsible because of negligence, we should probably pay her a settlement." That much was true, at least.

Wilson glanced up at the man in work clothes.

"I told them it was dangerous," the man said. "I told them if they didn't fix it, it was going to fall off and kill somebody."

CHAPTER TWELVE

"You knew it was going to fall?" Gideon asked in wonder.

"This is Alden Vickery, Mr. Bates," Wilson said. "He's one of our masons. Tell him what you just told me, Vickery."

"The gargoyle, the one that fell. They sent for us to take a look at it. The gargoyles are part of the gutters and that one was clogged up. I went out and I saw some of the stone had broken off and created a dam, so I opened it back up, but the water had been standing a long time, and the iron bolts holding it to the building were rusted nearly clear through. I told them they needed to repair it or it was going to fall."

The hairs on the back of Gideon's neck were standing at attention. "Who did you tell?"

"I don't know. Some gentleman. Said he was the club president, I think. I wanted to do it right away, but he said the club would have to vote or some such nonsense. He said they'd let us know. I tried to tell him—"

"When was this?"

Vickery blinked in surprise at Gideon's vehemence. "I don't know exactly."

"How long before the gargoyle fell do you think?"

"A week or two, I'd guess. Not long."

"So you see, Mr. Bates," Wilson said quickly, "Wilson Brothers is not responsible. We warned your club president or whoever he was—"

"Yes, yes, I know. You aren't responsible at all. Mr. Vickery, it's my understanding that the remaining three gargoyles were removed, even though they did not appear to be in danger of falling. Is that correct?"

"Yes. They said they didn't want to take any chances and the other members wouldn't feel safe until they were gone."

"They? Did you speak with more than one person that time?"

"I . . . Yes, I did. It was the same fellow as the first time and some other man was with him."

"Do you remember what the other man looked like?"

"I don't know. Ordinary looking, except he was a preacher. I could tell by his collar."

"I see. Thank you, Mr. Vickery. And thank you for your help, Mr. Wilson."

"You can't hold us responsible," Wilson said again.

"I don't, Mr. Wilson. You can rest assured of that. I know exactly who is responsible for this."

Consulting with the police was a bit more difficult than dealing with Wilson Brothers Masonry. Gideon began to regret not having a background in criminal law, because he would have been much more familiar with the police department, but eventually he was directed to the correct precinct and the detective who had investigated DeForrest Jenks's death.

Detective O'Reilly was a jovial, red-faced Irishman almost as big around as he was tall. He suggested Gideon treat him to a beer in a nearby bar so they wouldn't be interrupted. Gideon was only too happy to buy O'Reilly a beer or three if he could give him the information he needed.

"Oh yeah," O'Reilly said when they received their beers and had withdrawn to a booth. "I'll never forget that poor sod. What a terrible way to go. And if he'd been standing a few feet away, it would've missed him completely."

"Where exactly did you find him?"

"Under the big stone monster," O'Reilly said and laughed heartily at his own joke.

Gideon smiled politely. "I meant how close to the building?"

"Of course you did. Not far away. The . . . what do you call them things?"

"Gargoyles."

"Gargoyles." He gave a little shudder. "It didn't jump off the roof, you know. It just kind of let loose of its moorings and fell straight down from where it was."

"So Jenks must have been standing right next to the building."

"I guess so. That's where we found him. Flat on his face and the gargoyle perched on his back, so to speak."

"His back?"

"Yeah. It was almost funny. Would have been if the man wasn't dead, I mean. It was like the man had cushioned the gargoyle's fall, so the thing was hardly even damaged, just sitting there on him."

"Let me get this straight. Jenks was lying on the sidewalk, facedown, and the gargoyle was on his back."

"That's it." O'Reilly had drained his beer and signaled for another.

"What were his injuries? Jenks, I mean."

"His chest was crushed. The weight of the thing and the force of it hitting him did that, I guess."

"Not his head?"

"Oh no. His head wasn't hurt a bit, not even his face when he hit the sidewalk. I reckon they could have a viewing for him with no trouble at all. That's nice for the family. It's bad when they can't see the dead loved one. Makes it hard to accept they're gone."

Gideon could imagine. What he could not imagine was getting hit by a falling gargoyle and not having any injuries on your head. "Have you ever seen anything like that before?"

"A falling gargoyle? Not when it hit somebody."

"I'm just trying to figure out why the gargoyle

didn't hit Jenks in the head if he was standing up."

O'Reilly shrugged. "Maybe he ducked."

But even if he ducked, the gargoyle wouldn't have landed squarely on his back unless . . . "Could Jenks have already been lying down when it hit him?"

O'Reilly glanced around as if making sure nobody was listening. Nobody was, because nobody in the bar cared what they were discussing. "I don't like to speak ill of the dead, and I know this fellow was a friend of yours, but . . ." He glanced around again.

"He wasn't a close friend," Gideon said quite truthfully. "And I need to know if there was anything suspicious about his death."

"Not suspicious, but . . . They said he'd been pretty drunk when he left the club that night."

"So you think he'd passed out?"

"That's what we figured. I didn't tell the widow that, you understand. No sense making it harder for her. But we thought he was already down when the thing hit him."

"Do you usually find drunks lying facedown?"

"We find them every way. I even saw one poor sod who drowned when he fell in the gutter and then it rained."

But O'Reilly didn't know that DeForrest Jenks had not been a drunk and hadn't habitually passed out on public streets. Or that someone who had reason to wish him dead knew something heavy was ready to fall and kill him if only he were in exactly the right place.

"What if I told you that Jenks had enemies, someone who wanted to marry his widow?"

"You mean she had a lover? And they wanted this Jenks out of the way?"

Oh no, was that the first thing someone would assume? That Priscilla had been in on it, too? Of course it was, if Knight had killed Jenks and promptly married his widow, which was exactly what he'd done. "Not really, but suppose this enemy knew the gargoyle was ready to fall and only needed a push, so the enemy drugged Jenks and laid him down on the sidewalk, and then he went up on the roof and pushed the gargoyle off."

O'Reilly thoughtfully sipped his beer. "Did anybody see him do it?"

"No."

"Did he tell anybody he did it?"

"No."

"Any chance he's going to confess he did it?"

"I don't know. There were two of them, and one is already dead."

"Which means all the other one has to do is keep his—or her—mouth shut."

"Yes."

"Then I'd say you've got a snowball's chance in hell of proving it, Mr. Bates."

"But couldn't the police reopen the investigation and—"

"And what? Why would we reopen it a year later when it was ruled an accident and nobody even questioned it then and you've got no proof otherwise even now?"

"What would it take to reopen the case?"

O'Reilly shook his head at such an absurd question. "Your man would have to march down to the precinct house and confess and beg us to arrest him, because even then we'd probably just think he was drunk or insane."

"But—"

"Mr. Bates, thank you for the beer. I'm sorry your friend got killed, but if what you say really happened, you're going to have to figure out another way to get your revenge, because the police can't help you."

Daisy was enjoying an afternoon with no responsibilities. The maid had done the housework, and Daisy had no committee meetings or other church responsibilities, so she was free to sit back, put her feet up and read the latest salacious novel from the collection she kept locked in the safe in her husband's office. She had to replace the dust jacket with one from a more respectable book, in case someone happened to see it, but that rarely happened.

Today she appeared to be reading a book of

sermons when the maid told her there was a man at the door who wanted to see a Matthew Honesdale and he wouldn't believe no one named Matthew lived there.

"Should I send him away?" the girl asked.

"No, I'll see him," Daisy said, overcome with curiosity. She glanced down at her dress and sighed. She'd chosen her oldest gown today since she had not expected visitors, but it would take too long to change. The man might leave and she'd never find out what he wanted with Matthew.

She chose to stand in the middle of the modest parlor to meet him, and the maid ushered him in and announced him as Leonard Ross. She assumed her best lady-of-the-manor expression and signaled the maid to leave the door open.

She wasn't sure what she'd been expecting, but he was a pleasant surprise: young and attractive and a little puzzled, although his checked suit offended her sense of fashion. "Mrs. Honesdale?"

"Yes. I understand you're looking for a Matthew Honesdale."

"That's right. Your maid said he doesn't live here, but I was told otherwise."

"By whom?"

That stopped him and he winced slightly. "A friend. So you're not his wife, *Mrs. Honesdale?*"

"No, I am not. May I ask what business you have with Matthew Honesdale?"

That stopped him again. "I'm not sure I should discuss it with anybody except Mr. Honesdale. Are you sure you don't know him?"

"I didn't say I didn't know him. I said he doesn't live here."

To her surprise, he smiled. "Ah, that's different. So you do know him."

"Mr. Ross, perhaps we should sit down. Can I offer you something to drink? Tea or coffee?"

"I'd prefer something stronger, but coffee will do."

Daisy rang for the maid and offered Mr. Ross a chair near the gas fire. When the maid had gone off for the coffee, Daisy took the chair opposite his.

"Now, perhaps you'll tell me how you ended up here looking for Matthew."

He leaned back and studied her for a moment. "I was sent to find him. My . . . business associates are anxious to speak to him."

"And would Matthew be happy if you found him?"

"He might be *richer* if I found him, so I assume that would make him happy."

"So you have a business proposition for him."

"Yes, I do. Or rather Mr. Franklin does. Mr. Franklin is my, uh, associate."

This was the most interesting thing that had happened to her since Endicott Knight died. "What kind of proposition would that be?"

Ross gave her an apologetic grin. "I don't think I could discuss it with a lady like you."

"Oh, I know what kind of business Matthew does, so I doubt you could shock me."

"Really, Mrs. Honesdale, if you just tell me where I went wrong and where I can find Mr. Honesdale, I'll leave you to your own business. Believe me, you'll be glad I did."

"I don't think I will, Mr. Ross. I think I will worry and fret over whether I did the right thing or not, because I'm afraid I must send you away *unsatisfied* if you don't tell me more."

At her emphasis on the word "unsatisfied," his eyebrows had risen, and she saw the unmistakable glint of interest in his dark eyes. She hardly ever saw that glint in a man's eyes anymore, not since she'd let Matthew convince her that marrying Peter would mean a life of leisure and luxury. Before that, she'd seen it on every man who entered her house. Oh, maybe it wasn't for her specifically, but she could elicit it at will back then with just a swish of her skirt or a flutter of her lashes. That glint made a woman feel alive.

"I wouldn't want to be *unsatisfied,* Mrs. Honesdale, but what would your husband think?"

"He'll think what I tell him to think." Awareness flooded her veins. She was powerful and in control again. Oh, how she'd missed that feeling. "Now, tell me why your Mr. Franklin wants to see Matthew."

"You said you know about Matthew's business."
It was a question.

"Yes, I do. We used to be . . . partners." Only a
slight exaggeration.

"Partners, eh?" Now he was really interested in
her. "Then I suppose it wouldn't hurt to tell you.
It's not a secret or anything."

Daisy remembered the door was still open, and
she certainly didn't want the maid to hear what
Mr. Ross had to say. She got up and closed it.
When she was back in her chair, she said, "Tell
me."

"Mr. Franklin is looking to, uh, expand his
business interests into New York City."

"Where are his interests now?"

"Chicago."

"Then he must know what he's doing. Why
does he need to consult with Matthew?"

"He knows his business, but he doesn't know
the city. He needs a partner to introduce him to
the right people."

And, she knew, to help him figure out whom to
bribe and whom to intimidate. "And how did he
settle on Matthew?"

"Mutual friends suggested Mr. Honesdale
would have the right contacts."

"Does your Mr. Franklin actually know
Matthew?"

"No."

"So Franklin would be just as happy with

anyone who could give him the help he needs."

"Maybe. I'd have to ask him."

The maid tapped on the door and delivered their coffee. When she had gone, Daisy went to a cabinet and brought back a bottle of bourbon. After adding some to Mr. Ross's coffee, she did the same to her own.

She gave him a chance to taste his before she said, "Now tell me exactly what your Mr. Franklin's plans are once he's paid off the right people."

Gideon had resisted the urge to go to Elizabeth and tell her what he'd learned. What he'd learned was interesting but not helpful at all. In fact, it only confirmed her theory that the law offered no hope of justice, at least so far. So at the end of this very full day, he went to Priscilla's bank for his long-delayed visit to see Mr. Renfroe on the slim chance he might know something about how Endicott Knight had disposed of his money.

"What can I do for you, Mr. Bates?" Renfroe asked when Gideon was seated in one of the visitor's chairs facing Renfroe's massive desk. Renfroe was a portly man in an expensive suit he'd had made when he weighed at least twenty pounds less than he currently did. He wore a diamond stickpin and had a heavy gold watch chain stretched across his round belly, as if it were holding his vest closed against the pressure of his girth. He made up for having no hair at all on the top of his head by sporting enormous side-whiskers.

"Mrs. Priscilla Knight has asked me to help her settle her husband's affairs. She was quite confused and, I must say, alarmed when you informed her about the current state of her finances."

"I thought she might be, which is why I made a point of informing her. Of course, I only know about the funds she and her first husband had deposited with us. Perhaps Mr. Knight merely moved those funds to another institution, but I knew Mrs. Knight would assume they were still with us. I didn't want her to be surprised."

"That was kind of you, Mr. Renfroe. Do you usually take such an interest in your depositors?"

Renfroe shifted uneasily in his large leather chair. "No, I don't, but I do try to look after the widows. My father died young, and my mother had a difficult time of it, I can tell you. I wouldn't wish that on anyone, so I offer what advice I can and try to help them."

"If Knight really was moving her funds to another bank, how would we find out which one?" Gideon asked to see what he'd say.

"He would probably have documents from that bank. Checks and statements, that sort of thing."

"And if he didn't?"

Mr. Renfroe leaned back in his luxurious chair,

frowning. "Mr. Bates, may I be frank with you?"

"I hope you will be."

"I do not believe Knight was merely moving the funds."

"Why do you say that?"

"Because he withdrew them in cash. If he were merely moving them to another bank or investing them in something like stock or property, he would have asked for a bank draft or used a check."

"Some people prefer to deal in cash," Gideon suggested.

"That may be true, but I find that *legitimate* business rarely requires large sums be paid out in cash."

"What did you suspect, Mr. Renfroe? And please be frank, because Mrs. Knight's future depends upon it."

"I'm well aware of that, Mr. Bates, but I hesitate to say what I suspect because all of the possibilities are so distasteful and reflect very poorly on Mr. Knight."

"Then let's speak in general terms. In your experience, what are some reasons a man would need to withdraw large sums of cash?"

Renfroe sighed and shook his head. "As I said, all of the possibilities are distasteful. The usual one is gambling debts. Gambling has no appeal for me, but I understand it can become quite an obsession with some men."

"Except for an occasional game of cards at his club, I've never known Knight to gamble."

"I haven't either, although I never knew him particularly well. Another weakness that frequently drains a man's resources is women. I don't mean his wife, although some wives can be extravagant, but rather a kept woman who requires support over and above the usual costs of supporting a family, and whose demands can become excessive."

"We've found no evidence of another woman." Except for the one in the photograph.

"And some men prefer many different women and the variety found in brothels. Customers in such establishments are encouraged to spend lavishly on liquor and entertainments, I understand."

Establishments that catered to men with Knight's tastes would be more expensive than most, Gideon suspected as well.

"I know this only from hearing the lamentations of men ruined by such practices, you understand," Renfroe added.

"Of course," Gideon said, more than willing to believe him.

Gideon waited, but Renfroe apparently had nothing else to offer. "Is that all?"

"Probably not, but that is all I can think of at the moment."

"What about blackmail?"

Plainly, Renfroe had not considered blackmail. "Good heavens, do you think Knight was being blackmailed?"

"We have reason to believe it, yes. That is one reason I came to see you today. I wanted to know if you had any idea what Knight was doing with the money he withdrew."

"I told you, it was all in cash. If he had used a check or a bank draft, we would have records, but . . ."

"Can you remember anything at all about his behavior at the bank? Was he particularly friendly with anyone in whom he might have confided? Or even someone who might have overheard him say something or have seen him with someone who might have been the blackmailer?"

"Do blackmailers accompany their victims to the bank?" Renfroe asked, horrified.

"I have no idea, but if anyone was with Knight when he made the withdrawals, that person might know something, at least."

"Oh, I see what you mean. I don't think I ever encountered Mr. Knight when he visited the bank. He never asked to see me, and why would he if his main interest was simply withdrawing as much of his wife's money as he could?"

"You're probably right. Who else might have seen him?"

"Any of the tellers. The doorman."

"Shall we ask them?"

"No, I don't think that's wise, and I don't want to get them upset, either. I can call them in, one by one, and ask them over the course of the day tomorrow. If I learn anything, I'll let you know."

Gideon wasn't satisfied with that. He wanted to hear their answers. "I would be happy to sit in while you question them."

But Renfroe was shaking his head. "I said I don't want to upset them, and having an attorney present would do that only too well. No, I'll make it a matter of my personal concern. They'll be anxious to help Mrs. Knight if they can."

Gideon reluctantly took his leave with Renfroe's promise to send for him when he'd finished with his task. In the meantime, he had another death to investigate.

"He wants to open several houses in the city," Daisy told Peter that evening. "Each of them would specialize." She'd waited until after supper, when the maids had left for the day and they could speak privately, to tell him about Leonard Ross's visit. They were enjoying their after-dinner coffee in the parlor she hated so much.

"I don't understand," Peter said in that petulant voice that set her teeth on edge. "Why did he come here looking for Matthew?"

"He said someone told him this was where Matthew lives. Who cares why he came here?

The important thing is that we heard about this first."

"I don't know why that's important."

He wouldn't. She had to think of everything. "Because this is our chance."

"Our chance to do what?"

She managed not to snap at him. Patience was the key for dealing with Peter. "To finally have everything we want. Don't you see? This Franklin needs a partner, someone who knows the city. He wants to open the first house in a respectable neighborhood and cater to the carriage trade."

"Isn't that dangerous? The respectable neighborhood, I mean."

"Of course it is, which is why he needs our help. Don't you see? We can guide him. We can introduce him to the right people."

"And what do we get in return?"

"Half of the business. Maybe more than that. We can provide the house and the introductions."

"What house are you talking about? This house belongs to the church. We can't—"

"Knight's house."

He blinked stupidly. "But we don't own that house."

"Matthew does, or at least he owns the mortgage."

"What good does that do us, though?"

"We can buy the mortgage from him and then foreclose, because Priscilla won't be able to pay it and she won't care about holding on to Knight's house, in any case. Matthew won't think anything of it, either. He never wanted the mortgage in the first place. He only took it because I asked him."

Peter smiled at the memory. "And you did it so if Knight ever reported the blackmail, he'd be implicated. Matthew never suspected a thing."

"Of course not. He still thinks I'm his creature."

"That's been the most fun of all of this, knowing Matthew still thinks he's in control. He's going to be so surprised when he finds out what we've been doing right under his nose."

"Which is why we need to convince this Franklin to go in with us instead of Matthew. You have no idea how much a house like that can earn."

"And we'll be rich, like Matthew is."

"Richer," she assured him, glad to see he finally understood.

He considered the possibilities for a long moment. "I'll have to give up the church."

"You were going to anyway, when we had enough money."

"I'm glad we won't be doing the blackmail anymore."

"I know it was difficult for you," she soothed.

"Poor Jenks. I still dream about him sometimes."

She managed not to roll her eyes. "But it was necessary. And won't your father be furious when you leave the church?" she added to distract him.

He brightened instantly. "Yes. Yes, he will.

We'll have to make sure he knows about the house and what's going on there. Maybe we'll invite him for a visit. Can you imagine his reaction when he realizes what we've done?"

"That would be delicious," she said, although she knew Nathan Honesdale would never accept an invitation to *her* home, even if it weren't a brothel. They'd make sure the scandal touched him, though. Poor Peter didn't seem to realize that any scandal that ruined his father's name would ruin his, too, but she wasn't going to point it out. Ruining Nathan Honesdale had always been one of her goals, ever since he'd told her she wasn't welcome in his house, and she didn't care if Peter's good name got ruined, too. "I'll need you to help me with Franklin."

"Certainly, my love." He gave her the silly grin he thought was appealing. It wasn't.

If only she could get rid of him, but she would need him for a while yet. "Men like Franklin don't like doing business with women. I'll tell you what to say to him, but he won't want to think I'm making any of the decisions."

"You know you can depend on me. Haven't I proved that already?"

"Yes, you have." As difficult as it had been to convince him in the first place, she had to admit he had managed to follow her instructions so far.

"What do we need to do now?"

"This Ross fellow is going to let us know when

Franklin arrives in the city. Then we'll meet with him and find out exactly what he needs."

"And we'll make it clear he won't get it unless we're his partners."

"I don't think we need to be quite so uncompromising, darling. He could always seek out Matthew if we're unreasonable. We should be as accommodating as possible, I think."

"Oh, of course. You're right. What will he want from us?"

"He'll tell us, and we'll be only too happy to help."

"Can we trust a man like that, though?"

"Absolutely not, but he can't trust us, either, can he, darling?"

Peter smiled at that, because he didn't know he couldn't trust her, either.

In the light of day, Gideon observed the next morning, Death Avenue didn't look particularly dangerous. Pedestrians and vehicles, both motorized and horse-drawn, moved easily around and across the tracks that ran down the center of Eleventh Avenue. Even when a train came chugging along the tracks, no one seemed alarmed. In fact, they seemed almost oblivious to the danger such a huge vehicle could pose if one weren't quite careful enough. True, it chugged very slowly, but it also would stop very slowly if someone were to slip and fall at just the wrong time. Still, pedestrians crossed in front of it with impunity, allowing themselves just enough time to clear the tracks to avoid disaster as the train went by.

The now-legendary West Side Cowboy rode his horse ahead of the train to warn people and vehicles off the tracks. Dressed in a uniform coat of navy blue and sporting a large-brimmed Western hat, the rider held a red flag that presumably alerted everyone to the oncoming danger. Wasn't he supposed to be waving the flag or something, to be more noticeable? Gideon couldn't help observing, however, how many people and even vehicles hurried to cross in front of the train after the cowboy passed. So the cowboy's warning obviously wasn't as effective as it was supposed to be.

Gideon tried to imagine the street after dark, the time when Endicott Knight had been hit. The train would have a spotlight and the cowboy would carry a lantern, but Gideon imagined his warning would be just as ineffective.

Gideon had spent most of the morning trying to track down someone who could tell him about the night Endicott Knight had died, but the people in the office of the New York Central Railroad had claimed complete ignorance and referred him to the police. The detective who had investigated Knight's death wasn't on duty, and no one knew where he could be found. Finally, Gideon decided that the West Side Cowboy might know what had happened, since he'd undoubtedly been on the spot when Knight died.

Gideon waited until the cowboy took a break and led his horse into a livery stable for a rest. The stalls were all full of horses, who turned their heads lazily to follow Gideon's progress as he sauntered through. When Gideon found the cowboy, he had unsaddled his horse and was brushing him. Gideon introduced himself.

"A lawyer, huh?" the young man said with a frown. Gideon guessed him to be about twenty. "That can't be good."

"I'm just trying to find out some information for a friend of mine, about the man who got hit by the train a couple months ago."

"I don't know nothing about it."

"But surely you remember when it happened."

"We all remember when it happened. Not too many folks get hit by the train anymore, and even then, it's usually kids, fooling around. So for a grown man to get killed, that's something you remember."

"Were there any witnesses?"

"I told you, I don't know nothing about it."

"But if you were there . . . ?"

"I wasn't there. I only work in the daytime."

"Who works at night, then?"

"Lots of fellows. Lots of fellows work in the daytime, too. There's twelve of us cowboys."

Why hadn't Gideon realized that? It would take more than one person to guard the tracks twenty-four hours a day, seven days a week. "Do you know who was working that night?"

"I sure do, but why should I tell you?"

"Because the dead man's widow is still very upset, and she wants to know what happened to him." He glanced around to see if anyone was listening, and of course nobody was, but he lowered his voice just the same. "They said it was an accident, but some people think he committed suicide, and his widow thinks somebody might've pushed him."

The cowboy's eyes got big. "Pushed him? You mean on purpose?"

"That's exactly what I mean."

The young man whistled his amazement. "Sam was working that night. He says he still has nightmares. Your fellow got caught under the wheels. It wasn't pretty."

Gideon could imagine. "Where can I find Sam?"

"He'll be at home, probably still sleeping if he worked last night." The cowboy gave Gideon the address of Sam's rooming house. "Do you think he saw the guy get pushed and that's why he's having nightmares?"

Gideon had no idea, but he was determined to find out.

CHAPTER THIRTEEN

"It was an accident."

The West Side Cowboy named Sam hadn't been awake long. He was unshaven and had apparently just pulled his trousers on over his long johns when the landlady had summoned him to meet his visitor. Like the other cowboy, he was a young man, but without the uniform and cowboy hat he wasn't quite as impressive.

"Your friend said you were still having nightmares."

"Who wouldn't?"

They were sitting in the threadbare parlor of the boardinghouse, a room most notable for how many sprung chairs it harbored. Gideon shifted a little to see if he could find a more comfortable spot on his. He couldn't.

"Can you tell me everything you remember from that night?"

"Why should I? It wasn't my fault. I did my job. Couldn't nobody say I didn't."

"I'm sure you did, but you must know how many people don't pay any attention to you when you wave your flag."

"I use a lantern."

"Or your lantern."

"No, they don't pay any attention at all.

Sometimes I think people enjoy running out in front of the train after I go by, just to see how close they can come to getting run over."

"Do you think that's what happened to Mr. Knight?"

"Was that his name?"

"Yes, Endicott Knight. His widow is very anxious to find out what really happened." His widow and several other people.

Sam winced. "She wouldn't be if she knew."

"Why do you say that?"

"Did you ever see a man get run over by a train?"

"No, I'm happy to say. I imagine it's pretty gruesome."

"Cut his arm clean off. His legs was all twisted and mangled. The train dragged him for a ways before it could stop." He shuddered at the memory.

"Did anyone see it happen?"

"The engineer. There's a light on the front of the train, and he yells at people to get out of the way when he sees them. Like you said, some folks don't pay any mind to me trying to warn them off."

"And what did he see?"

"You could ask him, I reckon, but he said this Knight fellow just stepped in front of the train and there was no way he could stop in time."

"He stepped in front of the train on purpose?"

"That's what he told the police, but . . ."

"But what?"

"I don't know. I didn't see anything, remember? It was all behind me, and I don't turn around to make sure people don't act foolish. I got enough to do controlling the horse with all the traffic and the train and making sure *I* don't run over anybody. So maybe he did just step in front of the train or maybe the engineer just said that so the railroad wouldn't get blamed."

"Do you have a theory?"

Sam made an expression of distaste. "They said he was drunk."

"That could explain it."

"I didn't smell no liquor on him, though, and he was dressed real nice. Before he got blood all over him, of course, but you could still see he was wearing a nice suit, and his shoes was practically new."

"He could be dressed nicely and still be drunk."

"Yeah, but where did he get drunk? There isn't any saloons for swells like him down on Eleventh. Just some stale beer dives where he'd get rolled in about ten seconds."

Since Gideon had no idea why Endicott Knight would have been in that part of the city at that hour under any circumstances, he couldn't answer Sam's question. Unless Endicott had gone there to kill himself. "Did anyone else see it happen?"

"Nobody who came forward. The police got there pretty quick, but at night people can just slip away pretty easy."

"And what did the police say?"

"I think they thought he'd killed himself, but they never came right out with it. That's a tough thing to accuse somebody of when they can't defend themselves, and this fellow sure couldn't. Besides, he had that nice suit and those new shoes."

"So they didn't want to say something bad about him because he might be an important person," Gideon guessed.

"Yeah. So they said he was just careless and it was an accident."

"And you didn't see anybody with him? Or near him?"

"I didn't, but I wasn't looking. I told you."

Yes, he had. Sam didn't know the engineer's name, although he often saw him, and he had nothing else to add. Gideon thanked him and apologized for dredging up bad memories.

He considered returning to the railroad's offices but thought better of it. They weren't interested in talking about a man who'd gotten himself killed by one of their trains. Besides, if the engineer had seen someone push Knight, wouldn't he have said so when it happened? In that case, the railroad wouldn't have been responsible at all.

Maybe he'd try the police again, although he

suspected that even if someone really had pushed Endicott Knight in front of the train, no one else had seen it happen, either. Maybe Endicott Knight had simply reached the end of his rope. His fortune and Priscilla's were gone, so he had nothing left with which to buy the blackmailer's silence. He was facing financial and social ruin. And if what Gideon suspected about DeForrest Jenks's death was true, Knight also carried the burden of having committed murder. If any man had a reason to commit suicide, it was he.

The only question Gideon had now was what, if anything, should he do with this information? Normally, he'd go straight to Elizabeth with it, but would she even see him? And what would telling her accomplish when he couldn't prove anything at all?

Mr. Franklin was a tall, slender man with a shock of silver hair and bright blue eyes, and he wore a tailored suit in a pattern that was just a bit too loud for good taste. He and Ross came that evening after Ross telephoned to tell them Franklin had just arrived in the city and to make certain Daisy and Peter were available to meet with them. Daisy served them coffee in the parlor.

"Leonard, you should have warned me that Mr. Honesdale is a man of God," Franklin said with only a hint of irritation.

"In his defense, he didn't know," Daisy said quickly. "I hope that doesn't make any difference to you. It certainly doesn't make any difference to Peter, does it, darling?"

"Not at all," Peter confirmed obediently. "It's nothing more than a clever social disguise."

Franklin smiled and accepted the cup of coffee she offered. "It makes no difference to me, although it was a bit of a shock. I thought we'd come to the wrong house."

"Actually, we did. Or at least I did," Ross said. "Our, uh, contacts told me this was where *Matthew* Honesdale lives."

"Matthew is my cousin," Peter said. "More like a brother, really. My family took him in when his parents died."

"Then perhaps you'd like to include him in our discussions," Franklin said. "I know he's been very successful with his enterprises, which was why he was recommended to me."

"I'm sure you'll forgive me if I'm not anxious to include Matthew in our negotiations," Peter said, just as she'd instructed him. "Daisy and I have helped Matthew in his business for a long time, but we've been wanting to sever that partnership. We've just been waiting for the right opportunity."

"Tell me," Franklin said, "how does a minister manage to operate brothels?"

"Very quietly," Peter said with a knowing smile.

"I'm sure." He turned his razor-sharp gaze to

Daisy. "Mrs. Honesdale, you told Leonard that you and Matthew Honesdale were partners. Exactly what does that mean?"

"Just that I ran one of his houses."

"You were a madam," he said baldly. At least he didn't pretend to think he might have offended her.

She nodded her acknowledgment.

"Forgive me, Mrs. Honesdale, but I rarely see a woman in my business who is so obviously as, uh, well-bred as you are."

"Thank you, Mr. Franklin." How nice of him to notice.

"So naturally, I'm curious as to how you became involved."

"Not in the usual way, I assure you," Daisy said. She didn't want him to think she'd ever been a whore. "I was a widow operating a boardinghouse for young ladies, and Matthew Honesdale recruited one of my tenants."

"He was a cadet," Franklin said.

"Yes. He approached me about working together, and I saw the potential at once. Eventually, we opened a house together."

"I see. And you have a financial interest in his business?" Franklin directed this question to Peter.

"Not as big an interest as we'd like," Peter said. Franklin didn't need to know they weren't involved with Matthew at all.

"And are you thinking you'd like to have a financial interest in *my* business?"

"Yes," Peter said. "In exchange for our knowledge of the city and our connections with powerful people who can protect your business."

"I'm not sure that's enough to justify the kind of partnership you describe. I'd want to see some financial commitment as well." Franklin wasn't a pushover, but they'd expected that.

"What would you consider a reasonable *commitment?*" Peter asked.

"Let's see, how much to start? Hmmm, first I need to purchase a house—"

"We have a house," Daisy said.

Franklin expressed surprise, then glanced around the sad little parlor.

"Not this one," she assured him. "It was once the home of a society family. It's located in a very respectable neighborhood." She gave him the address.

"I'm not familiar with the city, but I'll take your word for that, at least until I've seen it for myself."

"That should cover our half of the partnership," Peter said.

"Half?" Franklin scoffed. "Hardly. Oh, your contacts will be helpful, but no one provides assistance without being well compensated, as I'm sure you know. A lot of palms will have to be greased. The house will need to be furnished,

too, unless it's already operating as a brothel. Is it?"

"No, it's not," Peter admitted reluctantly, which was technically true.

"And then we'll need the women. They must be top quality, which means we'll have to entice them away from wherever they are now."

"Won't you bring some girls with you?" Daisy asked. "Mr. Ross said you have establishments in Chicago."

Franklin smiled tolerantly. "I prefer to use local talent. They're much less likely to get restless and want to return home. So that means more expense."

Because he'd have to bribe the girls to leave their current positions and probably pay off their current pimps and madams as well. Local girls would often bring along their own clientele, though, which made them even more valuable.

"How much do you think it will cost in total?" she asked.

"I think around a hundred thousand, in addition to the house. If you provide the house, I can give you twenty percent."

Peter caught her eye with a questioning look. They'd wanted a much larger cut. Ideally, Peter should make the counteroffer, but he had no idea what she was thinking. She turned to Franklin.

"We'll provide the house and fifty thousand and I'll run it," she said. Because if she was running it, she would be the only one who knew how much money was actually coming in. "Then we'll get sixty percent."

"You'll run it yourself?"

"I'm very good at it. Matthew can vouch for me." He would, too, for a price, and because he had no idea this deal had originally been meant for him.

"I suppose you'll want a salary if you're running it."

"I'll settle for our sixty percent. That will give me an incentive to earn as much as possible."

He considered her offer for a long moment and apparently found no reason to refuse it. "I'll let you run it for the first three months and then we'll reevaluate. But before we settle anything, I'll need to see the house."

Peter cast her an alarmed glance, but she refused to meet his eye. "We have some engagements tomorrow, so I'm not sure when we'll be available. Can we send you a message to arrange a time?"

"Yes," Franklin said. He gave her the name of his hotel. He had a few more questions, but nothing they couldn't answer. After some pleasantries, he and Ross took their leave.

When they'd gone, Peter turned to her, his eyes shining. "We did it!"

"Not quite yet, but we're on our way."

"How will you get Matthew to give us the house?"

She smiled at such a notion. "He won't *give* it to us, but I'm sure I can convince him to sell us the mortgage."

"You'll pay him, then?"

"I'll have to, but it will be worth it."

"Are you sure you want to run the house yourself? When we get it, that is."

She'd have to, in the beginning, just to make sure Franklin didn't cheat them and to get everything organized. "Just to start, but I'll always keep the books. That way we'll get more like eighty percent." Then she'd truly be rich and would never have to lift her hand again. Or put up with Peter again, because as soon as everything was in order, she was finished with him.

"You're amazing, Daisy."

"Yes, I am."

"And we'll be rich, richer than Matthew."

What a beautiful thought. "And much classier, too. We'll buy a house on Fifth Avenue and get a box at the opera." At least Daisy would.

"My father will be furious."

"Which makes it all the sweeter."

He took her hand in both of his. "Daisy? Can we . . . ? I mean, you said after we made the deal, but it's practically made now and . . ."

He was so pathetic. He made her want to vomit. But she had to keep him in line for a while longer. "Of course, darling. Come along. I'll even show you something new."

• • •

"So she's going to send me a message and tell me when to meet them so I can see the house," the Old Man said. He'd stopped by Cybil's the next morning to tell Elizabeth about his meeting with the Honesdales.

"Where is she sending you a message?" she asked with interest.

"The Waldorf."

"How will you get it?"

"I'll go to the desk this evening. They can't keep track of everyone who's staying there. And if I can't get it from them, I'll just telephone Daisy and blame the hotel for not giving me her message."

"She's kind of in a mess because she gave Matthew the key to the house, so she can't even get into it. She doesn't know it, but he gave the key to . . . to Gideon." Just saying his name hurt her heart, but she swallowed down the pain. "So it's going to be harder than she thinks to get it."

"Should we warn Matthew?"

"It may already be too late for that. Gideon did tell him we'd be taking steps, though, so he may assume that's why she came to him."

"And if not?"

"Matthew doesn't know what we're doing yet, so he can't possibly give us away. In any case, he'll have to go to . . . to Gideon for the key."

"So we do need to inform Gideon. May I

316

assume from your expression that you haven't made up with him yet?"

"What do you mean, *made up with him?* You act like we just had a lover's spat."

"Didn't you?"

"I told you, I'm never going to see him again."

"I don't think you told me that, Lizzie."

"Then I'm telling you now."

"This sounds serious."

"It is very serious. I never should have . . . I was a fool to think . . . In any case, it's over."

He nodded sagely, which made her want to scream.

"Don't be understanding. It doesn't suit you," she said.

"I don't know why not. I understand everything."

"You should. You've made understanding other people your life's work."

He gave a long-suffering sigh. "Lizzie, my darling, I know I haven't been the usual kind of father, but I do care about you and want to see you happy."

"Then you should know I'd never be happy with Gideon."

"I do know that, far better than you, I'm sure."

For some reason that stung. Had she wanted him to deny it? To reassure her? To convince her she really belonged with Gideon? "Then why aren't you glad I broke it off with him?"

"Because I think you'll be even more unhappy without him."

"That doesn't make any sense."

"Yes, it does. Lizzie, if you don't marry Gideon, who will you marry?"

"I don't have to get married at all." She thought of the unmarried women she'd met in the women's suffrage movement. They were doing important work.

"No, you don't. You can spend your life alone and amuse yourself by grifting, I suppose."

"I don't have to grift!"

He shrugged that off. "The world is not a comfortable place for unmarried women. You know that, which is why you've been so interested in the suffragists."

"We're going to change all that."

"I know you want to try, but how long do you think it will take until women get all the rights they're fighting for?"

"I . . . I don't know."

"I don't, either, but I expect it will be a very long time. In the meantime, a woman can't support herself the way a man can or do most of the things a man can. You can't even be as successful as a man at the grift."

Which she well knew, although even that knowledge was grating. "Which is why you need to think about what your future will be. Do you want children?"

"I . . . I suppose I do." She'd only let herself think about having a family of her own after she'd fallen in love with Gideon, but now . . .

"Then they'll need a father. You can marry a grifter, but you already know from experience that grifters don't make very good fathers, and we make even worse husbands. How many grifters do you know who turn their wives out to sell themselves when times get tough?"

"Stop it! I'm not going to marry a grifter."

"Then who else can you marry? You want someone straight who'll stick by you, but how many men like that would forgive your past?"

"I don't need to be forgiven!" she cried, outraged at the thought.

"Overlook it, then. Accept you without judging or condemning you. And how many of those saintly men would really love you? Even more importantly, how many of them could you love?"

Rage bubbled up inside her. "You're a fine one to be giving advice!"

"I'm the best one to give advice, because I know how things can go wrong. I loved your mother. I gave her a home and supported her, but I still couldn't be faithful to her. She deserved better than me, and so do you."

"You're forgetting one thing. Gideon did not accept me without judging or condemning me. He's willing to *forgive* me so long as I never do anything the least bit shady again, but he's not willing to compromise his . . . his *standards* for any reason at all."

"Are you willing to compromise yours?"

"I don't have any standards! I'm a grifter!"

He frowned. "You have standards. They're different from Gideon's, but you're just as determined to stick by yours as he is to his."

"And since neither of us can change, we can never be happy together."

"Who said you can't change?"

She opened her mouth to reply, but she had nothing to say, so she closed it with a snap.

"People can change, Lizzie," he said so gently she could hardly believe it was her father saying the words. "It's not easy, but if they must, they can. You've already changed."

"No, I haven't."

He scowled as if he thought her crazy. "Of course you have. Those women changed you when you were in jail. You aren't even interested in grifting anymore."

"Of course I am! That's what we're doing right now."

"Yes, we are, but for all the wrong reasons."

"Wrong?"

"Well, most people would probably say it's for the right reasons. You want to get money from blackmailers to give it back to the innocent victim instead of wanting to keep it for yourself. That's unnatural."

She couldn't help smiling at his disgruntled frown. "I suppose it is, by *your* standards at least."

"You see, even I have standards," he told her with a ghost of a grin. "Would you have been so concerned about the widows and orphans of this world if you hadn't been locked up with those women?"

She sighed in defeat. "I wouldn't have even noticed them before."

"So you see, it is possible to change."

"But only if you want to. I don't think Gideon wants to change. He's convinced he's right." Which was so infuriating she wanted to scream again.

This time his smile was sad. "Love can make a man do amazing things."

"I don't want him to do amazing things. I just want him to accept me for who I am."

"In this case, that would be amazing."

He was right, of course. "Which means it probably isn't going to happen."

"Don't underestimate Mr. Bates, and in the meantime try to keep him from interfering with this job."

Gideon had spent the morning meeting with a couple who seemed determined to drive him insane. They wanted to disinherit all of their relatives while not appearing to be unkind. Since they also didn't want to leave their money to charity, he had been unable to provide them with an agreeable solution.

No sooner had they left than Smith handed him a note that Renfroe had sent over informing him that, according to his employees, Endicott Knight had usually arrived at the bank alone and never engaged in conversation with anyone, although they all agreed he always seemed a bit tense and oddly nervous. Only one clerk remembered ever seeing him with someone else, and that had been a minister. Which confirmed all of Gideon's suspicions but proved nothing at all.

Just when he thought the day couldn't get any more bizarre, Smith came in to tell him Matthew Honesdale was there to see him.

When Honesdale entered the office, he gave Gideon a knowing smile and waited until Smith had closed the door behind him before he said, "I see you didn't waste any time. Daisy called on me this morning."

Gideon gestured to the visitor's chair while he frantically tried to figure out what Honesdale was talking about. "She did? What did she want?"

"First of all, she wanted the key to Knight's house, but then she also happened to mention that she'd been feeling guilty about asking me to take the mortgage on it, so she and Peter had decided to buy it from me."

Gideon sank back down into his own chair as

he absorbed this information. "Did she mention how she and Peter could afford to do that?"

"I think we already know how they could afford it, but she did mention she had a nest egg she'd accumulated during the time she worked for me. She indicated she would use that."

So Peter and Daisy were suddenly interested in taking possession of Knight's house, and they wanted access to it immediately. "What did you tell her about the key?"

"I said I'd put it into my safe-deposit box, and I'd have to go retrieve it. She wanted to come with me. She was very eager to come, in fact, until she figured out that was making me suspicious. I'm supposed to drop the key off at the parsonage later today. So tell me what your plan is."

Gideon managed a smile that he hoped looked mysterious. What *was* their plan? He had no idea, but could he bluff his way through this in hopes of figuring it out? "I'm not sure it's a good idea for you to know the details."

"You're not afraid I'll tip them off, are you? I've got more reason than anyone to see them called to account. They tried to frame me for blackmail, after all."

"I know they did, and you have every reason to want to know what's going on."

"And every reason to help. Just tell me what you're doing. I can already see how it will benefit me. Daisy and Peter will buy the mortgage from me, so I won't have to bother the poor widow and her orphaned children to get my money back. But surely, you've also got a plan for getting Mrs. Knight's money back as well."

Yes, surely they did. Reimbursing Matthew for the mortgage would just be a side benefit. But Gideon had only witnessed one con in his life, and that one was very different from this one, whatever this one was, so he truly had no inkling.

Consequently, he was enormously grateful and completely astonished when someone knocked on his office door. No one at Devoss and Van Aken ever interrupted a partner when they were with a client unless the building was on fire. "Yes?"

Smith stepped in, his reluctance and mortification at breaking such a cardinal rule apparent in every line of his body. "Miss Miles is here to see you. I told her you were with a client, and when she learned you were meeting with Mr. Honesdale, she insisted that I interrupt you. She said you would *understand*." Plainly, he did not expect for one moment that Gideon would understand anything at all about this.

"Thank you, Smith. Would you show Miss Miles in?"

Clearly, Smith was flabbergasted. If he had not been so well trained, he might have fainted, but because he was well trained, he disappeared and soon reappeared with Elizabeth in tow.

She was a vision in a coat the color of burgundy wine that almost matched the auburn of her hair, which was mostly tucked up under a ridiculous hat. He'd never seen either the coat or the hat before, and apropos of nothing, he recalled her saying all of her clothes were new because he'd made her return the clothes she'd *borrowed* when they were in Washington City. The memory stung him, even though he was sure he'd been right to insist on it. "Miss Miles," he said, appalled to hear that he sounded as disconcerted as he felt.

"Mr. Bates," she replied stiffly. "Thank you for seeing me." She turned her beautiful blue eyes to Honesdale, who had also risen when she entered.

"Mrs. Knight?" he said in some confusion.

She gave him her glorious smile. "So much for my disguise. I should have known a mere veil would not fool a man of your perception, Mr. Honesdale. I'm Elizabeth Miles."

He took her offered hand, having obviously fallen completely under her spell. Gideon wanted to punch him.

"I hope you'll forgive us for our little subterfuge. The real Mrs. Knight does not know the true depths of her late husband's depravity, so we thought it best that she not attend the meeting with you."

"And yet you thought it best that you *impersonate* her at that meeting." The statement contained an unspoken question.

"We weren't deliberately trying to mislead you, but you will probably never have the opportunity to meet the real Mrs. Knight, and we did think you might be more kindly disposed if you came face-to-face with the unfortunate widow."

"An excellent strategy, because I did feel more kindly disposed, so I will forgive you, but only if you convince Mr. Bates to tell me all the details of your plan to bring down my cousin and his unholy wife."

"Unholy? Surely your cousin Peter deserves that title more than she."

"Perhaps you don't know her as well as I. In any case, someone will tell me your plan before I leave here."

"We would be happy to," she said and took the other visitor's chair, allowing both men to sit again as well. "What has Mr. Bates told you so far?" she asked, knowing full well he couldn't have told the man anything at all, since he probably knew even less about it than Honesdale.

Gideon couldn't help noticing that she had hardly spared him a glance since she entered the room, too, and even now was avoiding his eye.

"He hasn't told me anything," Honesdale said.

"Mr. Bates is the soul of discretion," she said, infuriating him. She made him sound like a stodgy old uncle. "May I assume that Daisy has called upon you, asking for the key to the Knight house?"

"Yes, and I have to confess to being annoyed that I wasn't warned ahead of time."

"Please accept our apologies. Things moved a little more quickly than we anticipated, and quite frankly, we didn't realize the house would come into play so early. I only learned this morning that our agents met with Reverend and Mrs. Honesdale last evening. I came here immediately to tell Mr. Bates, but . . ." She shrugged, and any man with blood in his veins would have forgiven her anything.

"The important thing is that I know now," Honesdale assured her much too eagerly. "Daisy also offered to buy the mortgage from me."

"I thought she might. That was to be your inducement to participate in the plan, although I believe that once you give them the key and accept payment for the mortgage, your part will be over."

"How disappointing."

"Don't worry, we'll allow you to know everything else that happens."

Gideon cleared his throat and then was sorry he had when she turned her cool, blue stare on him as impersonally as if they'd just met. "Mr. Honesdale wanted me to tell him the entire plan, but I wasn't sure if that was a good idea."

She turned back to Honesdale. "Mr. Bates is extremely cautious, as all good attorneys must be, but certainly you may know the plan. A gentleman who is in the same business as you in another city has approached your cousin and his wife—his *unholy* wife, was it?—because he wants to expand to New York City."

"Why would he approach a minister about something like that?"

"He pretended to be confused. He was actually looking for you and was misdirected."

Even Gideon was impressed by that detail, although he took care not to show it.

"And Daisy would have jumped at the opportunity," Honesdale said. "Being a minister's wife was beginning to wear on her."

"They apparently offered Mr. Knight's house as a location for the new business, and they claimed to own it."

"Which explains Daisy's visit this morning. So now I know how I benefit, but how will you get the widow's money back?"

"Reverend and Mrs. Honesdale will need to make a cash investment in the, uh, enterprise," Gideon said, surprising both of them. Did he catch a hint of admiration from Elizabeth that he had figured it out? Probably not, but at least he'd contributed something so Honesdale wouldn't think him a complete fool.

Honesdale turned to Gideon, and he did show some admiration. "A very clever idea. So all I have to do is give Daisy the key and let her buy the mortgage from me. Is that correct?"

Gideon glanced at Elizabeth who gave a quick nod. "Yes, that's all."

"That's easy enough. If you'll give me the key, I'll be on my way to do my part."

"And be sure to get your payment before you turn over the mortgage," Gideon said.

"Always the careful attorney," Honesdale said cheerfully as Gideon handed him the key he'd removed from his desk drawer. Once again Gideon managed not to punch him.

Honesdale went to the door, opened it and stood aside. "Miss Miles?" he said, indicating she should precede him.

But Gideon couldn't let her go, especially not with Honesdale. "Miss Miles, if you wouldn't mind staying, I have some more information for you. On another matter," he added for Honesdale's benefit.

She'd already turned to follow Honesdale. She stopped, and for a horrible moment, he was afraid she wouldn't stay. Then she turned, an artificial smile stiff on her lips. "Of course, Mr. Bates. I'm always happy to oblige."

CHAPTER FOURTEEN

Elizabeth waited until Honesdale had closed the door behind him, then walked the few steps back to Gideon's desk. She made a point of not sitting down. She didn't want him to think she'd sit still for another of his lectures on the rule of law. "What information did you have for me?"

"You asked me to look into DeForrest Jenks's death."

"Oh." Well, that was different. She sat down again, although she only perched on the edge of the chair, ready to jump up and escape at a moment's notice. She also kept her tone cool and disinterested, and steeled herself against his charm, just in case he tried to use it. "What did you find out?"

Gideon sat down again, too, but much more slowly. She didn't trust him. He was being too careful. "It looks like Jenks was murdered."

She shivered as a chill ran down her spine. "Murdered? Are you sure?"

"I found out from the club manager and the company that removed the gargoyles from the other three corners of the building that they had been called earlier to inspect the gargoyle that fell on Jenks."

"Inspect it? You mean before it fell?"

"Yes, it wasn't working properly. The gargoyles aren't just decorations. They're actually part of the gutter system, and this one wasn't draining. The company determined that it was loose and could fall at any moment."

"So they knew it was a hazard and did nothing about it?" she asked in outrage.

He seemed somehow gratified by her outrage. "Only the club president knew."

She needed a minute to make the connection. "If I remember correctly, Endicott Knight was the club president."

"You do remember correctly, and he probably confided in his good friend Peter, who immediately saw an opportunity."

"After what we've learned, do you really think it was *Peter* Honesdale who saw the opportunity?"

"Or Peter's unholy wife saw it," he said with a trace of his usual spirit. "In any case, I also talked to the police detective who investigated Jenks's death."

"But he must have thought it was an accident."

"He did, but he didn't know what we know about how much Knight needed Jenks's money and what happened after Jenks died."

"No, he wouldn't have, and it looked like an accident, so why would he have bothered to find out anything more?"

"He wouldn't and he didn't, but he did tell me

that Jenks was already lying on the sidewalk, facedown, when the gargoyle hit him."

"Already lying . . . ? How could they know that?"

"Because the gargoyle hit him on his back. Think about it. If he'd been standing on the sidewalk, it would have crushed his head or at least his shoulder, but his head wasn't injured at all. Just his back."

"That's . . ." She stopped, unable to think of the right word.

"Impossible," he supplied. "Yes, it is."

"And the police detective noticed this?"

Gideon nodded. She wished he didn't look so handsome when he was being serious. It was distracting.

"Then why didn't he investigate?" she asked, frustrated all over again.

"He'd been told Jenks had been drinking heavily that evening. They assumed he had passed out and just happened to be lying there in the exact right spot when the gargoyle fell."

"That's monstrous! You mean they just laid him out on the sidewalk and then . . . ?" She shivered again.

"The detective thought Jenks had passed out, and he probably had if he was drugged as we suspect, but the detective didn't want to add to the widow's burden by mentioning it. Either way, it would have been an accident."

"Except it wasn't an accident at all. Did you

tell him what we know? Did you tell him it was really a murder?"

"No, I didn't."

She gaped at him. "Why not? You're the one who wanted the law to take care of them. Now you have the proof and—"

"But I don't have proof."

Was he crazy? "Of course you do! You just told me!"

"I told you Knight was told the gargoyle was loose, and we know he was being blackmailed, and we know he married Jenks's widow. None of that proves he murdered Jenks."

"Yes, it does!"

"Not in a way that would stand up in a court of law. Not even in a way that would convince the police to bring charges."

"But—"

"And there's more, something we didn't even think of, something that will hurt Priscilla."

"What?"

"When I was talking to the detective, I mentioned that Jenks might have had enemies, someone who wanted to marry his widow, and he immediately thought I meant Priscilla had a lover and the two of them conspired to murder him."

"Oh no!"

"Oh yes. Don't you see? That's what everyone would think if they found out Knight killed Jenks."

"Especially because he married Priscilla just a few months later! Oh, Gideon, Priscilla would get all the blame, too, because Knight isn't even here to tell people she wasn't involved."

"Assuming he'd do that, and nothing we know about him indicates he was a gentleman."

"But even if he did try to take the blame, no one would have believed him. People are always willing to believe the worst about a female."

"At least Knight had the decency to kill himself."

"You sound very sure of that," she said, remembering that they had wondered if the Honesdales hadn't gotten rid of him when he was no longer of use to them.

"I found the West Side Cowboy who was on duty the night Knight died. As far as anyone can tell, Knight stepped in front of the train on purpose and of his own accord."

"So it was suicide."

"As far as we'll ever know. I also met with the manager of Priscilla's bank to see if they had any idea what Knight did with the money he withdrew from her accounts, but they didn't. The only interesting thing I learned is that a minister once accompanied Knight to the bank. So that's another dead end."

Elizabeth could only stare at him as the import of his words—all of his words—finally sank in. "You investigated all of this."

Some emotion flickered across his face, but his voice was expressionless when he said, "You asked me to."

Had she? So much had happened since then that she'd forgotten. But he hadn't forgotten. He'd remembered and he'd done it, because she'd asked him to, even though she'd sent him away and told him they were finished. But why? "Were you trying to prove you were right?"

He jerked back as if she'd struck him. "Prove I was right about what?"

"About the law being the only right way to get justice."

He considered her question for a long moment. "Yes, I suppose I was, but also . . . I wanted to impress you."

"Impress me?" she echoed in wonder.

He smiled bitterly. "Yes. I wanted to find out the truth that would bring the full weight of the law down on Peter and Daisy so you'd understand why I believe in it."

And he *had* found out the truth, for all the good it had done. "Oh, Gideon—"

He raised his hand to stop her words. "No, it's fine. I needed to do that. And we needed to know what really happened."

"Should we tell Priscilla?"

"No. Not yet, at least. It won't give her any comfort and might just make her grief harder to bear."

"You're probably right. Oh, Gideon, this is even more horrible than we suspected. I really do wish we could see the law punish them for this."

He raised his eyebrows in amazement. "I don't suppose your plan calls for anything like that."

"Not a punishment, no. Nothing that could compare to being put in prison. We were just going to get Priscilla's money back."

"That's something, at least."

She blinked in surprise. Was he actually expressing approval of their plan, however tepid and halfhearted? "I . . . Thank you for giving Mr. Honesdale the key and . . ."

"And what? Not trying to talk him out of helping you?"

"Yes, that, too."

"I don't think I would have succeeded in any case."

"But you didn't try, and I'm grateful for that. I'm also sorry I didn't give you fair warning. The Old Man really just told me this morning what he'd done, and I came right over to let you know."

"Will you . . . keep me informed?"

Oh dear, why did he want her to do that? "Are you sure you really want to know?"

"I won't help you, but so long as Peter and Daisy are the only victims, I won't interfere, either. I just think it will be easier not to interfere if I know what you're doing."

That made sense. "All right." Although that

meant she'd have to see him again. Would she mind so very much? Seeing him wouldn't change anything, after all. "I . . . The Old Man will get Daisy and Peter to take him over to Knight's house next. They think they are going to turn it into a brothel and Daisy will run it."

"Run it?" he echoed in astonishment.

"She was a madam before, remember? The Old Man thinks she wants to run the house so she can skim the profits, and he's probably right."

"What will Peter do?"

"I've been wondering that myself. Surely, he doesn't think he can keep on being a preacher."

"I imagine that's one of the attractions for him of opening your own brothel. You can't possibly have a future in the ministry."

She couldn't help smiling at that. "Matthew did say Peter resented his father as much as Matthew did."

"So this would cause his father the most embarrassment possible."

"Not as much as a murder would have, but enough, I'm sure."

Gideon rubbed his chin thoughtfully. "But they won't really be opening a brothel, will they? So there won't be any scandal. What will happen when it's over? When you've taken back the money, I mean."

"Nothing as dramatic as the last time, I promise," she said, remembering the scene in

337

Gideon's parlor when Anna shot her. "The Old Man and his cohorts will just disappear. Daisy and Peter don't know their real names or where to find them, and they'll just vanish."

"So aside from losing their ill-gotten fortune, nothing will really change for Peter and Daisy."

"I hadn't thought about it, but I suppose not. Peter will go on being a minister and Daisy will be his wife, but without any extra money to spend. That hardly seems fair, does it?"

"No, it doesn't."

She waited for him to say more, but he didn't, although she could tell he was thinking very hard about something. She should go, she knew. No use prolonging the agony that she felt every second she was with him. "I guess I should—"

"Of course," he said, rising to his feet so quickly she felt insulted. "I'm sorry to have kept you."

His formal tone cut like an icicle thrust into her heart, but she rose, too, and thanked him for his time.

"You'll keep me informed," he repeated as she turned toward the door.

"Yes, I will."

He must have pushed some kind of alarm button, because Smith opened the door from the other side before she reached it.

"Please see Miss Miles out, Smith," Gideon said.

Smith was the perfect gentleman, escorting her to the front door and wishing her a good day, but by the time she reached the sidewalk, she was blinking at the sting of tears. She wouldn't cry. That would be idiotic. She was the one who had ended it, after all. It was for the best. It was for her own good.

It was horrible.

"Smith!" Gideon called when he heard his clerk returning.

Smith stepped into his office. "Yes, sir?"

"Do we have any clients in the newspaper business?"

"One or two, I believe. We drew up a will for—"

"Can you give me their names?"

"I'm sure I—"

"I'll need them immediately. And I've written a note for Matthew Honesdale. I'd like to have it delivered as well."

If Smith was curious—and from his expression, he was almost insanely so—he said not one word.

When he was gone, Gideon sat back in his chair and remembered his conversation with Elizabeth. She'd seemed pleased to learn he'd investigated the two men's deaths, although neither of them could be pleased with the results of those investigations. And as much as she'd wanted justice for her friend, her father's con would still

339

leave Peter and Daisy free to destroy the lives of others, just as they had done to Jenks and Knight and Priscilla. The law couldn't touch them for the murders and punishing them for the blackmail would only hurt Priscilla and her daughters.

If he really wanted to impress Elizabeth, he needed to get true justice for Priscilla and stop Peter and Daisy from ever harming anyone else again. He wasn't sure he could actually do all that, but he was certainly going to try.

The next morning, Daisy and Peter met Franklin and Ross at Knight's house. Daisy was annoyed that Franklin had once again worn a suit with a slightly less-than-conservative pattern. Was he serious about opening his business in an upper-class neighborhood? If so, then he'd have to learn how to dress so he wouldn't draw attention to himself. Or else never show himself at all. She'd be sure to speak to him about it once the deal was made.

Using the key Matthew had delivered to her last night, she opened the front door. The place smelled dusty and musty, the way empty houses always smelled, and it was bone-chillingly cold. They hadn't used it since the last time they'd met Knight here for a session. He'd been such a fool, but she supposed sensible men didn't allow themselves to be photographed in compromising positions.

"What do you think?" Peter asked Franklin with the false heartiness he used when he was nervous.

"The neighborhood is just what I was looking for. I've had great success in Chicago with my place in Hyde Park, although you do have to be careful with the neighbors."

"I'm sure you do," Peter said, although he had no idea what it took to run a successful house.

"What precautions do you take?" Daisy asked. "Besides the usual ones, I mean."

"You mean besides paying off the police and the politicians?" Franklin asked with a knowing grin. "We make sure no one gets in without a referral. That keeps out the riffraff, so the neighbors don't have any reason for complaint."

"Do the neighbors know what's going on?" Peter asked with a frown.

"Some do. Most, I have learned, prefer not to notice, if you know what I mean. They refer to it as a gentleman's club or some such."

"Nobody wants a whorehouse on their street," Ross said, earning a chastening glare from Franklin. Ross merely shrugged, unrepentant.

So much for chitchat. "Most of the furniture will have to be replaced, of course," she said, leading the men into the front parlor. "It's not nearly flashy enough."

"Just tell me what you want, and I'll take care of ordering it," Franklin said. "Brass beds, I assume?"

"With feather mattresses," Daisy confirmed.

She led them through the rest of the house. Franklin occasionally pulled up the edge of one of the furniture covers to see what was underneath and frowned. None of the furniture seemed to meet with his approval.

Upstairs they determined the bedrooms would need to be divided. She claimed the master bedroom with its adjoining bath for herself.

"And what about you, Honesdale?" Franklin asked with a sly grin. "Will you live here, too?"

"Hardly, although I'll visit," he added with a sly grin of his own.

"Will you need any special equipment?" Franklin asked. "I have a man who makes mine for me. He can ship whatever you need."

"I already have what I'll need to start," she said.

Franklin raised one eyebrow. "Do you keep it at the parsonage?"

"Don't be silly. The servants would see it. No, it's in the attic for now."

"May I take a look?" Franklin asked. "Professional interest only," he added.

Peter took him and Ross up because Daisy didn't want to hear what the men would have to say. Men could be so tiresome, thinking their crude observations could somehow stimulate her to bed them.

She waited on the first floor for them, ready to leave now that the tour was over.

"May I compliment you on your creativity, Mrs. Honesdale?" Franklin said as he came down the stairs to find her in the foyer. "I find myself more and more pleased that Ross here found the wrong Honesdales."

She smiled graciously. "Thank you, Mr. Franklin. It's nice to see one's work appreciated."

"I'm sure your clients will appreciate it, although I'm afraid we may have to increase the amount of money allotted to bribes once word gets out."

Daisy wasn't worried. She'd make sure those bribes came out of Franklin's share.

"How did it go with Daisy when you dropped off the key?" Gideon asked Matthew Honesdale when he had been escorted into Gideon's office. Even though it was Saturday, Matthew had been only too happy to hear what Gideon had to propose.

"She was glad to get the key so quickly, and she wants me to sign over the mortgage as soon as I can."

"You won't be able to see an attorney until Monday, but that should be soon enough."

"Can you do the transfer for us?"

"They would probably be suspicious if I did. I'll have one of my partners help you with it. Be sure to get the money in cash."

"That's a lot of cash."

"Use a bodyguard. I'm guessing they keep the money in the parsonage, though. They wouldn't want some banker asking awkward questions about where they got so much cash on a minister's salary."

"I don't suppose they would." Honesdale stared at him across the expanse of his desk for a long moment. "All right, you've got a plan. Out with it."

"What makes you think I've got a plan?"

"You've changed since yesterday. All that talk about not being able to tell me, that was guff. You didn't know the plan then any more than I did, did you?"

"I knew some of it."

Honesdale gave him a pitying look. "That Miss Miles is an interesting woman."

"She's my fiancée." It wasn't a lie. Gideon still had every intention of marrying her. In the meantime, he didn't want Matthew Honesdale getting any ideas about her.

"You're a lucky man, although she'll lead you a merry chase, mark my words." She already had, but he wasn't going to admit it to Honesdale. "Now, tell me what the two of you have cooked up since yesterday."

"It will require your cooperation," Gideon said, although the words wanted to stick in his throat. He hated everything about Matthew Honesdale, but in this case, he was the lesser of two evils.

Gideon would have to dance with this devil if he hoped to defeat a worse one.

"I already said I'll help, and don't forget I have good reason."

"And I can give you an even better one. We think Peter and Daisy have committed murder."

Now he had Honesdale's complete attention. "Murder? Who did they kill? And don't tell me Peter did it, because I'll know you're lying."

"He probably did do it, just because it would have been too difficult for a woman, but he had help." Gideon quickly explained how DeForrest Jenks had died and what part Peter and Endicott Knight had played.

Honesdale gave a low whistle. "Daisy came up with that plan. Peter could never have thought of something that complicated."

"Unfortunately, we can't prove any of this unless one of them confesses, and that doesn't seem very likely. But the reason I told you all this is because if you get involved, they may decide to kill you, too."

For some reason, this seemed to please him immensely. "You have indeed given me an even better reason to assist you in your endeavors, Mr. Bates. If I had a conscience, it would be completely salved now. Since I don't, I have an excuse I can use if I ever need one."

Gideon wasn't quite sure what to make of Matthew Honesdale's exuberance, but he said,

"As you know, Miss Miles and her agents have a plan to trick Reverend and Mrs. Honesdale into returning the money they took from you and Mrs. Knight. The real Mrs. Knight, that is, who—I assure you—is more than worthy of our efforts on her behalf."

"I don't particularly care if she is or not, Bates, but go on."

"That plan will not punish them in any meaningful way, however, or ensure they won't try to blackmail some other poor soul in the future."

"I always assume that anyone who did something worthy of being blackmailed for isn't particularly deserving of my pity, but I am very interested in punishing Daisy and Peter, if only for the annoyance they have caused me."

"Then you should appreciate *my* plan." Gideon outlined it for him.

When he was finished, Honesdale sat back in his chair and smiled with satisfaction. "A good start, and it will totally humiliate them, but you've still left Peter and Daisy free to wreak whatever havoc their devious little minds can contrive in the future. If you'll allow me, I'd like to make a suggestion that will completely satisfy me, and probably you as well. May I?"

"Certainly," Gideon said and leaned back in his own chair as Honesdale explained his suggestion.

When he was finished, Gideon was smiling just as broadly as Honesdale.

● ● ●

"I hope you aren't insulted when I say I don't completely trust you, Mrs. Honesdale," Franklin said. They'd returned to the parsonage after touring Knight's house, and they had enjoyed lunch before sending the servants out so they could complete their negotiations. Now they were seated in the parlor.

"And we do not completely trust you, either, Mr. Franklin," Daisy said. "We are, after all, still strangers to each other."

"And yet we will be partners, so how will we manage to do business together?"

Daisy smiled sweetly. "Very carefully."

"Exactly, which is why I have come up with a plan for combining our financial contributions and ensuring that neither of us can cheat the other."

Daisy exchanged a glance with Peter, who seemed as intrigued as she. "Do tell us, Mr. Franklin."

"I have rented a safe-deposit box at the Safe Deposit Company of New York. I chose that company because it is the oldest one in the city and you know it is reliable."

Daisy nodded, although she had never heard of the company. She had little use for such a thing as a safe-deposit box.

Peter said, "My father uses them." As if that were important.

"Good. I propose that we each put our fifty-thousand-dollar contribution into the safe-deposit box. Each time we have an expense, we will both go to the box and withdraw the necessary amount to pay that expense. That way we will both know only that amount is being withdrawn."

"But what is to stop you . . . or me for that matter . . . from going to the box alone and withdrawing all the cash?" Daisy asked.

Franklin smiled his charming smile. "I'm crushed that you would suspect me of such a thing, Mrs. Honesdale," he chided with amusement, "but I was also going to propose that we give the key to a third party, someone we can both trust, and who has been instructed not to give access to the box unless both parties are present."

"Where on earth would we find such a trustworthy person?" she asked.

Franklin shrugged. "I am new to the city, so I thought perhaps you could suggest someone. It would have to be someone so painfully honest and incorruptible that he would never dream of violating his instructions." He turned to Peter. "You're a minister. Surely, you know such an individual."

Peter's forehead wrinkled with the effort, but after a moment, he brightened. "Gideon Bates."

Daisy inwardly cringed.

"Who is this Bates?" Franklin asked.

"He's an attorney," Peter said.

Franklin frowned. "In my experience, attorneys are not particularly trustworthy."

"This one is," Peter assured him. "He's from one of the old Knickerbocker families, and he's the biggest Goody-Two-shoes you'd ever want to meet."

"What kind of attorney is he?"

"Estates, mostly. People have to trust you when you do that work, and they all rave about how Gideon always makes sure their interests are protected."

"Mrs. Honesdale, what do you think?" Franklin asked.

How nice to be asked her opinion. "He is certainly painfully honest—disgustingly so, in fact—but won't he also be suspicious? He'll at least wonder what we're doing."

"What if he does?" Franklin said. "And quite frankly, everyone will know soon enough. Meanwhile, he must maintain our confidentiality, but actually, we won't have to tell him anything at all. He'll have no idea what we're putting into the box or taking out, and we'll pay him a handsome fee for his trouble. I've found that usually satisfies even the most curious."

"And you're willing to accept our choice of . . . ? What shall we call him?" Daisy asked.

"Holder of the key? I'll have to meet him, of course, but if I'm impressed, then yes, he can hold the key to the box."

"How soon can you have your half of the money ready?" Daisy asked, already planning how she would outsmart Gideon Bates.

"I transferred some of my funds to a bank here in the city. I can withdraw the fifty thousand on Monday and meet you at the Safe Deposit Company. Will you be able to access your funds by then as well?"

"Oh yes," Daisy said, thinking of the safe in Peter's study, where they kept the cash. "Monday will be just fine."

"But what about Gideon? He'll have to be there, too, won't he?" Peter said.

"Yes, he will," Daisy said. "You will see him tomorrow at church. Ask him then."

"Shall we say one o'clock on Monday, then? Unless Mr. Bates has a conflict?" Franklin asked.

"I'm expecting a visitor later this afternoon," Gideon told his mother when they had retired to the parlor after Sunday dinner.

"Not Elizabeth, I assume," she said. She still blamed him because Elizabeth hadn't been at church that morning.

He tried a smile, although he suspected it didn't make him look especially happy. "I don't expect we'll see Elizabeth for a while yet."

"Really, Gideon, all you have to do is apologize to her."

"If you believe that, you don't know Elizabeth at all, Mother."

"It would at least be a start."

"Don't worry. I'm . . . Well, I have a plan for winning her back."

"*Winning?* Is that what you think it will take? And if you win, does that mean she loses?"

"Maybe that was a poor choice of words."

"I hope so. Now, tell me about your plan."

Before he could figure out how to refuse to explain, they heard the doorbell ring. Gideon managed not to sigh in relief even while his pulse soared. He'd been hoping for this.

"Is that your visitor?" she asked.

"I don't think so. He wasn't coming until later." No, this would be a much more welcome guest.

They waited for the maid, who stepped in to announce that Mr. Miles had come to call. This was not the Miles Gideon had been hoping to see. They both rose to greet him, although Gideon's mother was much happier to see him than Gideon was.

"Mr. Miles, what a pleasant surprise," she said, offering her hand.

To Gideon's dismay, he kissed it. "You are looking very well, Mrs. Bates. What a lovely gown."

"Thank you, Mr. Miles." Dear heaven, was she blushing?

Gideon stepped forward and offered his own

hand, so Miles had to release his mother's. "To what do we owe this honor?" he asked grimly as Miles shook his hand.

Miles seemed not to notice Gideon's lack of enthusiasm. "I need to speak with you on a small matter, Gideon. Lizzie said she had promised to keep you informed."

"And she sent you in her stead?" he asked, trying not to show his crushing disappointment.

"Oh no, not at all," he assured Gideon heartily. "I am the one who needs your assistance, so it was easier for me to come in person to explain."

Gideon didn't believe him for a moment, but he said, "All right. Won't you have a seat?"

"And I'll leave you gentlemen to your business," Mrs. Bates said.

"This won't take long," Miles said, bestowing upon her his most charming smile. "Then perhaps you'll rejoin us."

This seemed to please his mother far more than Gideon thought appropriate. Gideon pretended not to notice, though, and saw Miles settled and served him a drink. He even took one for himself, figuring he would need it to deal with whatever Miles wanted.

"You said you need my assistance," Gideon prompted when they were both seated again.

"Yes. Lizzie said you know the plan."

"She explained it to me, yes, and this morning at church Reverend Honesdale asked me to meet him at the Safe Deposit Company tomorrow at one o'clock. I'm assuming this has something to do with your plan."

"Yes, it does. We have convinced the Honesdales to place their share of the, uh, investment in a safe-deposit box along with my share. We will withdraw funds from it jointly as our expenses arise."

That didn't sound like a very good plan. "What's to stop Daisy and Peter from just taking all the money out and disappearing?"

"If they did, they'd just be stealing their own money."

"But you said you were putting your own share in as well."

"Oh no. We're just using boodle."

"Boodle?"

"That's what we call it. We use stacks of paper cut in the size of a greenback. Then we put a real twenty-dollar bill on the top and bottom and band them the way banks do."

Which was pretty clever, although Gideon didn't mention it. "I see. But if Daisy and Peter don't know it's boodle, what's to stop them—"

"We have agreed that we cannot trust each other and a third party should hold the key to the box, someone whose honesty is above reproach. That person will be instructed not to open the box unless both the Honesdales and I are present."

"Where on earth will you find someone like that?"

"Obviously, the Honesdales have selected you."

Which was why Peter had asked to meet with him. "But why would they choose me?"

"Your reputation, my dear boy. You should be honored."

"Did *you* suggest me?" he asked, not honored at all.

"Certainly not. They would never trust my choice, and they have no idea that we are even acquainted. I merely described all your attributes as the ideal candidate, and Peter Honesdale thought of you immediately."

"What if he hadn't?"

"I would have accepted whoever he chose, although I do feel more comfortable with you holding the key."

"And you expect me to violate my instructions and open the box for you so you can steal their money?" he asked, outraged.

"'Steal' is such an ugly word. And no, I do not expect you to violate your instructions. We chose you for your honesty, and that is all we will require of you."

This didn't make any sense. "How will you get the money, then?"

"You needn't concern yourself about that. All you have to do is follow your instructions."

CHAPTER FIFTEEN

Daisy carried the satchel into which they had put the money. She'd draped the strap across her body and then put her coat on over it, on the off chance that someone decided to snatch it as they made their way through the city. Not that such a thing was likely to happen. She and Peter hardly looked like the sort of people to be carrying a fortune in cash through the streets. Still, she felt safer knowing no one could even see the bag, much less easily jerk it away from her.

Gideon Bates was waiting for them in the lobby of the building, looking as smug and self-righteous as always. What a pity that such a handsome man was so virtuous.

The Safe Deposit Company looked a bit like a bank, only without the teller windows. It had a soaring ceiling with ornate plaster designs and mahogany wainscoting along the walls. Several clerks sat at desks around the edges of the room and various doors seemed to lead to the storage areas of the large building. Peter had explained that the company had been formed to provide safe storage for people who didn't have safes in their homes or who had valuable items too large for a safe that they didn't want to keep in their homes. Banks didn't have room for storing these items, so someone had seen the need for secure storage and filled it.

Gideon greeted them with more courtesy than enthusiasm, and Daisy made a point of being warm and friendly, just to shame him. He seemed unmoved, however.

"Mr. Carstairs told me the rest of our party is already in the vault waiting for us," he said.

Mr. Carstairs was an officious-looking man of middle age with a broad stomach and thin hair combed carefully over a bald spot. He greeted them cheerfully.

"Mr. Franklin asked me to escort you to the vault. This way, please."

The three of them followed him through one of the doors and down a hallway to a large vault. The heavy steel door, which had an impressive locking mechanism, stood open, and inside the long walls were covered by dozens of compart-ments that looked like the mailboxes at the post office but larger. Each had a handle and a keyhole. A plain wooden table sat in the middle of the vault. On it was a long, oblong metal box that appeared to have been pulled from one of the spaces on the wall, which now stood empty.

Franklin and Ross stood by the table. Today Franklin wore a conservative suit, thank heaven, although Ross still looked like a pimp. Or a pimp's assistant. Franklin greeted them. "And this must be Mr. Bates," he added, turning to Gideon and introducing himself.

"Yes. Pleased to meet you." Bates shook Franklin's hand with the same haughty disdain he used on everyone. He always thought he was so much better than everyone else.

Franklin introduced him to Ross, and they shook hands as well.

"Thank you, Mr. Carstairs," Franklin said. "You've been a great help."

Carstairs sketched a little bow. "I'm happy to be of service. I'll be in my office if you need anything. Just take care that your box is securely locked in place before you leave."

He stepped out of the vault and pulled a curtain across the opening, giving them privacy in the event anyone happened by.

"Has Reverend Honesdale explained your role in all this, Mr. Bates?" Franklin asked.

"Not exactly," Bates admitted, glancing uneasily at Peter.

Peter opened his mouth to rectify his oversight, but Franklin raised a hand to stop him.

"It's very simple," Franklin told Bates. "The Honesdales are investing in a project of mine. We have some valuable documents that need safekeeping for a period of time. To ensure these documents are kept safe, we will place them in this box, and we will ask you to hold the key."

Bates didn't like this. He didn't like it at all. "Why can't one of you keep it?"

"Because if anything happened to the documents, the person holding the key would naturally be suspect."

Bates smiled mirthlessly. "So you want to be able to blame me if anything happens to them."

"Not at all. Even though you have the key, Mr. Carstairs and his staff will never allow you access to the box since you are not listed as an owner. Only the Honesdales and myself are allowed access, and only you have the key."

"So one of you would have to be with me," Bates guessed.

"Yes," Daisy said, impatient with the wrangling. "Except that we are going to instruct you to never unlock the box unless both Mr. Franklin and at least one of us is present."

Now he understood, although he still wasn't happy about it. "This seems very convoluted." He turned to Peter. "If you don't trust this gentleman, may I suggest you shouldn't be engaging in business with him?"

Peter chuckled and slapped Bates on the back in an awkward show of camaraderie. "I appreciate your concern, old man, but we know exactly what we're doing."

In Peter's case, that was an exaggeration, but Daisy didn't bother to correct him. "Is that acceptable, Mr. Bates?"

"We will pay you for your assistance, of course," Franklin said quickly, in case there was any doubt.

"I'm sure my firm would insist on it," Bates said. "I am also available to advise you, and you may rely on my discretion," he added solemnly to Peter in a last effort to persuade him.

"We'll keep that in mind," Daisy said before Peter could say something stupid. "Now if you'll step out, Mr. Bates, we can conclude our business."

She could see Bates hated all of this. Men like him always liked to be in control, so this had to be galling to him. Daisy enjoyed his discomfort for a few seconds before he walked with notable reluctance out of the vault.

"He seems like a nice young man," Franklin said.

"Which is exactly what we need," Daisy said.

"Did you bring the, uh, documents?" Franklin asked, taking note of their empty hands.

Daisy gave him a mysterious smile and began to remove her coat. He watched with appreciation as she slipped it off and handed it to Peter. Then she lifted the strap of the satchel over her head and set the bag on the table. "Did you bring *your*, uh, documents?" she countered.

"They're already in the box."

She hadn't known exactly what to expect, probably that they'd have to stuff the bundles of cash into the small end of the box with the keyhole, which must swing open somehow, but Franklin stepped aside so Ross could flip open the top, which was hinged to provide complete access to the box.

Franklin's money was indeed already inside, stacked neatly at one end. She opened the satchel and pulled out their twenty-five neatly stacked and banded bundles of twenty-dollar bills. "It looks so small to be worth so much," she said when she'd carefully placed their contribution into the other end of the box.

"Most truly valuable things are small," Franklin said.

"You're a philosopher, Mr. Franklin," Daisy said.

He laughed at that. "Hardly." He reached in and tore the band off one of the bundles and counted out five twenties. At her shocked expression, he said, "For Mr. Bates."

Then he nodded to Ross, who flipped the lid closed, picked up the box and slid it neatly back into the opening from which it had come. The key was still in the lock, and he twisted it, setting the tumblers in place, then removed it. After giving the box a good yank to verify it was secure, he held up the key from which hung a brass circle stamped with the box's number, 406.

Daisy let Peter help her put her coat back on, and then she led the men through the curtain, out of the vault and into the hallway. Bates had walked down to the end of the hallway in an apparent effort to give them some privacy. Daisy wondered if he had heard the "nice young man" comment from Franklin. She smiled at the thought.

When they reached him, he opened the door to the lobby and held it for them all to exit. Carstairs must have been watching for them, and he bustled up to meet his newest clients. He thanked them for their trust in his establishment and wished them well, then left them standing there.

Franklin nodded at Ross, who handed Bates the key.

"And you won't open the box unless I and at least one of the Honesdales are present," he reminded Bates.

"I haven't forgotten," Bates said a little testily.

"And this is for your trouble." Franklin had folded the twenties in half and stuffed them into Bates's coat pocket as if he were tipping a doorman. Bates looked as if he'd like to murder Franklin, and he made a point of putting the key into a different pocket.

"Call my office if you need . . . anything," he said through clenched teeth and strode out of the building with a stiffness that betrayed his fury.

Franklin's smile never wavered. He either

hadn't noticed or didn't care that Bates had been offended.

Franklin turned to Daisy. "I'm looking forward to working with you . . . with you both," he added, glancing dismissively at Peter. "I'm returning to Chicago this evening, and I'll be gone for a few days, but Ross will be staying at the Waldorf if you need anything before I return. I'll let you know when I'm back so we can begin preparations."

They exchanged pleasantries and shook hands all around, and then Franklin and Ross left.

Peter turned to her, his face alight with pleasure at how well everything had gone. "It was so easy."

"That part is always easy. Now the real work starts." She'd already made up a list of people Franklin would need to buy off. She was thinking she would start recruiting the girls. She knew where Matthew's best ones worked, and poaching them would be a sweet form of revenge. And it would be so much easier than the old days, when she had to bring in drugged girls who cried and carried on until they finally accepted their fates.

She could move the new girls into the house, and they could keep seeing clients while Daisy got things ready. And she would have expenses. Lots of expenses. She would soon have skimmed a tidy sum from the unsuspecting Mr. Franklin.

But Peter was babbling, disturbing her train of thought. "Let's go out this evening and celebrate."

"You have a meeting of the church council this evening," she said. "Don't worry, though. We'll have plenty of time to celebrate after you resign from the church."

They had started walking toward the door. "How soon can I do that?"

"A few more weeks, I should think."

"I can't wait to tell my father." He held the door for her.

"I'll go with you. I can't wait to see his face."

Elizabeth had decided to remain in her room that evening instead of attending the salon. She didn't feel much like socializing, especially when she knew Gideon wouldn't be there. She could tell from the rumble of voices that the guests had begun to enjoy themselves when someone knocked on her door.

Probably Cybil or Zelda wanting to lure her downstairs so she wouldn't brood. They always assumed that social interaction was the cure for whatever emotional travail one was suffering. She opened the door to find Anna smiling widely.

"Did you come alone?" Elizabeth asked in surprise. Anna's mother would never have allowed that, she was sure.

"And hello to you, too," Anna said, making no

move to step inside. "No, I did not come alone. Gideon escorted me, as always."

"He came?" She laid a hand over the fluttering in her stomach.

Anna rolled her eyes. "I'm not sure which of you is the bigger idiot. Of course he came. Not showing up for church yesterday was a masterstroke, by the way. He could hardly sit still through the entire service. He kept looking around to see if you'd somehow snuck in without him noticing."

"But I . . . We . . . Why is he here?"

"Because he's madly in love with you and can't stand being away from you. He didn't say that, not directly, but I know it's true."

"What did he say *directly?*"

"He said he knew how much I wanted to come and that my mother would never let me come unescorted, so he'd make the sacrifice."

That didn't sound like "madly in love" to Elizabeth. "And I suppose you think I should go downstairs and talk to him."

"Or you could go downstairs and not talk to him, which might actually be better. At this point, you're obviously trying to drive him insane and—"

"I'm not trying to drive him insane!"

Anna just smiled knowingly. "Let's go downstairs."

For reasons Elizabeth did not examine too

closely, she checked her appearance, pinched some color into her cheeks and smoothed her hair before following Anna down the stairs. Just as they reached the bottom, Cybil opened the front door and Jake stepped in.

"Oh no, I forgot it was Monday night," he groaned when he noticed the crowd in the parlor.

"I don't believe that for a moment," Cybil said, giving him a kiss on the cheek. "You had a wonderful time last week."

"No, I didn't, but I needed to see Lizzie." He turned to her, looking desperate for rescue.

She took pity on him. "Come upstairs."

Anna sighed with long-suffering but left them to it after greeting Jake, and wandered off to find some other friends to converse with.

Elizabeth led Jake back up to her bedroom. "What is it?" she asked when she'd closed the door behind them.

"The Old Man thought you should know we got your fellow involved."

Elizabeth didn't know which part of this statement was more surprising. *"We?"* she asked first.

"Yeah, I'm the steerer." He said it almost defensively. So the Old Man had taken her suggestion. He must be doing all right, too, or he wouldn't be bringing her messages.

She decided not to comment, though, because Jake would probably take offense no matter what she said. "And what is Gideon doing?"

"He's holding the key to the safe-deposit box."

Which made no sense. "What are you talking about?"

Jake explained.

"He won't open the box for the Old Man, you know," she said, completely mystified.

"We know," Jake said with complete confidence.

"Then why . . . ?"

So Jake explained that, too.

"Oh, that does make sense." Although Gideon would probably be furious when he figured it out.

"The Old Man thought you should know."

"Why should I care? Gideon and I have broken it off."

Jake looked as convinced of that as Anna had.

"Really! Why won't anyone believe me?"

"The Old Man told me to tell you, so I did. Can I leave now?"

"Don't you want to get something to eat before you go? Zelda will be crushed if you don't."

"I guess that wouldn't hurt."

They went back downstairs, although with each step the flutter in Elizabeth's stomach grew stronger. How silly! She shouldn't be worried about seeing Gideon. She shouldn't care at all. He was nothing to her now.

Except then she saw him waiting at the bottom of the stairs, and she knew he was not nothing to her and never would be. She managed a polite smile. "Gideon, how nice to see you."

"Yeah, nice," Jake said and slapped him on the back a little harder than he should have. Ignoring Gideon's black look, Jake strolled off in search of Zelda and something to eat.

"It's nice to see you, too." Gideon looked completely at ease, much to her annoyance. "I was just about to give up and go sit beside Miss Adams and mention Wordsworth."

She couldn't help smiling at that. "You make it sound like a suicide attempt."

"It would have been, since I surely would have died of boredom. Thank you for saving me."

She glanced around to make sure no one was paying them any attention. "Jake told me about . . . that you're holding the key."

"Apparently, I'm the most honest person the Honesdales know."

"It's . . . a compliment," she said lamely.

"So I've been told. Tell me, do you have any part to play in all of this?"

"No," she was happy to say. "I'm completely reformed."

He raised an eyebrow at that but didn't challenge her. "Elizabeth, I need to apologize to you."

For some reason, her heart started thudding against her ribs in an alarming manner. "For what?"

"For having the arrogance to judge you."

She had to put a hand on her chest to keep her

heart from leaping right out. "I . . . I don't know what to say."

"You don't have to say anything. And I don't expect you to forgive me. I just wanted you to know I was sorry for it, sorrier than you will ever know."

"I don't think I want you to be quite that sorry."

He smiled at that. "Why not?"

"Because . . . you're the most honest person I know, too. That's one of the things I lo . . . I like most about you."

"And one of the things I like most about you is that you aren't completely honest."

"Really?" She could not have been more shocked.

"Really." His smile nearly melted her heart, and she wished so fervently that things could be different that she could hardly get her breath. "And don't worry, I won't bother you anymore. I just wanted you to know how sorry I am. I hope we can still be friends."

She didn't want to merely be friends with him, but she nodded because that was so much better than never seeing him again. "That would be . . . fine."

"Good," he said and motioned for her to precede him into the parlor, where several small groups of people were apparently enjoying whatever topics they were so enthusiastically discussing.

Gideon stopped to greet Miss Adams, although Elizabeth noticed he didn't sit down but rather moved on to another group. Elizabeth didn't stop at all, instead going straight through to the butler's pantry, where she could have a moment alone to compose herself.

What was Gideon *really* sorry for, and did he really mean it when he said he liked her dishonesty? And what did that actually mean? And what difference could it possibly make?

The day after they had put the money in the safe-deposit box, Daisy was making a list of all the furnishings she wanted to order for the house, when someone pounded on her front door with an insistence that alarmed her. She didn't wait for the maid to come but hurried to answer it herself.

The assistant pimp, Ross, stood on her doorstep looking impatient.

"What do you want?" she demanded.

"I need some money."

"Money? For what?"

"A delivery. There's a delivery at the house, and you need to pay for it."

"A delivery of what?"

"I don't know. Furniture, I think. Beds or something." His smile had become a leer.

"I didn't order anything yet."

"Franklin did. He ordered them before he even

369

met you. I telephoned to tell him it arrived, and he said to get the money from you and we'd reimburse you from the box when he's back in town."

This was outrageous. "How dare he do such a thing?"

"I don't know, and it's none of my business. My business is that there's a truckload of brass beds that needs to be unloaded and paid for, so if you give me the key to the house and the cash, I'll take care of it."

"I'm not giving you anything. How do I even know what you're telling me is the truth?"

Ross shrugged, unconcerned. "Come and see for yourself, then. But you better bring the key and the money."

That was exactly what she would do. "How much is it?"

"Ten thousand dollars."

"*Ten thousand!* That's absurd!"

"Oh, well, I guess it is." He patted his pockets and managed to come up with a packet of papers that proved to be a bill of lading. "It's really just $9,876.32. See for yourself."

She looked at the papers and saw the merchandise listed was indeed brass beds and feather mattresses at prices she never would have paid. "I'm not going to pay this!"

Ross shrugged again. "So I should tell Franklin the deal is off, then?"

"No, of course the deal is not off!"

"Then you'll give me the key and the cash?"

"No, but I'll go myself. Wait here." She left him standing on the front stoop.

She punished Ross by taking her time changing into something more presentable and retrieving what was almost the last of the blackmail moneys. She'd invested some of the early money in jewelry, and paying Matthew for the mortgage had taken much more than it should have, since he'd sensed their desperation and demanded almost twice what he'd originally paid. But she'd get it all back and much, much more when they opened the house. In the meantime, she'd give Franklin a tongue-lashing he'd never forget for this inconvenience.

Ross had left a cab waiting, which he'd neglected to mention, and she was expected to pay that as well. At least he hadn't lied about the delivery. A truck full of wooden crates stood at the curb outside Knight's old house, and three deliverymen piled out of it when the cab pulled up.

She unlocked the door for them and watched as they brought in crate after crate. Because they still needed to divide the bedrooms upstairs, she had them jam the crates into the downstairs rooms in between the furniture that was already there. When they were finished, she paid them, carefully counting out the bills while the workmen stood patiently by. As they left, Ross snatched up the small stack of twenties remaining from the ten thousand she had brought.

"I need to tip them," he explained cheerfully, and followed the men out. Only after the truck had rumbled off and the house became completely still did she realize Ross had also left.

What had she expected? That an assistant pimp would wait around to see her safely home? Muttering curses down on both him and Franklin, she locked up the house and went out to find a cab.

Sometimes Gideon hated being right. He'd told his mother that simply apologizing to Elizabeth would not be enough, and it hadn't been. What had he expected, though? That she'd fall into his arms when he said he was sorry? Well, he'd hoped, even though he'd had no reason to and even though he'd already predicted it wouldn't solve anything. And now he had the coid satisfaction of being right.

For the past hour, he'd been trying to read over the last will and testament that he had prepared for a client, and he had no more idea now than he'd had an hour ago if it was correct or not. He looked up with relief when Smith knocked and stepped into his office.

"Although he does not have an appointment, Mr. Matthew Honesdale is here to see you."

"Send him in," Gideon said, unreasonably glad to hear it.

Honesdale looked almost as pleased as Gideon felt.

"Do you have news?" Gideon asked when Honesdale was seated.

"I have news and more." He reached into his inside coat pocket and pulled out an envelope, which he laid on Gideon's desk.

Gideon looked at it curiously but made no move to pick it up. "The mortgage?"

"I drove a hard bargain. Peter tried to pretend they were doing me a favor, but he had no idea I knew how desperate they were. I got almost twice what I had given Knight for it."

Gideon nodded his appreciation. "Congratulations."

"I kept the original amount and the interest, but . . ." He grinned sheepishly. "Maybe Uncle Nathan's Bible lessons stuck a little. I couldn't keep it all." He gestured toward the envelope. "That's the rest. Give it to the widow, will you?"

Gideon looked at Honesdale with admiration. "I certainly will." He took a moment to savor this small victory. "Did you have success with the police?"

"Oh yes. They're always happy to make an arrest that won't interrupt their flow of income. This will make them look like they're protecting public morals without offending anyone who is actually corrupting public morals."

"That's a sad commentary on our criminal justice system."

"Because our criminal justice system is very sad. But then I've never believed we should punish people for what they do in the privacy of the bedroom."

Gideon could think of a dozen reasons why someone should be punished for what happened to the women in Matthew Honesdale's brothels, but he didn't bother to mention them. Instead, he would somehow manage to be grateful for Matthew's assistance and happy that he'd never have to see him again. "Thank you for your assistance in this matter. You didn't have to do what you did, and you certainly didn't have to be so generous to Mrs. Knight," he added, nodding at the envelope.

"My pleasure. This was the most fun I've had in a long time, and the show isn't over yet. When can we expect the next act?"

"I'm just waiting to hear from my associates before setting things in motion."

"Be sure to alert me, too. I wouldn't miss this for the world."

"What do you mean all the money's gone?" Peter nearly shouted at Daisy

Fortunately, the servants had left for the day. "I didn't expect you to be so *generous* with Matthew," she nearly shouted right back.

"But we had to get the mortgage and he wouldn't take any less!"

"And I had to pay for the beds today."

"I don't understand why you didn't just go down and get the money out of the box," Peter grumbled.

"Because we told Gideon Bates not to open the box unless Franklin was there, too," she said, trying hard not to scream at him. Was he really that stupid?

"I know, but you could have at least tried."

"Are you serious? With Gideon Bates? We chose him because he's intractable!"

"Couldn't you have used your charm or something?" Peter whined.

"You mean seduce him? Hardly. In any case, Franklin will be back soon, and we'll get the money then. We can certainly survive for a few days."

"I don't like it. When did Franklin say he'd be back?"

She started to reply and realized she had no answer. "I don't think he said exactly."

"But he did say we could send him a message through Ross."

"Yes, and Ross already told him about the delivery. I'm sure—"

"Well, I'm not sure about anything, and I won't be until I've talked to Franklin."

That was fair enough. "Why don't you go to the

Waldorf tomorrow, darling, and have Ross send Franklin a message?"

How long did it take to con someone out of their entire fortune? Gideon realized he had no idea, and while it had only been two days since he'd seen the Honesdales put much of their fortune into the safe-deposit box, it felt like a century. He'd often thought his work a trifle dull for the most part, but now he found it impossibly tedious, as the minutes dragged by at a glacial pace. He couldn't even muster much relief when Smith tapped on his door with what surely would be welcome interruption.

"Although he does not have an appointment," Smith began, but the rest of his announcement died in his throat when Peter Honesdale burst into the room, shoving Smith aside to make way.

"Franklin has disappeared!" Peter cried.

"Thank you, Smith. I'll just . . . I'll take care of Reverend Honesdale."

Smith discreetly and quickly took his leave while Honesdale stood there looking half-crazed.

"Sit down, Peter, and tell me what's wrong."

He sat with a thunk, dropping the hat he'd been holding to run his hands through his hair. "Franklin has disappeared," he repeated.

Just as Elizabeth had said he would. "What do you mean?"

"I mean he said he was going back to Chicago—that's where he lives, Chicago—for a few days, but that we could reach him through his man, Ross."

"Have you tried Ross?"

"That's just it. They were staying at the Waldorf. That's what he told us. We'd even left him messages there. But I went to the Waldorf this morning, and they never heard of either one of them."

"Maybe they just moved to a different hotel."

"Except they were never staying at the Waldorf at all. I made the desk clerk check. I made them go back a month. Neither of them was ever there!"

"That's curious. Don't you have an address for him in Chicago?" This seemed like a logical question to ask, even though Gideon knew Franklin didn't live in Chicago.

"No, we don't," Peter said. His anger was burning out, and now he just sounded petulant.

Gideon couldn't help himself. "You'll remember I warned you about this Franklin."

"Don't go all righteous on me, Gideon. Don't you think I feel enough of a fool without you rubbing it in? And there's more."

"More of what?"

"The delivery! We paid for the delivery out of our own pocket!"

"What delivery?"

"Uh, furniture. Franklin had furniture shipped to the house."

"The *parsonage?*" Now Gideon really was confused.

"No, to . . . to the other house. And we had to pay for it. Ten thousand dollars! And there was nothing in the crates."

"What crates?"

"The furniture crates. When I couldn't find Franklin, I got suspicious, so I went to the house and broke some of them open, and there was nothing in them but some trash. No furniture at all!"

"Peter, I have no idea what you're talking about." Which was the gospel truth.

"It doesn't matter. What matters is you have to open up the box and give us our money back."

Gideon had to remind himself that he wasn't supposed to know anything about the money. "Money? You told me you were putting important documents in the box."

"Yes, and the documents are money. There's a hundred thousand dollars in that box, and I want to get it out."

"A hundred thousand dollars? Was it *your* money?"

"Half of it, yes."

Gideon leaned back in his chair. "Peter, you are the one who told me I was not, under any circumstances, to open the box unless you and Franklin were both present."

"I've changed my mind. Can't you see that no longer applies? Franklin has run out on our deal."

"I'm not sure you can assume that. It's only been two days. You said he went back to Chicago, and he's hardly had time to get there, much less get back again. Maybe there's just some misunderstanding about what hotel he was staying at. You had some sort of business agreement with him, didn't you? Surely, he wouldn't run out on that. And the money in the box. You said only half was yours. Was the other half his?"

"Yes," Peter admitted with great reluctance.

"He's hardly likely to leave that behind. I think you need to give him time to get back and straighten all of this out."

"But what about the crates and the furniture?"

"I don't know anything about that, but like I said, you need to give him time to answer all your questions. And in the meantime, or until I hear from Mr. Franklin himself, I can't open the box for you."

"I told you he wouldn't do it," Daisy said, fighting the urge to slap the stupid expression off Peter's stupid face. "That's why we chose him. We didn't want Franklin bribing or threatening someone into opening the box. And now look at us."

"I even told him about the empty crates, and he didn't care."

"You told him about the crates?" Daisy cried. "Did you tell him about the house, too, and what it was for?"

"No! I'd never—"

"Shut up about what you'd never do, Peter." She slammed out of the parlor, where they'd been arguing, and marched up the stairs to their bedroom.

Unfortunately, Peter, still whining, followed on her heels. She wanted to push him down the stairs, but she marched on resolutely, knowing it was up to her now to clean up this mess.

"You should have looked in the crates before you paid for them," Peter said.

Maybe she *would* push him down the stairs.

Ignoring him, she went to her dresser and pulled out the bottom drawer. There was the lovely leather case that held her lovely little pearl-handled revolver. She'd carried it in a pocket every day when she'd had her own house and people called her Mrs. Grayson and treated her with respect. She'd never actually fired it, but she'd pulled it out a time or two to subdue rowdy customers.

"What are you doing with that?" Peter asked in alarm.

"I'm going to convince Gideon Bates to open that box."

"Do you think he'll do it just because you point a gun at him?"

"No, but I think he'll do it if I point a gun at Miss Elizabeth Miles."

CHAPTER SIXTEEN

"Remind me again, who is Elizabeth Miles?"

Peter really was hopeless. Maybe she'd shoot him when this was over. "She's the little chippie Hazel Bates has been bringing to church."

"Oh, right. Priscilla's helpful friend. Why should Bates care if you point a gun at her, though?"

"Because his mother likes her, and Bates loves his mother. I'd prefer the mother, but she'd be much harder to control, and I've developed a definite dislike for Miss Miles. She's entirely too nosy for her own good, and Bates is such a gentleman, he'll certainly want to save his mother's protégée, so she'll do nicely."

"Are you sure? Why should he even care about her?"

"I've seen the way he looks at her, Peter," she explained in exasperation. "And his mother has been dragging her around to visit people so she'd be accepted into society, so Mrs. Bates has also noticed. Other people at church have noticed, too."

"I haven't," Peter insisted.

"Everyone but you, then. In any case, all I need is her address."

"I'm sure Gideon knows it."

Not while I have a gun in my hand, Peter! "And so does his mother, I'm sure, but they're likely to wonder why we need it. I was thinking I would check the city directory first."

The Old Man had sent Elizabeth word yesterday that things were going as planned. Hopefully, Matthew Honesdale had successfully sold the mortgage to Daisy and Peter, so he'd gotten his money back as well. Maybe by the weekend, she'd be able to tell Priscilla the good news.

Cybil and Zelda had left for Hunter College, where they taught, and Elizabeth was looking over the newspaper when someone rang the doorbell. Even though it was unlikely Gideon would be calling on her on a weekday morning— or quite frankly, any time at all—she couldn't help the little skitter of excitement she felt at the possibility. But she was sorely disappointed when she opened the door.

"Mrs. Honesdale," she said warily, glancing around to see if anyone was with her. "What a surprise." How had Daisy found her?

This wasn't good. It wasn't good at all.

"Hello, Miss Miles," Daisy said, forcing her way inside by the simple method of walking forward until Elizabeth had to back up or be knocked over.

"Did we have an engagement?" Elizabeth asked, knowing full well they had not.

"In a manner of speaking. I need your company on an errand I must run."

"What sort of errand?"

"It's nothing, really. Nothing for you to be concerned about, at least."

"Then why do you need my company?"

"For insurance."

Elizabeth had a very bad feeling about this. Daisy seemed calm enough, but her eyes had a determined cast that made Elizabeth's skin crawl. She obviously knew or at least suspected that something had gone wrong. But why would she come here? "Insurance against what?"

"Against disaster. Let me tell you what we are going to do. You are going to put on a coat and hat, and we are going to get into the cab I have waiting. You will sit quietly and say nothing at all in the cab. We will drive to a business called the Safe Deposit Company. When we get to the Safe Deposit Company, we will meet my husband and Gideon Bates."

Elizabeth couldn't help her reaction. Everything was crystal clear now. Daisy wanted Gideon to open that cursed box, and he wouldn't do it. Of course he wouldn't do it. He had given his word. And Daisy thought she could force him by threatening Elizabeth.

But Elizabeth shouldn't know any of this, so she had to pretend complete ignorance. "Why would we do all that?"

"Because . . . Well, you don't need to know all the details, but we need Mr. Bates to open a certain safe-deposit box for us, but he has refused to do that, so we wanted to give him an incentive, as it were."

Elizabeth feigned confusion. "Do you think he's more likely to do it if I ask him to?"

Daisy smiled, an expression that chilled Elizabeth's blood. "I think he's more likely to do it if I have a gun pointed at you." With that she slipped her hand out of her coat pocket to show Elizabeth exactly what she meant.

"Oh dear" was all Elizabeth could think to say.

"Yes, oh dear. Now get your coat on, Miss Miles. We have work to do."

This time, Smith was obviously at the end of his patience. Never in the history of Devoss and Van Aken had he received so many visitors without appointments. He could hardly force himself to say the words. "The Reverend Mr. Peter Honesdale," he announced without even moving his lips.

Gideon sighed and prepared himself for another hysterical rant, but this time Peter appeared perfectly calm and perhaps also a bit gleeful, if the sparkle in his eyes was any indication.

"What can I do for you today, Peter?"

He waited until Smith had closed the door behind him. "You can go with me to the Safe Deposit Company and open the damn box."

"We went through this yesterday, and I thought I made myself clear. I can't ethically open the box unless Franklin is present as well."

"Can you ethically open the box to keep Miss Elizabeth Miles from being shot?" he asked.

Gideon had been sorely mistaken. The glitter in his eyes wasn't glee. It was madness. "What are you talking about?"

"My wife has gone to fetch Miss Miles and will bring her to the Safe Deposit Company. I will bring you there as well. If Miss Miles's safety is of concern to you, you will open the box. If you do that and allow us to reclaim what is ours, we will release you and Miss Miles, no harm done."

He surely must be out of his mind, although the threat sounded very real. Horror turned his blood to ice. "And if I refuse?"

"Then Daisy will shoot her."

Gideon could hardly think as he relived the moment when he'd actually seen Elizabeth being shot once before. "Your wife has a *gun?*"

"A pistol. Yes. She's had it for years. For protection, you understand. She was a widow with no one to take care of her."

"And I'm supposed to believe that she would shoot Miss Miles if I refuse to open the box?"

"Are you willing to doubt me at the risk to Miss Miles's life?"

That, of course, was the really important issue

here, and Gideon had a really important answer. "No, I am not."

"Good. Then get the key and let's go. The ladies will be waiting."

If time had been dragging before, it had stopped completely now. The ride to the Safe Deposit Company took forever in the afternoon traffic, and Gideon was nearly paralyzed with fear during the entire trip. The office probably closed at three, just like a bank, and they would barely make it in time.

Indeed, when they rushed in, the clock on the wall said 2:58. Gideon would have bet his heart couldn't beat any harder, but it did when he saw Daisy and Elizabeth were already there. Daisy looked strangely calm, and Elizabeth was pale, but no one had shot her, so he could at least take a breath again. She smiled when she saw him, although it looked a little stiff. Gideon instantly noted the way Daisy kept her right hand in her pocket and held Elizabeth slightly in front of her. Judging from the careful way Elizabeth moved, Daisy really did have a pistol.

"We're so glad you could make it, Mr. Bates," Elizabeth said with just a trace of sarcasm.

At least she hadn't lost her sense of humor. "You must have known nothing would keep me away."

"Ah, just as I suspected," Daisy said with satisfaction. "Gideon will do whatever it takes to protect you, Miss Miles. Let's just get this over with, shall we? Did you bring the key, Gideon?"

"Yes."

"Peter, tell Carstairs we're ready to go to the vault. I already told him we were just waiting for you to arrive."

Peter did as he was told.

"Won't Carstairs be suspicious, since Franklin isn't here?" Gideon tried while Peter was gone, wondering if there was any way to protect Elizabeth and keep them away from the money, too.

"Carstairs knows nothing about our little agreement with you, and Peter and I have every right to open the box. I told him we're signing some papers and you two will be our witnesses."

Before Gideon could think of anything else, Peter had returned with Carstairs.

"We're almost ready to close for the day," Carstairs said, torn between pleasing his customers and knowing his employees wouldn't be happy.

"And we really appreciate your bending the rules for us. This won't take long," Peter assured him.

If Carstairs noticed the tension between his visitors, he didn't let on. He led them back the way they had gone before and left them alone in the vault.

When he had gone, Daisy said, "Open it."

"I'm sorry, Gideon," Elizabeth said, and to his amazement, her eyes filled with tears.

"It's all right. Nothing is more important to me than you are."

"Really? Nothing?"

"Nothing at all," he assured her, knowing for certain now that it was true.

"Stop this nonsense and open the box," Daisy cried.

Not wanting to antagonize a woman holding a gun on his beloved, Gideon pulled the key out of his pocket and went to the box that bore the number 406.

It should have been easy. Just put the key in, turn it and pull the box out. Except . . .

"It doesn't fit."

"What?" Peter said, hurrying over to see.

Gideon tried again. "The key. It doesn't fit in the lock."

"You must have brought the wrong one," Peter said, snatching it from him to try it himself.

"How could I bring the wrong one? I only had one key. Look at the tag. Do the numbers match?"

Peter had tried the key himself, also without success. He looked at the tag and compared the numbers. "It's the same number, but it won't go in the lock."

"Do I have to do everything?" Daisy asked, and forgetting Elizabeth completely, she pulled her empty hand out of her pocket and snatched the key from Peter. But she had no more success than the men had. "It's the wrong key!"

"How could it be?" Gideon asked. "You saw Franklin give it to me."

"Ross gave it to you. He was the one who locked the box, too," Daisy remembered.

"Whoever it was, it has to be the same key."

"Get Carstairs," Daisy told Peter, putting her hand back in her pocket. "And you two, don't get any ideas. Just keep your mouths shut."

Gideon turned to Elizabeth, hating the fact that she was here because of him. "Does she really have a pistol?"

"Oh yes. It's lovely, too. Pearl handle. Very feminine."

Daisy sighed in frustration and pulled her hand out of her pocket again, only this time she held a pistol. Pearl handle. Very feminine. She wasn't quite sure where to point it, though. Gideon was closer, but Elizabeth was the one he cared about.

"This is very irregular." Carstairs's outrage echoed in the hallway, and Daisy automatically turned toward the sound.

"Get down!" Gideon shouted and lunged for Daisy.

He grabbed her wrist with both hands and jerked her arm up. She screamed, but he threw his weight against her and she fell—they both fell—as the gun exploded. She thrashed and kicked, but he wrestled the pistol out of her hand

390

just as Carstairs and Peter burst through the vault door.

"What on earth is going on here?" Carstairs demanded.

"That man attacked me!" Daisy cried from where she lay, holding her wrist as if he'd injured her.

Gideon bounded to his feet, pistol in hand. "Elizabeth!" he called frantically.

She was gone—but no, she was on the floor, where she'd dropped on his command. Dear heaven, had she been hit? His heart stopped dead in his chest.

"Elizabeth, are you hurt?"

He was beside her now, and she was trying to sit up. "I don't think so, except for a terrible ringing in my ears."

Gideon realized his hearing was a bit distorted as well. The vault's walls had magnified the gunshot.

His heart had started to beat again, and he helped her to her feet.

Peter had rushed to Daisy. "What did he do to you?"

"He tried to attack me!"

"Was that why you pulled out your pistol and tried to shoot us?" Elizabeth asked with an angry smile.

"Will someone tell me what's going on here?" Carstairs asked again, obviously at the end of his patience and eying the pistol Gideon held with deep distress. "And if you're thinking of robbing us, you should know that everything of value is locked securely away and only the owners of the property have a key."

"No one is going to rob anyone," Gideon said. At least not today. He flipped open the cylinder and removed the bullets. Then he put the bullets into one pocket and the pistol into another. When he looked up again, he was gratified to see Elizabeth had been suitably impressed by his gallantry.

Daisy and Peter, however, were not. "What did you do with the real key?" Daisy demanded.

"Nothing. This is the key Ross gave me on Monday. Mr. Carstairs, this key does not open Reverend and Mrs. Honesdale's box." He picked it up from where it had fallen to the floor in the excitement and handed it to Carstairs.

"Nonsense. The key works perfectly." He checked the number on the hanging disk, then went to box 406 and tried to unlock it. He tried far longer than Gideon and Peter and Daisy had, but he still had just as little success. "That's impossible."

"You must have given us the wrong key," Peter insisted.

"I certainly did not. And the key worked perfectly when Mr. Franklin used it on Monday."

"We know. We were here," Gideon said.

"No, I mean when he returned later."

"What do you mean, when he returned later?" Daisy asked warily.

"He came back shortly after all of you left. He said there was a document he'd forgotten to put in the box."

"What did he use for a key?" Gideon asked, because he'd had the key in his possession by then.

"I assume he used the key I had issued him when he paid for the box," Carstairs said.

"He couldn't have," Peter said, rising and helping Daisy to her feet as well. "This is the key you gave us, and Bates here has had it all along. Or did you give it to Franklin?" he added to Gideon with growing outrage.

"No, I did not give it to Franklin. This is the key I was given on Monday in front of all of you, and it's been locked in my office ever since."

"Then how—"

"He switched keys," Daisy said.

"Who did?" Carstairs asked, thoroughly confused now.

"Franklin," she said, furious now. "He kept the real key and gave Bates here a phony one."

"But why?" Peter wailed.

"So he could come back and empty out the box," Daisy said. She turned to Carstairs. "Open it."

"Open the box?" he repeated in confusion. "I

can't. Not without the key. The proper key, I should say."

"But surely, people sometimes lose their keys and you have to get into their boxes some other way," Gideon said.

Carstairs cleared his throat. "It does happen. Rarely, you understand."

"Do you have a pass key? Or duplicate keys?"

"That would defeat the whole purpose of our institution," Carstairs said, thoroughly insulted. "No, when someone loses their key, we have to drill the box open and then replace it with a new one."

"Drill it then," Daisy said.

"You will be charged for replacing the box," he warned. "And there are some papers to sign . . ."

"Drill it!"

This would take some time, and Gideon insisted that Elizabeth go home. She argued with him, but he finally convinced her when he said, "I don't want to have to worry about you while I'm dealing with them, too. Please, I need to know you're safe."

A workman had to be summoned to open the box, and then he had to do the work, but eventually he got the box loose from its moorings and pulled it out. He set it on the table, obviously very interested to see what had been inside that was worth so much trouble, but Carstairs sent him on his way disappointed.

"Mr. Carstairs, would you stay as another witness, please?" Gideon asked.

Plainly, Carstairs was more than happy to do so. He was now as curious as the workman had been. After a moment and at Daisy's urging, Peter stepped forward and flipped the lid of the box open.

It was empty.

"I didn't know that it's illegal to put money in a safe-deposit box," Peter said as the cab carried them back home. As if that was the worst thing they had learned that day.

Daisy was too numb to even be angry with him anymore. How could they have been so stupid? She'd been so excited at the prospect of cheating Franklin, she'd completely ignored the possibility that he could be cheating her.

At least Carstairs hadn't called the police about anything. He could have done so over their having put cash in the box—which he never would have known if Peter hadn't started babbling when they saw the box was empty—but especially over her shooting the gun. For some reason Bates had convinced him the gun had been a stupid accident, though. She hated pretending she hadn't known the gun was loaded or how it worked and that she had inadvertently pulled the trigger. Carstairs hadn't even believed it, but he'd been willing to avoid any trouble by pretending to.

And Bates wouldn't even give her gun back.

"What's going on?" Peter said, sitting up straight and peering through the windshield of the cab.

"Looks like there's some trouble," the driver said, slowing because the street was blocked. "That's quite a crowd. Do you know who lives in that house?"

"*We* live in that house."

The driver had to let them off on the corner. Too many people had spilled off the sidewalk and into the street, and traffic had stalled.

Daisy took Peter's arm and they pushed their way through the crowd. No one paid them any mind until they turned up the front walk.

"Reverend Honesdale? Are you Reverend Honesdale? Is that your wife?" someone shouted.

A dozen voices called out a dozen questions.

"Were you really a madam, Mrs. Honesdale?"

"Did you really drug those girls and force them into prostitution?"

"Were you really planning to open a brothel in the church parsonage?"

Daisy saw her own horror reflected on Peter's face. Somehow they managed to get inside the house. Their maid greeted them with a tear-stained face.

"They been out there since right after you left. They pounded on the door and wanted to know was you here, and I told them to leave, but they didn't. They give me this."

She handed them a newspaper. The headline said, "Brothel in Church Parsonage."

"It wasn't at the parsonage," Peter said, outraged by the error. As if that mattered.

"I won't stay here if it's a brothel," the maid said. "I'm a good girl!" No one paid her any heed.

Daisy peered out the window at the crowd. "Are they all reporters?" Not all. She saw one familiar face. "Matthew is here."

"Matthew? Why would he be here?" Peter asked just as the doorbell rang.

The maid, who was now openly weeping, admitted Matthew Honesdale. He held several newspapers and wore a disgustingly satisfied grin. "What on earth have you two been up to?" He turned the newspapers so they could see the one on top, which said, "Minister Recruiting Prostitutes."

"Nothing!" Daisy said, furious. "Where could they have gotten this information?"

"And it's all wrong," Peter said. "We haven't even opened the brothel yet."

"Is that what you wanted Knight's house for?" Matthew asked, still enjoying himself far too much.

"You did this," Daisy said. "You betrayed us!"

He seemed genuinely shocked by the accusation. "I didn't tell them *this*." He pointed to the newspapers. "How could I? I didn't even know about it. Besides, why would I betray you?"

Daisy could think of many reasons, but all of them would require that Matthew knew she'd turned on him and tried to frame him for the blackmail. But how could he have known that? She and Peter were the only ones still alive who knew that.

Someone started pounding on their door again. Peter actually screamed.

"Don't answer it!" Daisy called to the maid, who was now sobbing in the kitchen.

"Police!" a voice shouted from the front porch. "Open up!"

"Why would the police be here?" Daisy cried in panic, looking first to Peter, which was a waste of time, and then to Matthew.

"Have you done something illegal?" he asked with interest.

They couldn't be here about the brothel. They hadn't even gotten the girls for it. No one even knew about it. She thought of the blackmail, but no one could have known about that, either. "Not yet." Not recently at least.

"Is there anything incriminating in the house?" Matthew asked. "You'll want to get rid of it before you let them in."

"What would be incriminating?" Peter asked, nearly hysterical now.

"I don't know. Documents of any kind? That

mortgage, maybe. It would tie you to the house if that's really where you were going to open the brothel. I just wish you'd consulted with me first, though. That's a terrible location—"

"The mortgage!" Daisy ran to Peter's study and quickly opened the safe while the police continued to pound on the door.

By the time she pulled out the mortgage documents, Matthew had caught up to her. "Is that it?"

"What should I do with it?"

Matthew shrugged. "No use hiding it. They'll search the entire house. You should probably burn it."

Daisy cast about for something to use. Matthew sighed and pulled a matchbook out of his pocket. "Here."

The pounding continued and her hands were shaking too badly to even tear out a match. Matthew took everything from her and easily lit a match and held it to the corner of the documents until they caught. Only when he dropped the last, black ash onto the floor to keep from burning his fingers did Daisy happen to wonder if burning the mortgage was really a good idea.

"You can let the police in now," Matthew called to whoever might want to follow his orders. "I'm afraid I'll have to leave you, Daisy. I'll just go out the back. I don't really want to speak to any policemen today. I wish you the best of luck."

Before she could think, Matthew had slipped away and the police were swarming everywhere. Someone grabbed her and locked her hands behind her back in handcuffs.

"You're under arrest," a snaggletoothed fellow in a cheap suit told her.

"For what?" she tried, using her haughtiest voice.

"Procurement. I was really surprised by how many whores claimed you'd drugged them and sold them to a brothel," he said with a leering grin. "You should be ashamed."

Procurement? They weren't arresting her for opening a new brothel at all, which made sense, because they hadn't actually done that. But who knew about her past?

No one but Peter and Matthew.

As two uniformed officers dragged her down the hall to the front door, she saw Peter still standing in the parlor, tears streaming down his face. "No! You can't have her!" he cried when he saw them taking her away.

"Hire a lawyer for me!" she called to him, but she didn't think he'd understood.

"My father is here," he called back, his horror at the thought plain on his tear-ravaged face.

And sure enough, Nathan Honesdale nearly collided with her and her escorts as he barreled in the front door. "Peter, what has this Jezebel made you do?"

"So that's why they arrested Daisy," Elizabeth told Priscilla the next morning. She'd known Priscilla would have heard—the scandal of a minister's wife being revealed as a former procuress and madam was being covered in every New York newspaper, in addition to being passed along what was normally the church's prayer chain—and would want to know the whole story.

"What a horrible woman. How on earth did she end up married to Peter Honesdale?"

"It seems he was one of her, uh, customers."

Priscilla was suitably shocked. "Which one of them thought up the blackmail scheme, do you think?"

Elizabeth was pretty sure it was Daisy, but she didn't want to let Peter off the hook. In any case, Peter was equally guilty of killing DeForrest Jenks. "We'll probably never know. The important thing is that they won't be blackmailing anyone else."

Priscilla sighed. "I don't suppose there's any chance that . . . But no, it's too much to hope for, I'm sure."

She was thinking about her lost fortune, naturally. Elizabeth wanted to tell her everything was going to be all right, but she hadn't heard from the Old Man yet, and if there'd been any kind of glitch, she didn't want to give Priscilla false hope.

The doorbell rang.

"Who could that be at this time of day?" Priscilla wondered.

Elizabeth wondered, too, but she didn't dare get her own hopes up, until the maid announced Gideon Bates.

As always, her heart beat a tattoo against her ribs when he stepped into the room. He was already smiling, and he smiled even more when he saw Elizabeth.

"Miss Miles," he said with mock formality once he'd greeted Priscilla. "I thought you might be here."

"Did you?"

"Well, I hoped you would, at least. I knew you'd want to be present when I shared the happy news with Mrs. Knight."

Priscilla invited him to sit down, and when all the social niceties had been dealt with, she said, "What happy news have you come to share with me, Mr. Bates?"

"I assume you've heard that Mrs. Honesdale has been arrested."

"Yes, I think everyone in New York knows by now, and Elizabeth was just telling me what wasn't in the newspapers."

"Yes, we were fortunate that several of the women Daisy Honesdale had forced into prostitution stepped forward and accused her."

"Very fortunate," Elizabeth said knowingly.

Who had known about them and who had convinced them to charge Daisy? But Gideon didn't acknowledge her unspoken question.

"We were hoping to bring Reverend Honesdale to justice as well, but the only thing we could accuse him of was the blackmail of Mr. Knight, and we couldn't do that without damaging your own reputation."

"I know, and I appreciate your discretion, Mr. Bates. Still, it's difficult knowing he will go unpunished."

"I'm not sure that's entirely true. We knew the scandal would mean he would have to give up the ministry, but that didn't seem like enough weighed against what the Honesdales did to you."

"No, it didn't," Elizabeth said, remembering how Peter had also helped murder Priscilla's beloved husband. They hadn't told Priscilla this and never would, but Priscilla still had many reasons to hate them.

"Sometimes a higher power takes a hand, though," Gideon continued. "It seems Peter Honesdale had some kind of breakdown when his wife was arrested, and his father has seen fit to put him into an asylum."

"An *asylum?*" Priscilla said. Such things rarely happened to people like the Honesdales.

"Yes. He didn't see fit to pay for Peter's care, either, and since Peter couldn't pay for himself, he has fallen on the mercy of the state."

"The state's mercy tends to be rather harsh, doesn't it?" Elizabeth said.

"Indeed it does, and the Reverend Mr. Nathan Honesdale's desire to prevent Peter from causing any more scandal is even harsher. I'm very much afraid Peter Honesdale will never be released from this asylum."

Elizabeth waited for Priscilla's reaction. If she felt sorry for Peter, she would be forced to reveal how Peter had killed DeForrest Jenks.

But Priscilla simply shook her head. "At least he'll never be able to hurt anyone else."

"No, he will not. Neither of them will. And I am also happy to report that we were able to recover the money that they and Endicott Knight stole from you."

Priscilla's reaction was everything they could have wished. "Recovered? How on earth . . . ? What did you do? How did you persuade them?"

Elizabeth exchanged a glance with Gideon and was happy to see the sparkle in his dark eyes.

"We didn't exactly *persuade* them," Elizabeth said.

"And you needn't worry about the details," Gideon added quickly, "but I wanted you to know that I saw Mr. Renfroe this morning and deposited almost eighty thousand dollars in your account."

"Eighty? But that's even more than DeForrest left me."

Elizabeth held her tongue, anxious to see how Gideon would explain it. He cleared his throat. "We also recovered some of the money Knight had paid them as well, which should have been yours as his widow."

"That's . . . wonderful," she managed a little breathlessly.

"And I am also happy to tell you that the mortgage Mr. Matthew Honesdale once held on Endicott Knight's family home has been forgiven."

"What does that mean?" Priscilla asked.

"It means you have a free title to that house, and you can do whatever you want with it."

"You mean I can sell it?"

"Yes."

Priscilla's eyes filled with tears. "Oh, Gideon, how can I ever thank you?"

"Don't thank me at all. I had very little to do with any of this." He glanced at Elizabeth again, but she saw no trace of bitterness or anger or even disapproval.

"But you were the one who—"

"I only told a few people that you needed help. You have many friends."

"Then who should I thank? I feel like I owe them that at least."

"I'm sure they've been adequately repaid," Elizabeth said quite truthfully. The Old Man would certainly complain that in the end he'd only cleared the ten thousand he'd bilked Daisy out of for the bogus furniture delivery, but he'd had very few expenses, too. She also knew he'd thoroughly enjoyed involving Gideon in a con. And helping a widow would earn him some credit on Judgment Day. He'd have to be satisfied with that.

Gideon had been worried about how he would get Elizabeth to leave Priscilla's house with him, but she graciously accepted his offer to see her home. When they were on the sidewalk, he said, "Why don't we go to my house instead? We can tell Mother what happened."

She held his gaze for a long moment, so long he was afraid she would refuse, but she said, "All right. I haven't seen your mother in a long time."

"She missed you in church last Sunday."

She did not reply to that. The walk to his house was only a few blocks, and Gideon let the first one pass in silence. Then he said, "I was angry when I realized your father had tricked me into holding the key to the box."

"You had every right to be. I had no idea he was going to involve you at all."

"Maybe I should say I was angry *at first*. Because I thought he expected that he could get me to break my word and compromise my sense of honor by opening the box for him."

"Could he have done that?" she asked with genuine interest.

"I didn't think so, but you'll notice how easily the Honesdales accomplished it."

She pressed her lips together, and he could see she was trying not to smile. "But you said you were only angry at him *at first*."

"Yes. When I realized the key they'd given me didn't fit the box, I understood everything. He'd never intended to ask me to open the box at all."

"The Old Man may be morally corrupt, but he's not a fool."

They had reached his door, and he ushered her inside. The maid came to help them with their coats.

"Would you tell my mother that Miss Miles is here?" Gideon asked her.

The girl frowned. "Mrs. Bates is out, sir. She told you she would be at breakfast this morning."

Found out, Gideon felt the heat rising in his face, but when he glanced at Elizabeth, he saw only an amused smile.

"I'm sure Mrs. Ordway has something to say about this," she said, strolling into the parlor instead of slamming angrily out of the house, as she should have done. "Perhaps she has a chapter on how to avoid seductions that I missed."

"I'm not going to seduce you," he said, carefully leaving the parlor door open.

"That's disappointing. What *are* you going to do now that you have me in your clutches?"

A very good question, and Gideon realized he

wasn't quite sure himself, although he knew what he wanted the outcome to be. Sadly, he had no idea of exactly how to get there. "I wanted to talk to you."

She sat down on the sofa, leaving plenty of room for him to sit beside her, so he did. "All right. What did you want to talk about?"

"I told you a lie the other night."

That had the desired effect. "You did?" Was she surprised or delighted? Perhaps a bit of both.

"Yes. I said I hoped we could be friends, but I don't want to be friends with you."

"I don't want to be friends with you, either."

Not the reaction he'd expected, but he soldiered on. "I knew I had to apologize to you. I'd treated you very unfairly."

"I treated you unfairly, too."

"You did?"

"Yes. I expected you to change who you are."

"And I expected you to change who you are, too."

"Yes, well, who I am is sometimes illegal."

He smiled at that. "I thought you said you'd completely reformed."

"That was probably a lie, too. You see? You can never trust me."

"I'd trust you with my life."

Her beautiful eyes widened in shock. "You would?"

"Of course I would. I've never known anyone

more faithful or more loyal and determined to see justice done. Look how you fought for Priscilla."

"I thought you didn't approve of how I fought for Priscilla."

"I didn't. At first," he added when she frowned.

Now she was suspicious. "When did you change your mind?"

"I don't know exactly. It was a long process."

"All right, then *why* did you change your mind?"

He hadn't really thought about it, so he needed a moment to figure it out himself. "The reason I love the law so much is because I love justice, and I finally realized my sense of justice was too limited."

"Probably because you're a man."

"You may be right. Because the world is different for women than it is for men. For example, I'll never have to worry about my spouse dying and leaving me penniless and helpless."

"That's why the Old Man taught me the grift, you know."

"It is?" he asked, although he remembered a conversation he'd had on this very subject with the Old Man himself.

"Yes. He didn't want to, but if he did, I'd never have to depend on a man to take care of me."

And she'd never end up in a brothel, but he didn't say that. It was too painful to even contemplate. "Is that why you wanted to help Priscilla?"

"I don't know. I didn't stop to think about it. I just wanted to help Priscilla because she needed help and it was the right thing to do."

"Even if you had to break the law to do it."

He loved the way her eyes sparkled when she was angry. "Yes, even if I had to break the law to do it.

"And that's why I changed my mind. I finally realized that if justice is what we're fighting for, then we shouldn't be afraid to break a few rules along the way, especially if following the rules means there's no justice at all."

Now her eyes were just sparkling, because she didn't seem angry anymore. "Do you really mean that?"

He had to smile. "I never lie."

She smiled back. "Except about being friends."

He shrugged.

"The Old Man gave me some advice."

Gideon wasn't sure he wanted to know what it was. "Did he?"

"Yes. He said he thought we'd never be happy together."

Gideon almost choked on his outrage. "He did?"

"Yes, but he also said he thought I'd be even more unhappy without you."

Hope bubbled up, fragile but determined. "Do you think he's right?"

"Yes."

Not "I think so" or even "Maybe," but "Yes."

"I *know* he's right. Elizabeth, when I thought you were in danger, I knew I'd do anything to protect you. Nothing else mattered, not truth or the law or my honor, nothing at all. I finally figured out what was important."

"That's . . . wonderful."

"I love you more with every day that passes. I can't imagine a life without you, and I wouldn't be interested in living it even if I could."

"Oh, Gideon, we'll probably fight all the time and disagree about everything."

He took her beautiful face in both his hands and kissed her soundly.

When they were both breathless, he broke the kiss, and she said, "Well, maybe not about *everything*."

"We'll certainly never argue about the rule of law again. Or justice. Or how best to help other people."

"Are you sure?"

"I'm positive." He slid off the sofa onto one knee and took her hand in both of his. "Elizabeth Miles, will you do me the honor of becoming my wife?"

"Yes! Oh yes!"

Gideon started to get up so he could kiss her again, but he caught himself. "Wait, should I have asked your father for permission first?"

"You didn't the other time you asked me."

"That was an emergency, and besides, I didn't even know he was your father then."

"Mrs. Ordway says that, in America, that's just a formality, since my father wouldn't have let you court me in the first place if you weren't suitable."

"I don't think he *let* me do anything."

"Gideon," she said in exasperation, "I thought you weren't going to worry about following the rules anymore."

"It's a hard habit to break. I may need some help along the way."

Elizabeth gave him her most dazzling smile. "I'll give you all the help you need."

AUTHOR'S NOTE

This was such a fun book to write, and I hope you enjoyed reading it as much as I enjoyed figuring out all the twists and turns of the story. The book to which Elizabeth often refers, *The Etiquette of Today* by Mrs. Edith B. Ordway, really did exist and went through several revisions over the years. It makes for amusing reading by modern readers.

You are probably wondering how Priscilla Jenks Knight was able to live the rest of her life on a fortune of $80,000. At that time, this would have been the equivalent of about a million dollars in today's money. Priscilla wouldn't have been extremely wealthy, but since her house was paid for—it would have been in her first husband's family for generations—she and her children could have lived a comfortable middle-class life.

The Safe Deposit Company of New York, the first independent safe-deposit company, opened in 1865. At that time, banks would sometimes keep valuables for their big depositors at no charge, but they didn't really have the space for that or the ability to keep them truly secure in their large, open vaults. Someone figured out this was a need and developed a safe-deposit business. They would provide safekeeping for trunks and packages, but they also invented the safe-deposit box for smaller valuables. This was possible because James Sargent, a young employee of Linus Yale Jr., had invented the first key-changeable combination lock in 1857. By the 1920s, banks saw the profit potential and began offering safe-deposit boxes themselves, as they do today.

Please let me know how you liked this book. You may follow me on Facebook at Victoria. Thompson.Author and on Twitter @gaslightvt and visit my website at victoriathompson.com to sign up for my newsletter, so you'll always know when I have a new book coming out.